Worldwide acclaim for _____ ___
The Company

"An engrossing debut novel. . . . Cornelisz is both a memorable Faustian monster and . . . a nightmarish incarnation of the ruthlessness and avarice at the heart of the Dutch mercantile culture. A stimulating mix of *Oliver Twist* [and] *Lord of the Flies*. . . . A stunningly original triumph for a brilliant newcomer."
— *Kirkus Reviews* (starred review)

"Powerful. . . . A harrowing meditation on the nature of evil. The settings are vividly imagined . . . the imagery is breathtaking . . . never less than fascinating."
— *Milwaulkee Journal Sentinel*

"Robinson Crusoe was lucky to be marooned alone. . . . A mixture of classic sea-adventure yarn and grisly thriller."
— *Publishers Weekly*

"Disturbing. . . . Those who can stomach the violence will be drawn in."
— *Library Journal*

"Powerful historical fiction. . . . The story line is frightening because it is based on a true incident and person. . . . Genre fans will have a field day with this novel, especially comparing this diabolical individual with some of history's charismatic but deadly tyrants."
— Harriet Klausner

"[A] striking first novel . . . gripping historical novel . . . chilling portrait of evil."
— *The Age* (Australia)

THE
COMPANY
Portrait of a Murderer

Arabella Edge

SIMON & SCHUSTER
NewYork • London • Toronto • Sydney • Singapore

SIMON & SCHUSTER
Rockefeller Center
1230 Avenue of the Americas
New York, NY 10020

First Simon & Schuster trade paperback edition 2003
First published in 2000 in Picador
by Pan Macmillan Australia Pty Limited

Line drawings courtesy of the State Library of New South Wales

SIMON & SCHUSTER and colophon are registered
trademarks of Simon & Schuster, Inc.

For information regarding special discounts for bulk purchases,
please contact Simon & Schuster Special Sales at 1-800-456-6798
or business@simonandschuster.com

Designed by Gayna Murphy, Greendot Design

Manufactured in the United States of America

1   3   5   7   9   10   8   6   4   2

The Library of Congress has cataloged the hardcover edition as follows:
Edge, Arabella.
The company: the story of a murderer / Arabella Edge.
p. cm.
1. Netherlands—History, Naval—17th century—Fiction. 2. Survival after airplane accidents, shipwrecks, etc.—Fiction. 3. Western Australia—Fiction. 4. Shipwreck
victims—Fiction 5. Batavia (Ship)—Fiction. 6. Shipwrecks—Fiction. 7. Murderers—
Fiction. 8. Mutiny—Fiction. I. Title.
PR 9619.3.E245 C66 2001
823'.92—dc21   2001027009
ISBN 0-7432-1342-4
0-7434-1918-9 (Pbk)

*In memory of my
mother,
Marianne Berthiez Edge*

This is a work of fiction inspired by and based on the wreck of the *Batavia* off the western coast of Australia in 1629. Despite my reliance on historical sources, I have taken considerable liberties with the historical facts to suit the purposes of the novel's narrative, namely to explore the mind of Jeronimus Cornelisz, a psychopath and the perpetrator of the crimes.

Those interested in finding out more about the exact nature of the events surrounding the *Batavia* may wish to seek out the following historical accounts on which I have relied heavily: Henrietta Drake-Brockman's *Voyage to Disaster*, Western Australia University Press, 1995, to which I am indebted; Philippe Godard's *The First and Last Voyage of the Batavia*, Abrolhos Publishing, 1993; Hugh Edwards's *Islands of Angry Ghosts*, Angus & Robertson, 1989; and Rupert Gerritsen's *And Their Ghosts May Be Heard*, Fremantle Arts Centre Press, 1994.

Readers wishing to investigate Dutch life in general during this Golden Age period are directed to Simon Schama's *The Embarrassment of Riches*, Fontana Press, 1991, and C. R. Boxer's *The Dutch Seaborne Empire*, Hutchinson, 1965.

I could not have written *The Company* without these excellent and riveting sources and any mistakes are all my own.

Acknowledgments

I would like to thank several people for their support during the writing of *The Company*.

First, all my thanks to my husband, Nick Gaze, who told me the story of the *Batavia* and inspired me to write this novel; Glenda Adams, my supervisor at the University of Technology, Sydney, for her generosity and advice in steering me through the writing of *The Company* from its inception; my agent, Lyn Tranter, for her encouragement, enthusiasm, and patience; Nikki Christer at Picador for her belief in this work; Judith Lukin-Amundsen for her sensitive and perceptive editing; and Sara Douglass for putting me right on historical matters.

I would like to thank everyone at UTS, including Jan Hutchinson, Joyce Kornblatt, Stephen Muecke, and Graham Williams; and the UTS MA writing group: Rowanne Couch, Belinda Alexander, Pat Cranney, and Brian Purcell.

I also thank the New South Wales Government Ministry for the Arts for awarding me the Writers in the Park New Writer's Fellowship which helped me to complete *The Company*.

Many thanks also to my high school English teacher, John Fielding, who taught me a love of words.

And last but not least, thank you, Zoe, for enduring the sound of me reading my manuscript out loud whenever you returned home from school.

MY CHILDHOOD echoed with the sound of whispering. *The servants believed that I was conceived by the moon, born in the thirteenth lunar month. How the wet nurses feared me. Crossing themselves, garlic cloves pinned to their aprons, they would watch me creep about my cot, eyes still closed, mewling like a newborn pup.*

During her confinement, the servants said, my mother filled the rooms with armfuls of lilies and white lilac. She craved ewe's milk, warm and frothing straight from the teat, and took to gazing at the full moon through latticed windows.

Some explained she was frightened in her fourth month by the luminous reflections in the eyes of a white cat; others remembered the occasion of the bats, circling and swooping the terrace with red and flaming eyes.

My mother became distant, distracted, silent. At last refused to leave her room at all. Her harpsichord remained unplayed by the window and spiders wove intricate looms between the curled pages of her open music book.

They said that, teeth clenched, twisting her silk shawl into tourniquets, sweat beading her brow, my mother clung to the midwife. A sulphur-yellow moon rose outside the window and turned my mother's skin a deathly white.

The midwife swaddled me in rough flannel and pressed me into the reluctant arms of the wet nurse.

From an early age, I imagined I could hear the halting

tread of my mother's footsteps in the corridor outside and her voice calling to me. But no one ever came.

As a child, restless and insomniac, I waited for the rise of Sirius—the dog star, my only sun—and the white night of the moon.

My wet nurses were raw-boned recruits of peasant stock whose newborns had either died or were farmed out to the foundling hospital in exchange for bed and board, four-year contracts in the fashionable district of town.

I have a faint memory of one, head bent over her Bible, murmuring prayers, not once looking up from the pages.

I remember chapped red-fisted hands buttoning me in a coat of taffeta, folding me in a satin mantle, and another woman's voice, harsh, scolding, telling her to wipe the nipples of her dugs before putting them in my mouth. But then again, it could have been a childhood dream.

When it was time, the wet nurse would sigh, untie her apron, and unfasten the buttons of her chemise with trembling fingers. As she reached for me, her blue-veined pendulous breasts swung above my face, proffering their dark puckered fruit. My earliest memories are filled with the sour-sweet taste and the warm flesh smell of her.

So I am told, for one so slight I was an eager feeder and sometimes she would cry out if I nuzzled too hard. It was a long time before I was weaned.

Even now I still dream of my nurse. She holds me against her heavy breasts, her right nipple in my mouth. My hungry mouth. I suckle. Fresh blood warm as ewe's milk spills down my chin and stains my white silk shirt.

PART
ONE

AMSTERDAM, 29 October, *Anno* 1628.

I stand alone on the spice wharf and inhale the cinnamon salt-sweet fragrance that lingers still. Once again I check my papers. All in order, no detail gone unnoticed. Tutt did well. I admire his meticulous work in forging the Company seal on my accommodation pass to the officers' cabins. At last it is final.

Strange that Torrentius—my mentor and only friend—being an acclaimed Hollander miniaturist, was offered temporary refuge at the court of King Charles, whereas for certain beliefs of mine, I have to scuttle underground like a rat, board the ship *Batavia*, and adopt the crisp, moneyed manners of Dutch East India merchants bound on a five-month voyage to the Indies.

I'm no mariner. I can't even swim. I fear death by drowning, the cold touch of water on my skin. I, Jeronimus, am a man of phials, a measurer of powders on bronze scales, a potion brewer, an opium and arsenic merchant. The primped and perfumed Amsterdam burghers came to me in droves requiring cures for fevers, love balms, the miscarriage of a bastard child, and, of course, poisons. Ah, poisons. And there are many. Dusting an ostrich fan, the rim of a claret glass, the bloom on a summer rose—beware the innocent whose lips brush his lady's lace-gloved hand. Witchcraft I leave to the crones, the illusionists in market squares, the card shufflers, the crystal ball gazers, the decipherers of strangers' shadows in cracked teacups, reminding me of that other sorcerer, the lost prophet, who divided fishes and loaves, turned water to wine, spun tall tales to fisherboys and netmenders by the riverbanks.

Torrentius's hospitality knew no bounds. My friend's mansion was one of the most magnificent residences in the town. Furnished with every conceivable luxury, the salons were designed for pleasure. Nightingales sang from the orangerie, and in the summerhouse by the ornamental lake there were frescoes of pucks, centaurs, satyrs, priapic in the Arcadian style.

There were studios dedicated to the pursuit of knowledge. One devoted to natural history held my attention for a while, the accidents of nature in particular, coiled in jars of preserving fluid.

Another was a scholar's study of Zodiac charts, almanacs, the rarest of Tarot cards. These, day after day, I would play, until the worn emblems became intimate as friends.

The mansion also housed a large library of curiosa,

and it was there that I spent most of my time. In addition to Greek and Latin authors, my fingers roamed the works of Shakespeare and other moderns.

Bent over his desk, in silence and solitude, my friend deciphered his family's genealogies, transcribed them from Latin to Dutch on finely calligraphed sheets of parchment in a beautiful, unhurried hand.

Under his guidance, I began my study of the humanities and explored every part of the library, the trompe-l'oeil panels which slid open at a single touch. Among this secret archive of wax-sealed documents I found a precious collection of licentious literature. Bound in yellow calf vellum, *The History of the Flagellants*, a translation by an Abbe of the fifteenth century, was the first to catch my eye, and there was much to be learned from this tract.

~⟡⟐

My friend had a talent for masked balls. His guests would be asked to dress for the occasion, each request sending the district for miles around into a fever of anticipation. The delivery of those black scrolls caused considerable agitation among the jaded aristocracy, who, at the first sight of Torrentius's carriage in the streets, dispatched their servants to wait by the gate. And beware the hapless footman who returned to a house empty-handed. Not for my friend pastorals of goatherds and shepherdesses or seraglios of silken slaves—he preferred more demanding themes. Guests arrived as inquisitors, executioners, Satan's angels, pagan kings and queens. For him life was a game, his theatricals a play within a play.

Torrentius liked to teach his disciples in rented wharfside brothels. There he orchestrated secret pagan rites, choreographed magnificent still lifes, made lean street boys pose in supplicating attitudes of the bordello and desire.

One evening, when the moon crept smoothly across the parquetry floor, ruffling sighs among the shadows, my mentor took me to one side.

"I will make you an object of terror," he whispered. "You will not exist. People will look for you and never find you again."

I smiled, knowing it to be true. For I was different from the others, the fashionable, languid cherubim of his flock, with money and time on their hands, hoping to forge new lives among old gods, reciting the Lord's Prayer backward, slitting a goat's throat, desecrating tombstones in abandoned cemeteries, the usual delinquent stuff.

My friend found me firm in my principles because those I had were formed early. Always I had acted in accordance with them. Above all, I understood the nullity of virtue, for I was still very young when I learned to hold religion's fantasies in contempt, being convinced that the existence of a creator was an absurdity in which not even children should believe.

There is no need to flatter one new young god. Not when others clamor to be served.

As for this puny planet, I've been here before in many guises and Torrentius, who compiled my charts, has foretold I will return again. Paris. Raconteur, boulevardier, scratching memoirs on slivers of parchment, inciting revolutions from a Bastille cell.

Were it not for the indiscretions of Torrentius's disciples—those fools who escaped and ran screaming to their mothers—and the pleasure-denying Calvinist magistrates of this town, I would not be here, forged ticket in one gloved hand, condemned to Batavia.

At the heart of this city's pulsing roar of trade sits my keeper, the Honourable Company in East India House, a palatial agency which entangles every man in speculative ventures, and honeycombs the world from the Americas to Formosa with a multitude of enterprises. An oligarchy of seventeen councillors has decreed gold the Company's god and raised a veritable sovereign state, their kingdom of Batavia, into which flows all the sewage of Holland—buccaneers and bankrupts, disgraced corporate servants, idle noblemen bored of roaming the continent on the

Grooten Tour. The Company's new empire needs people, but show me one honest burgher who would volunteer for it. No, instead they apply for desk jobs as clerks, seek safe sinecures in the echoing marble chambers of India House. There, they pore over the great journal books dispatched from Batavia, compose minutes to be read by the Grand Council of Seventeen and prepare orders to be posted to chief ministers.

When a Company ship drops anchor, the mercantile clamor shrills. Precious cargoes of indigo, cardamom, saffron, rolls of raw silks are lowered from the hold and wheeled along the wharves to bolted emporiums, impregnable magazines, the Company warehouses built like forts, where armed soldiers patrol the battlements, defending these goods which will wait a seller's market and keep prices high.

~※◎

Now in the guise of salaried servant, I await exile, for the ship to sail, for the solid bricks of Amsterdam to dissolve and dim as if eroded by the mists of this land.

There are plans for our city, talk of constructing a municipal hall with a dome and a bell turret in the French style, widening the cramped alleys and waterways, connecting the islands to the town, building mansions on reclaimed land, even turning the medieval ramparts into grassy promenades and tree-lined malls. I wonder if I shall see my home again.

The Honourable Company's flagship, the *Batavia*, looks sturdy enough. A varnished timber leviathan, all six hundred gross tons of her. If one is to believe the Company's latest announcement, the *Batavia* has been built to the most modern design, heralding a new generation of retourships, faster, sleeker, more hand-some; at least three times the size of the caravels that sped Christophe Colombe to the shores of the West Indies in 1492. The *Batavia* is rigged as a three-master with a bowsprit, capable of spreading over a thousand square feet of canvas to the trade winds when all ten sails are set; she is even equipped with two officers' privies projecting from the stern and a well-stocked library. In this new life as corporate undermerchant, who am I to doubt the Company's word, its faith in figures, its proud measurements of the *Batavia*'s length, depth, height between decks and beam?

All around peddlers, porters, pickpockets, hawkers, painted courtesans accost the merchants and sailors spilling onto the wharves. Families everywhere, streaming past anchor smithies, ship chandlers, sail-cutting workshops, point at the crimson pennants fly-ing from the *Batavia*'s mainmast, each emblazoned with her figurehead, the red Lion of Holland. Chil-dren ride their parents' shoulders, blowing whistles and banging toy drums.

Above the stall vendors' ceaseless chant rise the

squeals of pregnant sows being hoisted into the *Batavia*'s hold. On the jetty, roosters shriek in their pens, unsettling the hens which, beaks open in fear, jostle for space and flap their wings. Now a bull is winched aboard, snorting with rage and bucking the gray hoary air with its hooves.

Unlike the crew who swarm the main deck and swing from the rigging like untamed monkeys, the merchants and their families teeter aboard, frightened of losing their footing, unsure of the harbor's shifting equilibrium.

One by one, the crew and passengers board: the butler's mate, the cook, the cabin servants, the chief trumpeter, the carpenters, the gunners, the soldiers, the merchants, the blacksmith, the cooper, the tailors and sailors. Trust no more in man. He has but a breath in his nostrils. How much is he worth?

News carries fast in Amsterdam. They say the *Batavia*'s hold is crammed with gold and silver, both coined and uncoined, money chests stashed with corporate cash, precious artifacts to trade with plump sultans of Mogul courts. All that wealth. Whereas I stand here on the quay, my last few guilders clinking in my pockets.

I watch the fat Predikant, his sullen wife, and six plump daughters scramble aboard. The Predikant's sallow sick-visitor, his *krank-besoeker*, follows like a shadow. The Predikant clasps his Bible to his chest and begins to pray.

Dressed in all his finery, breezes riffling the ostrich

plume in his hat, the Commandeur stands on the poopdeck, surveying the chaos below him. The skipper marches fore and aft, shouting commands to his men.

I turn to farewell Amsterdam, beloved city of linden trees and gray-green canals spread like a fan around the harbor, the narrow lanes packed with warehouses, the islands hidden behind forests of ship masts and spars.

Amsterdam, amphibious, slippery city, wreathed in flooded marshland mists, floating on foundations of Norwegian pine daily defeating the ebb tides. A city of secrets and business assignations along footpaths beside the canals, in the shadows of the colonnaded markets, the timber wharves, the doorways of brothels, among the fetid steam clouds of the *bagnios*, where maidenheads can also be exchanged for small favors of bone lace, silver bodkins, hooped rings.

City of trade, where all businessmen and bureaucrats are hot to buy and sell and the world's commodities are consigned to warehouses only to go out again at higher prices.

Founded in the last decade, monstrous cathedrals of wealth now soar against the skyline: the Exchange Bank, the Lending Bank, the Bourse, securing gold ingots, silver bars, piastres, ducats and ducatons, coin and bullion, making payments quick and trade feverish, protecting investors against loss from false or clipped money.

Stashed in labyrinthine networks of locked vaults,

the King of Sweden stores his stock of copper, the Hapsburg Emperors their assets of quicksilver from Idrian mines, the Tsar of Russia his ermine furs, the King of Poland his saltpeter.

In no other city is the bill of exchange used so freely, the weekly published exchange rates read so avidly and receipts for merchandise passed so swiftly from hand to hand. At rush hour, between noon and one o'clock, the Bourse and the Stock Exchange are packed with traders of all nations shouldered in a heaving hubbub of bargaining. Low interest rates at three percent for an entire year without pawn or pledge send merchants into a trading frenzy buying produce in seasons when prices are lowest—or as they say in the mercantile vernacular, out of the first hand. They even lay ready money for future commodities and sell them on trust. They buy entire forests in Germany to be felled on order, purchase grain before the harvest, wines before the vintage season, and trade with neighboring nations at prices which cannot be equaled.

Amsterdam, treacherous, lawless, lowlife city, munitions center of the world, which profits from financing rather than fighting with the Spanish enemy, furnishing warring naval supplies of muskets, buff coats, belts, gunpowder, arming ships of fighting strength, supplying corn to troops on the Iberian coast in Dutch ships sailing under false Flanders flags.

Crazed city, where a rare horticultural disease can topple the rose in favor of a tulip. An epidemic which inflames curious streaks of color in the tulip's corolla also infects the minds of men who haggle to sell three *Semper Augustus* bulbs at the price of waterside mansions and guard flower beds with guns and knives.

—⟨⟩—

Trade—what will a man not give in exchange of his soul?

Yet I have had to pack my worldly possessions in a sea chest like a common mariner, inventory my medicines and carry them like the cheapest of charlatans. I was ordered by the magistrates to discard my pointed hat, my black apothecary robes, remove my green crocodile sign from its hinges, and close a lucrative, if clandestine, business in medical consultations.

As for my valuable collection entombed in green glass jars of preserving fluid—the aborted, the two-headed, the horned and hooved, twins and triplets locked at the hips at birth, those pale curled worms of humanity—the magistrates consigned these to the gutter and the crows.

The vulgar mouths call me necromancer. The very name of chemistry sounds so deadly in their ears that many suspect I busy myself in the art of sorcery. I am feared by ignorant physicians and practitioners who never think seven years' study is enough, who never improve or bring any discoveries or inventions to their profession, but plod the common road of tradition and feed on the antiquities of long-dead masters, primitive herbalists, Galen, Hypocrates, whose prescriptions of hellebore and colloquintida are without result.

And yet I had clients in plenty. Many a veiled lady was turned from my door, having to seek uncertain remedies from the market herb woman and a season later taking her chance in the midwives' hands.

I have discovered drugs to fit all purposes, perfected each potion and greatly extended my stock of poisons.

As in any trade, fads and fashions govern my elixirs of mortality. Last year, the town's cuckolds favored powders which mortified the flesh, loosened gums like the scurvy, and turned faithless wives bald as scarecrows. This season, fashionable ladies driven to distraction by whoring lovers requested my lozenges, which if administered before the act of carnal copulation would ejaculate a mortal fountain of blood instead of seed from the victim's yard. My more conventional stock imitates disease, pockmarks fair skins with rashes and blisters, swells abdomens with sure signs of the dropsy, mimics brain fevers and heart seizures, ulcerates limbs.

Often during my consultations I would be struck by the fact that planning a lover's death was in many ways more intimate than the act of love itself. I was impressed by my clients' attention to detail, the way they leafed through my recipe books, carefully calibrating levels of pain, inquiring the precise time when the poison would strike and how long to expect before death. I think they enjoyed playing God for the day.

Now I await exile; let all Amsterdam's bastards be born and the city's cheating population soar. Let wives, cuckolds, and courtesans squander guilders on comfrey roots, sweet Juleps, licorice water, and oil of roses. Let them be duped by the efficacies in earthworm ashes, marshmallow ointments, sea-horse pizzles, dried frog spawn, the hollow promises of quacks and herbalists.

※

I draw my astrakhan cloak closer. I farewell the gulls diving for dabs in the cold gray waters, the *louche* smile of an autumn crocus vendor, the flames unfurled from a fire-eater's tongue. I hand the bosun my papers. He unfolds and inspects each page, then scrawls his signature beneath the Company seal and my name.

Balancing my luggage on their shoulders, the porters nudge their way through the crowds. And, steadying myself, I follow. I place the sole of one boot on the *Batavia*'s gangplank and shed my old life like snakeskin.

NEARLY TWO WEEKS at sea and never once in sight of land. I do not trust the *Batavia*'s straining tack nor the mainsail with her billowing belly of canvas. The officers' cabins are cramped. Damp furs, filthy woolens, cast-off boots, tobacco smoke, the stench of vomit, sick men, hour upon hour, with only a bunk in my cabin to lie on and a felt curtain to hide me—these make up the reality of my home.

Each morning, I wake to uneasy pinks and greens smeared against the sky. My porthole looks out onto the quarterdeck where the soldiers on duty march up and down. Beyond, the crew swarms the main deck and forecastle. Some lay cables, others splice and coil ropes. It is a dull scene. All day long they call to one another in a litany of nautical tongues which I cannot follow: sheet in the top gallants, put her about, clew the fore and lower sails in the buntlines, heave here and avast there. I also have to endure their endless banter, their volleys of oaths and curses. All the while the wind whistles tunes about the rigging and the ship's bell strikes the half-hour when sand in the watch glass runs out and is turned.

I am nauseous with the sea's restless swell, the ceaseless pitch. First the stern lifts and with a wallowing rush plummets each wave face. Then a broken mass of white water runs alongside the *Batavia's* length until foam spills around her bows.

I was unprepared too for the sour vinegar residue from washed beams, the mustiness in hemp and canvas, the acrid smell of paint and varnish, the vile, rotten stench from water swilling the bilges.

Nor did I expect the teeming, crowded conditions we now find ourselves in. There is barely an inch on deck a man can call his own. Even the heads at the *Batavia's* bow are crammed with men pissing through the deck slats or sluicing their vermin-infested shirts. Any attempt to move about the ship is like being compressed in a perpetual fairground throng, jostled and shoved in a heaving, seething, sweat-soured mass of humanity. Why, just to reach the main saloon, you have to wait your turn. Each time the hatches are opened, a fetid reek rises from the orlop deck where the soldiers are crammed two to a hammock. Wherever you look, there are sailors everywhere, agile and sure-footed as goats, scampering across the rigging, swinging like trapeze artists from rope to rope, or shimmying down the mainmast, gripping the rough tarred ropes with prehensile toes.

Gazing up now, there are ten of them leaning over

the yards of the mizzenmast to unfurl the top sails, the soles of their bare feet continuously shifting and balancing on strands of knotted rope. It makes me dizzy to watch them for long. Day and night, they go about the ship's business, hurling oaths, pushing past any passengers in their way.

Above this raging pandemonium, the captain surveys the oceans from the steep ledge of the poopdeck at the ship's high-backed square stern.

—ᘜᕙ⊙

Each morning, I master the sloping deck, eyes fixed to my feet, taking care not to trip over rigging ropes encircled in their cleats.

Pushing my way to the saloon, I pass the sows sprawled in their pens, suckling blind newborn piglets on swollen teats. I recoil from the sight of their pale, hairless flesh, the soft, squirming nakedness of them. Soon it will be time for the cook to sharpen his knives.

Autumn and the month of swallows is gone. The seasons unwind and we drift in an endless summer. The heat has come upon us gradually. First the water in the casks turns fetid, then vermin begin to appear in a creeping march across the cabin walls. Always a sea-damp wind coats the air. I dream often and sleep less.

Most days I lie on my bunk suspended in an eternity of boredom, waiting like a spider in the darkness, weaving idle webs from my past.

I LOOKED TO TORRENTIUS as the one masculine authority in my life, my father having died when I was young.

My father was a gambling, fox-hunting, claret-drinking man, a frequenter of concert halls, assembly rooms, and trotting races, with a pleasure in the solo soprano of a servant's song.

My childhood was spent in a spacious town house, being coddled and candy-fed by a collection of pious nurses while my mother wandered from church to cloister seeking relief from a nervous condition, hallucinations of a religious kind.

Most afternoons, when shadows slanted across the lawns and my nurse dozed beneath the elderflower and foxglove shade of the shrubberies, I, a precocious, solitary child, far older than my twelve years, soon wearied of chasing my hoop, or kicking a ball, and I would gaze at the blank windows of our house, tremulous that spring with the scented blooms of woodbine. Always at the siesta hour, a shutter from the library on the second floor would bang shut. Sometimes, I glimpsed the lace cuffs of Father's sleeve, the gold glint of his wedding ring, his long, thin hands fastening the catch.

One interminable afternoon in the garden, I allowed the string of a crimson kite to trail through my fingers. I let it go and watched it spiral into the air. When it began to float toward the house, I followed, my black leather shoes going clickety-clack along the paths, past trellised orchards of pear, peach, and apricot, the statue of Pan in the rose garden, until I stepped within the house itself, that dazzling region of blue gauze.

From the drawing room, I could hear the familiar clink of pewter, the squeak of a trolley wheeled by a maid onto the terrace.

I climbed the main staircase and paused outside the library, where the walls seemed to expand and contract to a stranger's breath.

I kneeled at the keyhole. On a velveteen *chaise-longue* in the library half-lit, Father reclined with Marie, the housemaid. He arranged her skirts this way and that, slowly unfastened her chemise, the satin ribbons of her stays, parted her thighs, stroked her unformed breasts with the ivory handle of his riding crop. Then he forced her, shivering and naked, to her knees.

"Bend over," he entreated. Each swift swish of leather made me catch my breath.

"Salvation is all of grace," Father said beneath his

breath. "Here you will understand the yoke of discipline. Upon my word you will be chastised and corrected." And he yanked her lovely long red hair back.

I almost cried out, and dug my nails into the palms of my hands until they bled.

—◦◦◦—

All summer long, Father's games became my afternoon ritual. I wonder now if he knew that outside, I was watching in the dim light.

I could barely sit still through the endless soup lunches in the schoolroom, barely tolerate the slurps and hiccups of my nurse, dabbing her moustached mouth with a napkin. It was then that I longed to punish her.

I'd stare at her swollen breasts straining against the starched fabric of her apron and have to squeeze my hands beneath my thighs in order not to reach out and touch them. I imagined Father sinking his riding crop into the soft white folds of her flesh and the raw crimson weals striping her broad creamy back.

Then, once again, I would become breathless at the thought of Marie cowering naked at my feet, her hair falling forward, exposing russet curls twining the pale nape of her neck. Like Father, I too would stroke her tear-stained cheek with the tip of my pigskin boot.

All summer long I was enfevered. On our afternoon

promenades through the garden, my nurse and I would pass the laundry house where the women bent, legs astride, to spread linen over the bushes. I almost swooned at the sight of their blue-veined thick ankles.

Once I whittled a birch stick and thrashed the gardener's greyhound to within an inch of his life, just to see what it was like. But it was not the same and never would be the same as the games Father played with Marie, hands tied above her head, thighs splayed.

Soon I became jealous of him. My dreams were lust-drenched, fever-soaked. Not even my ceaseless solitary touch could ease the pain.

Crouched at the keyhole, my jealousy knew no bounds. I wanted to swing open the library door, declare myself, and snatch the whip from Father's hands. Soon I began to loathe not only him, this father of mine who daily devoured soft fruit flesh, while I, Tantalus, slavered at the keyhole exiled from his Eden, but also my nurse, my frumpish, fretful guard, my lumpen watchkeeper at Heaven's Gate.

I also disliked the greyhound, which ran away squealing at my approach.

Although she never knew, I haunted Marie's every step. My only solace was to become her shadow, sliding from scullery to wine cellar, kitchen to larder, the stern housekeeper's parlor and the attic warrens of the servants' quarters, where peals of laughter sang from room to room.

By her heavy tread, her hair scraped back from her

face, pale and expressionless beneath a black cotton cap, I could tell my Marie was a sad girl. Although he paid her well, she did not love Father, and his games lacked the tenderness which only I could provide.

I longed for her then. Longed to dress her in lace and watch her shudder.

In the evenings, Father sat at one end of the vast oak dining room table and my nurse and I at the other. He rarely spoke to me but sometimes would question my nurse, who stammered and squirmed throughout the interview, saying that to be sure it was a quiet life for Master Jeronimus, who must miss his mama, but Mr. Chimes in the schoolroom believed he was a gifted boy, reading the way he did, tracts and treatise, which, dearie me, few could understand, and excelled at chemistry. Here she would pause and beam at me.

"You'd be proud to see his little head bent over all manner of phials and flames," she said.

Father would sink into his usual silence, satisfied with her answer.

I remember it was almost the end of summer when I devised my plan.

The schoolroom was a light, airy place of chalk dust, bookshelves, and polished pine. When first employed, Chimes, my tutor, would hide flagons of Rhenish wine behind the shelves where the chalk was kept, beneath three loose floorboards, the box of firewood, and his desk. But, as I had pretended not to hear the clink of his glass, liquor poured in fast furtive glugs, surreptitious sips whenever Chimes thought me absorbed in my books, he now kept a tumbler more or less filled by his feet and soon after breakfast fell fast asleep, leaving me uninterrupted in the pursuit of my studies.

How I loved to sit at the marble-topped table where, poised between copper buttresses, my glass cathedral soared, tier after tier, each phial, tube, and pipette enveloping sulfuric vapors while below, the scarlet-tipped flames of the burners raged.

In miniature, I had re-created the city of my dreams, municipality of fire and brimstone where Satan reigned, our fallen Company man, unceremoniously retrenched from Eden, those dull verdant vales, from former employment as God's agent spelling out the fine print in celestial contracts involving free will and predestination.

Each morning, I worked my alchemy, watched rainbows flare in bursts of steam, sparks gleam from heated measures of laburnum seed, baneberry, and belladonna. I pounded heart-leaf, darling pea, delphinium and listened to their dry pods crackle. I distilled essences of toadstool and stavesacre and marveled at those dark gases unfurling serpent tails within my glass architecture of pumps and pulleys.

All the while Chimes slept, oblivious to the combustion roar of my concoctions, painstakingly prepared through trial and error, until at last I was ready.

I decided to spare Chimes, who had offended no one in the world, whose only sin was to seek oblivion in Rhenish wine.

But one afternoon I threw the greyhound a fine mutton bone. Would he have it? The wretch cringed in the vegetable garden, ears flat against weasel head, teeth bared. I flung the meat after him and the ingrate ran off, tail between his legs.

The following day when I returned, I found the bone uneaten, yet was pleased to discover one dead raven among the sweet peas, a lump of gristle gripped in its beak. It proved that my experiment had worked.

It was autumn, my favorite season with its hint of frost and bonfires in gardens, when my nurse complained of a strange pink rash appearing on her arms, throat, and belly.

The local doctor was called in. A hesitant, uncertain man with a tense bedroom-manner smile. Although he probed, swabbed, uncorked a jar of leeches and held them squirming between tweezers, his prognosis was vague. He could not identify the cause of my nurse's affliction, yet by then her entire body boiled and blistered.

"It is definitely not the plague," he whispered.

How the very utterance of that word seeped like a pestilence throughout the house. To my dismay the servants began to leave in droves. From the schoolroom, I watched them bundle ragged possessions into covered carts and whip their mules into a canter through the gates of the grounds—Chimes bringing up the rear on a donkey.

I thanked the gods that Marie was not among them. She was a hard worker and Father rewarded her well. He gave her clothes in the latest fashion, even paid the rent for her mother's small cottage on the outskirts of town.

Through the keyhole at the siesta hour, I continued to watch Father's games, but these days they lacked their former luster—even my darling's seductive poses seemed wooden, yet, at his orders, she still kneeled or reclined legs apart on a chair. I noticed too that Father was becoming clumsy in his caresses and paused every now and then to wipe sweat from his temples, although it was unseasonably cold that year and frost had blighted the rose trees.

Surely it was only a matter of time before I could claim Marie as my own, confess my desires, make her love me to the end. Father's face was chalky white, and an angry purple rash had spread from both wrists to the back of his hands.

—≈≈≈—

The death of my nurse cast a pall over the house. Lonely in the schoolroom, I now spent most of my mornings in our labyrinthine kitchens of sandstone and green tile, helping Cook prepare her repertoire of rich, fragrant meals. Although at first surprised by the offer of my services, she was flattered to have the company, and perhaps she thought that I missed Chimes and my nurse.

Cook was touched by my filial devotion, the careful way I sliced apples for Father's compôte, a dish recommended by the doctor to reduce fever and animate the appetite.

While I grated ginger and cinnamon, Cook grumbled beneath her breath and heaved huge copper cauldrons onto the stove.

"There's disease in this house," she confided to the gardener who delivered baskets of beets, turnips, and shallots by the back door.

"Now the master's sick," she whispered to the

gamekeeper who threw down a sack of pheasants and made off without a word.

"The doctor said it started with a spreading rash," she told the laundry maids who rushed squealing to the washtubs to scrub their pink young hands.

The doctor instructed that no one except himself should visit Father, now confined to his bed, and all meals be left outside the bedroom door.

One night in the dining room where I alone presided, I saw Marie glide past, carrying a wooden dish of stewed apples made by myself that morning, lovingly prepared and intended for no one but Father. Throwing down my napkin, I rushed after her.

"Marie," I called.

She froze on the stairs, quite frightened by the urgency in my voice. Then she looked at me and smiled. The first time I'd ever seen her smile. I was struck speechless by her radiance. I wanted to embrace this alabaster angel, give her the kisses she desired.

"You're a good son," she said. "Although we promised not to, Cook and I couldn't help ourselves." She jerked her head toward the dish which she carried in strong capable hands.

"We had a taste and it ain't half bad."

I opened my mouth to scream but no sound came out. And then I knew, finally I understood. Apples were a cursed fruit.

When I lost my first and only childhood love, when Marie died, it could be said that my heart forever hardened against false prophets and that traitor Jesus who stole her from me. But in revenge, my own dark angels delivered me to Torrentius, my friend.

I call for Tonks, the galley servant, to bring me a glass of brandy. It makes me sick to think of my squandered past.

THE BELT OF CALMS is upon us. This uninterrupted monotony of ocean meeting sky offers little diversion. The *Batavia*'s convoy of seven ships attempt to scoop the listless wind in their sails. The man-of-war, the *Buren*, tacks alongside. Three retourships are also making the voyage, the *Dordrecht*, *Galiasse*, and *Gravenhage*. They say the *Batavia* is a palace compared to them. Two store ships, the *Assendelft* and the *Sardam*, bring up the rear, with the yacht *Kleine David* lagging behind.

Beneath the shade of a faded olive-green canopy, the passengers recline on folded rolls of canvas in the ship's waist. Deck games are abandoned. Cards listlessly shuffled. Pages flutter from unread books. A tattered, dog-eared Bible slides from someone's lap.

In the interminable stretch between luncheon and supper, the ship constricts. There is the ocean ahead. The sharp blue sky above. Shadows slant across the sunbleached deck. Not even a fly to brush away or a cloud to landscape the horizon. The ship glides. Days slide. Napkins are unfolded. Menus read. Today fish, tomorrow mutton, the day after boiled bully beef. I watch my fellow passengers alternate between sea sickness and gluttony, furtive flirtations and matrimonial bickering, and now a torpor is descending. Who are these strangers who mop their brows and fight their way into the saloon squabbling for tables beneath the great stern window? Surveyors, speculators, buccaneers, Company men, who have placed their trust in a world elsewhere, trusting the creaking worm-eaten planks of the ship against which every slap of a wave, every rush of the wind carries them farther from the place they used to call home.

When a tall woman strides into view and leans against the rail, arms outstretched, russet hair flying in the face of the wind, her velveteen cloak billowing behind her like a flag, I find myself taking in every detail: her absorbed gaze seaward as if expecting something to happen, her alabaster complexion, the mole on her upper lip, the gold glint of a wedding ring—she has slender, harpsichord-playing hands, scholar's hands accustomed to lifting nothing heavier than ink-soaked quills. This woman refuses to seek shade like the others and stands hatless in the full glare of the sun, buffeted by the hot dry trades. There is something imperious and defiant about her. Still she stares out to sea. Strands of her long red hair whip across her face and eyes. What is she waiting for?

A shoal of porpoises bursts from the waves in a swift plunging flight, their sleek arched backs silhouetted against the smoking spray.

Clapping her hands in delight, she hops onto the first rung of the rail and leans as far as she can without losing her balance to get a better look. Several of the traders lower their books to stare. They seem to enjoy this woman's recklessness. Their wives, on the other hand, exchange disapproving glances and click their tongues.

From the poopdeck, the skipper too is appraising her closely, while pretending to look through his glass.

Our skipper is a sly, slippery man of fat pensions and thin scars, a rum drinker, slave trader, seducer of women with rouged lips and dimpled thighs. This lady is too elegant to be his type.

I scan the crowded decks in an attempt to identify her husband. Surely no man would allow his wife to place herself in such a precarious position, the tips of her yellow satin slippers now perched on the rail's second rung, foaming glaciers of spume surging beneath her. It gives me vertigo to think of it. I close my eyes and press a lavender-scented handkerchief to my lips.

When I look up again, I see she is joined by a young, plump woman carrying a parasol and a black-veiled crimson toque. By her white lace cap and apron, the clogs on her stockinged feet, she must be some maid.

She would be pretty, but there is something sullen and sour about her expression which I don't like.

Her mistress is laughing and pointing at the shoal skimming across the surf-flecked flanks of a wind shadow. The maid entreats her to climb down and flicks open the parasol, which immediately blows inside out. Some of the traders snigger among themselves. Even our hardfisted skipper guffaws at the scene, then recovers himself by barking orders at a terrified midshipman unraveling a cat's cradle of lines in the mainsail rigging. The maid tussles with the parasol and almost loses her mistress's hat to the winds. Ignoring her, the woman jumps lightly onto the deck and hurries toward the ship's stern, to watch the porpoises cavorting in the *Batavia*'s wake. The maid trails behind her, a picture of bored dejection, until she catches sight of our Captain and darts him a sly, shy smile followed by a low reverential curtsy. This takes the skipper by surprise and he observes her progress across the main deck.

It seems this lass is determined to forfeit her maidenhead and better her fortunes before the journey is out.

In exchange for a guilder, I will ask about this mistress of hers, for my curiosity is aroused. Perhaps this voyage will not be as dull as I first thought.

MOST NIGHTS in the saloon, a drunken group of corporate boys toasts the Company with the finest French wines.

"*Vereenigde Oost-Indische Compagnie,*" they cheer. Filling my glass from a jug of brandy wine, I listen to one imitate the Commandeur's thin fluting voice when reciting his account of corporate grievances. Although drunk, the boy is a virtuoso mimic.

"From repeated personal experience," he shrills in a high falsetto, "it is more profitable for the Honourable Company for buyers to keep quiet. Goodness knows the Armenians do quite enough running and racing about the country from one village to another, making as if they would buy the whole indigo stock, raising prices, losing a little themselves, and causing great injury to us and other buyers who purchase large quantities."

He bows with a flourish. The saloon tilts to one side like a wine-soaked dream. Laughter from them all.

Like these corporate lads, I've always found the Commandeur a bore. His talk of the Company, the weft and woof of the indigo trade, his endless mercantile observations: that the ziarie indigo is superior in quality to the nauti in giving a violet infusion, that its quality can easily be judged for it is lighter in the hand, but in order to judge with certainty it should be looked at before midday in the sun, and if it is pure, it will glisten and show various colors like a rainbow. And so on.

How to describe these offspring of buccaneers and opportunists, raised in opulent waterfront mansions? Perhaps I should document an inventory of these drunken corporate boys.

Clever, handsome Wouter—at eighteen the eldest and already master of a colossal fortune, a speculator's son, dispatched by the Company to report on the Indian camphor trade.

Mattys De Beere, charmer, dapper, dandy, and like his illiterate forefathers an astute and nimble salesman.

Pelgrom, a bookish Latin-spouting linguist, engaged to the Company director's daughter based in Masulipatam.

Jacop, the poet laureate's son, dreamy, romantic, seeking adventures in exotic lands.

Andries, gambler, fearsome chess player, juggler of shrewd sums, appointed chief accountant in the Governor-General's office.

Hans, orphaned, inheritor of vast indigo plantations south of Surat.

And last, the youngest at just fourteen, Carp, who having failed his school examinations, is apprenticed to learn the trade of a cotton merchant.

—⟡⟨⟩

The *Batavia* is pushing south. The wind over our starboard quarter has increased the unsteadiness in the deck. But I am gradually growing accustomed to its constant slope to the left.

This morning, stepping out of my cabin, I was almost blinded by the dense blue zone that has become our world, stretching all around, infinite and without end. The pared, naked sky arches above in a seamless azure swathe stripped of all clouds. It would drive you mad to look at it for long.

Then there is the ocean below. The ship surges on a vivid vertiginous swell, which rises and falls beneath the stern without breaking. Both elements conjoin in an improbable indigo curve informing the blue frontiers of the horizon.

At times like this, miniaturized by this vastness like an ant on a leaf, I long for the wreathed mists and rolling cloudscapes of home, which tamed and veiled the vaulting heavens, weighed the skies with rains and vapors, gave the civilized world its rightful perspective.

Wearied by the stream of people pushing and

jostling their way to the saloon, I am tempted to return to my cabin, when on the starboard side of the ship's waist I see her in her usual stance, leaning against the rail, hatless, her hair streaming in the wind.

Yes, who could not take notice of Lucretia Jansz, naïve young bride, finally freed from the fear of spinsterhood which whistles through parlors in the fashionable districts of town and retires many good ladies to prudery and lace.

Married at last, journeying across perilous seas to join her dull husband, the uppermerchant Boudewijn van der Mijlen, dispatched by the Honourable Company with a cargo to Batavia where he is to remain until further orders.

I can just see this husband of hers, ever patient, ever faithful, pacing a cedar veranda in Batavia's scorched hinterlands.

Tell me, Lucretia, is he young or old? Tell me you married too late. No, let me guess, your honeymoon would have been a Venetian tour, punting gondolas on sunnier canals, but the Honourable Company sent him away on a tall ship. Not one night together, nor a single dawn caress. Tell me you were his only love, but not his first wife; she is buried on the outskirts of town, a swaddled stillborn child at her feet. He took you there once and you trod softly on the moist mown grass between graves in the cemetery, where alabaster angels spread their wings to touch the sky, where you mouthed a silent prayer and read the inscription—1610–1628. Yes, like you, she was young. At the age she reached, you too were cupped, blistered, wrapped in hot flannels before a fire. Remember the sound of a cart outside and a single bell.

Did you cry, Lucretia, when you farewelled your husband on the teeming docks? Did you shed bitter tears? For those ships departing over the seas, they are always the same, leaving the land in sorrow and despair.

You see, Lucretia, there is so much about you I already know. Your maid Zwantie earned her guilder well.

YES, WHO COULD NOT admire Lucretia Jansz, born in one of those fine mansions on the Herenstraat, her father a renowned physician, a brother also apprenticed to the medical profession. From an early age, she too shared similar scholarly aspirations, neglected harpsichord practice, *petit point*, her sampler, to suck the marrow out of the best in her father's library and satisfy her curiosity. When she almost died nursing victims of the plague, it was time to marry her fast before she disgraced the family name with unseemly ambition.

Poor clever Lucretia Jansz. Perhaps she never wants this journey to end, is condemned to a marriage of convenience, traded to one of Batavia's wealthy merchants, those universal landlords of cotton fields and indigo plantations, corporate agents all, awaiting the Honourable Company's orders, using profits in shipping slaves to Amsterdam.

Yet, how new and exciting this voyage must seem, released from the shackles of dull balls and assembly rooms, the whispers of dowagers and chaperones sizing up young protégées in the marriage markets.

As if aware she is being watched, Lucretia slowly turns and catches sight of me standing on the quarter-deck beneath the shadow of a sail. Ah, lady, you are fair. The sun has set your hair ablaze, see how it flickers like flames. I give a low, courteous bow and smile. You barely nod your head in return. At the very least I was expecting a curtsy.

"Madame," I call, descending the wooden steps to the main deck, "allow me to introduce myself, Jeronimus Cornelisz, undermerchant and former apothecary from Amsterdam."

At my approach, I notice Lucretia seems to shrink a little beneath my gaze. Recollecting herself, she nods, but I discern no warmth in the haughty, imperious set of her face.

"Lucretia Jansz," she murmurs and extends one hand.

When I stoop to kiss the family crest on her signet ring, her fingers tremble beneath the brush of my lips and she snatches away her hand.

What can be the matter? For I've always prided myself on being a lady's man.

Once again Lucretia contemplates the ocean. I am not accustomed to such disdain but I'll thaw this ice queen yet.

"I hope you're not finding the voyage too arduous," I begin.

She shakes her head, eyes still fixed on the horizon.

By her slightly clenched jaw, the way her hands flutter toward the pearl-beaded neckline of her gown and to the rail again, she seems ill at ease in my presence. I cannot fathom it. Yet when I bow to take my leave, she decides to speak.

"You say you were an apothecary, sir." Still she refuses to look me in the eye. "Tell me, what made you abandon your profession?"

I smile for I see a chink in this lady's heart.

"Oh, I would not say I've forsaken it," I reply. "Quite the contrary in fact."

I explain: my sole purpose on this voyage is to return to Amsterdam with an untold wealth of exotic drugs and remedies from the Indias, priceless cargoes of cardamom, saffron, cochineal, musk and spermaceti, poppy seeds, Indian hemp and opiates, precious gold and silver to be sold by the leaf or in the shell— all of which, through various chemical trials, will explode the herbalist principles of the ancients and elevate all those in my profession to messiahs at last having in their possession a fantastical repertoire of miracle cures.

I so warm to this theme that I almost believe it.

"This talk of chemistry unnerves me, sir," she says. "I'm told it's a necromancer's art."

"Only by herb women in market squares afraid of losing a profit."

Lucretia wheels around to face me. Her cheeks are

flushed. At last a reaction. I like to see my words quickening her pulse.

"Why, standing here in the *Batavia*'s waist," I say, "we're poised on the cusp of change. All ages have their inventions and why not we ours?"

She graces me with the briefest of smiles.

"Indeed, sir, but I believe the pestilences of this world are best vanquished by modest, learned, compassionate men who have no desire to become messiahs."

This is said with so much fervency and conviction that, for the first time in a long time, I find myself at a loss to reply. My, this lady is fierce.

I look at Lucretia, trying to find out who she is. I've watched her walk through the swarming chaos here, the crowds, the heat, the noise—yet she walks on unseeing, detached, aloof as a queen.

I take a step toward her. Is it my imagination or did she flinch?

"You must excuse me, sir," Lucretia says, gathering her cloak about her. "I must find my maid, she's been away too long."

I bow. "Perhaps we could meet again tomorrow in the same place?"

An alert, wary expression flits across her face. But she returns my gaze undaunted.

"I am married, sir," she says in a quiet, firm voice. "Forgive me, but it would not be proper."

And she is gone.

Snubbed, rebuffed, I seek solace in watching her maid flirt with the skipper on the poopdeck. She peeps at the tilting horizon through his glass, giggles each time he measures the inclination of the sun through the backstaff.

Now the skipper places one arm around her waist and gives it a firm squeeze. But when he sees Lucretia walking rapidly across the main deck, he releases the maid and gapes with rapt wonder at the mistress instead, lips curled in a wolfish lustful leer. Zwantie laughs uncertainly, then, espying Lucretia, falls silent. There is something pitiful in the expression of a woman scorned. She tosses back her hair and smiles bravely at her Captain. Yet her eyes darken with resentment and fear.

Like a stallion led to the breeding paddock, our skipper lusts after the prime mare, only to impregnate her lesser sister trotted out and paraded from the stables for the purpose. I pity him.

RETURNING TO MY MISERABLE hutch of a cabin, I find the air is closer than before and I call for Tonks to fill my basin with water.

Despite the primitive conditions I now find myself in, I am exacting, fastidious about my toilette. Each day, admiring my reflection in a pewter hand mirror, I smooth my eyebrows into swallow wings, rub my lips with cochineal, inspect the faint blond shadows of a moustache on my upper lip, stroke the beginnings of a beard.

Naked, I am but a man, thin, stooped, bony-hipped, slight as a boy, but I've inherited my father's piercing violet Viking eyes.

Holding up the mirror, I appraise my profile, the graceful almost feminine line of my jaw, the fine-boned aquiline nose, the high sculpted cheekbones, those fleshy incarnadined lips.

Studying my image, even I'm bewitched by the narrow, clever face of a faun.

Out of daily habit, I practice my trick with the eyes, the one I taught myself at an early age when I discovered that by rarely blinking you can hold some-one spellbound in your gaze. Stoat eyes on rabbit. Old as the Devil himself, giving you the power to persuade.

I count to twenty. I can count to one hundred if need be and not a flutter of an eyelash will you see.

I look into the mirror and try to fathom Lucretia. She dismissed me like a servant—who ever heard of such a thing?

Beneath Lucretia's frosty demeanor, I detected a strange, awkward reticence. Yet she was curious enough about my trade and questioned me outright. I am baffled, and if you asked me plain, I would say there was something in her attitude that came close to dislike. Yet was I not courteous and kind? Even lied to impress her. Besides there was a kernel of truth in my reply. These spice voyages to the Indias will bring great power to the apothecary's art.

I purse my lips into a seductive pout and once again admire the faun face smiling back at me in the glass.

Torrentius once said all discourse with the fairer sex was steeped in code and, once deciphered, each word, every quizzical lift of an eyebrow, the faintest of smiles, the flutter of a fan were none other than invi-tations to pursue the chase at a stately, decorous pace, leaving not one blemish or bruise on matrimonial reputations. He said he knew the game well.

Maybe I mistake Lucretia. Surely that strange shy-ness of hers, the sudden quickening of heart and pulse, the way her fingers trembled beneath my touch, can

also be read as classic symptoms of love made mani-
fest in young lovers unable to meet each other's ador-
ing gaze, the tremor in their hands opening a
billet-doux, their rapid exits to private chambers to
compose themselves. Perhaps this poor doomed wife
feels the same for me, has been watching me all this
time. That might explain it.

Dusting rouge on my cheeks, I decide to observe
Lucretia and see this theory proved right. And I'm
prepared to wait for time—we have that in plenty.

Turning my head sideways, I notice the brine-
coated trades have coarsened the ringlets and curls on
my wig. It has a limp, tattered look and will need another powdering before the day is out.

THE WIND HAS INCREASED on our starboard side and the *Batavia* now swiftly rides the waves, retiring many to their cabin quarters. The horizon has lost its blue sharpness and the decks are swamped in spray from time to time.

I have not seen Lucretia since that first meeting.

This morning, stepping out of the saloon, I pass Zwantie on her way to the poopdeck and ask if anything ails her fair mistress.

One eye on the Captain, she gives me an impatient look.

"Oh no, sir," she replies. "My lady is in the pink of health but busy, sir."

So some suitor demands her time. Surely she would not spurn me without a trial. But when I slip Zwantie a guilder and enquire further, it seems her mistress is indeed occupied.

There are others who need Lucretia, who call for her. Others not as strong. There was the gunner's wife, bled and blistered, port wine and water her only nourishment these last few weeks. Wasting from a strange sea-consumption. Day by day, her baby grew weaker, smaller, puckered lips pulling at her breasts. Dying of colic and not even all the opiates in the world would help, nor the women who tried to nurse him while their warm, plump babies sleep on their laps. Except Lucretia, who took him in her arms, administered arrowroot, brandy wine, whatever he could take.

The baby whimpered and plucked at her gown until his eyes were wide and staring, hands curled and clenched.

Survivors and victims.

Each time, clutching the rail the Predikant climbs, fearful and reluctant, onto the poopdeck. He snaps open his little black book and clears his throat. Another sea burial. Once more at dusk, the ship's bell tolls. Poor brave Lucretia.

Then there is Claudine Patoys delivered of a healthy blue-eyed girl in Lucretia's strong hands; Sussie Fredicxs suffering severe contusions from a knock to the head on the forecastle hatch door; countless other wounds and abrasions requiring a woman's touch with ointments and plaisters.

"When not looking after the women," Zwantie confides, "she writes a journal long into the night."

A journal. Not like an explorer taking notice of lands, shallows, cliffs, inlets, bays, and capes, but a lady's log no less. I wonder how much I can bribe this maid to steal it from her. For I would part with several guilders to read the workings of Lucretia's mind.

 WE ARE OUT OF THE TRACK of other ships and the convoy has been days rolling on the backs of the waves. The rigging casts fretworks of shadows on sunlit, wind-curved sails.

Beneath their shade, seamen sit in groups on the main deck picking oakum. There is continual talk of hogging the ship, for thick spongy weed now clings to the bow and dark tendrils stream greenly from the *Batavia*'s waterline. "Hogging the ship." I've never heard of such a term. On his rare constitutionals, even our Commandeur looks baffled.

Our corporate leader spends most days confined to his cabin, sick with the flux, leaving the skipper the highest authority on board. Rumor has it among the crew, the Commandeur suffers from seasickness, *mal de mer*, is as faint-livered as the merchant wives, who slump on the deck, handkerchiefs pressed to their lips. The Predikant too is rarely seen, except of course at mealtimes, when he wolfs his rations like a dog. His endless psalm recitals and whispered prayers at table begin to grate on my nerves.

The Commandeur should take a triple dose of laudanum. Regain control. The skipper loathes him beyond measure for petty rules and trade regulations concerning ale rations, private deals, and Amsterdam port brothels. How the skipper despises his mean-spirited abstemiousness. Whenever the Commandeur orders the skipper to retire to his cabin and sleep off the brandy, our hard-drinking Captain just laughs in his face. There is scant loyalty there. And, it seems to me, the crew has grown irritable, testy of late. The Commandeur is weak. He should not be in control of the Company's gold, its convoy of ships.

Often I like to imagine myself in his position, Captain-General of this flagship, promoter of the Dutch seaborne empire to the world. Yet I, who am born to rule, whose charts have foretold I will receive fortunes and be elected an emperor among men, must swelter in this vermin-infested cabin and each day in the saloon take my place among vulgar rabble, while our peruked Commandeur mocks the very name of authority to us all.

TODAY TAKING MY MORNING promenade along the main deck, I pass the uppersteersman, sitting cross-legged in the shade of a sail, engraving the *Batavia*'s bow on the yellowed fang of a whale. At my approach, he darts me a cunning look.

"I don't recollect having mentioned my cape pigeons," he says, squinting in the sun. "As plump as ducks, slate in color, with a vermilion crest and feathers spread like a fan."

I give him a curt bow and walk on. But this curious carver rises to his feet and keeps pace with me.

"But in my opinion," he continues, "the most beautiful in the ornithoid race are my two paroqueets from Panama."

He polishes the whale tooth on the back of his sleeve.

"Their heads are of the finest purple, their necks a crocus yellow, not to mention the exquisite plumage of their crimson breasts, scarlet tails, and green wings."

He smiles in delight. "They will fetch a pretty price when I'm done."

He scans the deck. This is the languid hour. In groups and pairs, the soldiers exchange listless banter and games of piquet.

"The name is Fitz, sir," he whispers. "Birdstuffing is a hobby of mine."

There is something dreamlike about this new life I am leading.

"Although potassium bichromate might toughen the tissues without rendering them brittle, and glycerine keeps the eyes, bills, and legs both fresh and damp," he says with one quick glance over his shoulder, "in my opinion nothing works quite as well as Preservative Arsenic Powder."

Arsenic. So this fool squanders the powder's secrets on drowned gulls.

"Why are you telling me this?" I ask.

"Why, sir, my brother the skipper is most interested in your profession," he hisses. "He wants to see you, sir."

And he's gone.

―✳︎―

Later, in the solitude of my cabin, I prepare myself a small opium pipe. So the skipper requests an appointment. Seeks the advice of an apothecary and arsenic merchant. Signor Syphilis must be stalking this ship. Unless, of course, the skipper and his men dream of acquiring the gold stashed in the hold. Maybe they yearn for a new life in America, Brazil, Valparaiso. They must hate the situation they are in. Answering to the prim and petty Commandeur, who does not know aft from fore. Valparaiso. Who of sound mind would give it a moment's thought?

Yet arsenic I have in plenty. More than enough to preserve a thousand birds and sleeken feathers on countless albatross wings.

Strange, this encounter with Fitz. It seems the man was trying to tell me something. His talk of birdstuffing sounded rehearsed, staged like a conversation in code. And that mention of arsenic. Dropped in almost as an afterthought. Then his blue beady eyes fixed on mine, reading my face for a reaction. But I am not one to give much away.

There is certainly division on board ship. Any fool can feel the strain of it. Despite the protection from the *Buren*, and the soldiers' patrol, their day and night watches in the hold, the unprecedented value of the *Batavia*'s treasures represents a temptation to us all. Those hardened seamen in particular, who return to their wives with barely one guilder in their pockets, whose overpriced ale allowances and store rations are docked from their pay at each voyage end. No wonder most mariners are press-ganged to serve these Company ships. Only the greenest of runaways would volunteer for a life such as theirs. Yet just one fistful of coins would keep their families in capons and wine for years at a stretch.

As for myself, reaping as I would the greatest share of the profits from my arsenic were it to be sold at a premium on this unsettled ship, I could retire with Lucretia perhaps to a fair citadel at the world's end. There, I would repair Torrentius's shattered dreams, recruit young disciples and spread my friend's gospel to enjoy pleasure in all its forms without censure or hindrance.

~❀~

I mull over this matter for several days. The skipper is a proud man. He refuses to approach me directly and sent Fitz instead as his enigmatic envoy. Our conversation was heard on deck yet at no time aroused the soldiers' suspicions. The skipper must be cleverer than I first thought.

The more I consider it, Fitz has placed a brave new plan in my mind. Beneficial to us all.

I should meet the skipper and sound him out. I will explain that for a substantial share of the corporate cash, I will divide my arsenic powder. Three lots could be distributed among the soldiers, merchants, seamen, all those not wanted on the final voyage.

I will tell him—that the hatch must be nailed at first signal and he should take the precaution of distributing swords to several of his trusted men which they will hide in their hammocks.

The grateful skipper will grasp my hand like a true friend and reply that he is capable of commanding the *Batavia* to any part of the world, that it would only take about thirty men to rise on her.

—⫸⫷◎

Not for me the flux, the malarial fevers, the decayed unwalled cities of the Indias, the stench of plague in every street, the dust, the heat, the flies. Give me instead citrus night scents off some pirate coast and more Company cargo to seize.

I am certain the outcome of my plan has even been foretold. "Though you are a man and not a God," Torrentius used to say, "consider yourself the equal of God for you will amass great piles of gold and silver."

 WE ARE ON THE LINE or within degrees of it. Again, days drift in equatorial doldrums. Flying fish, large as herrings, streak past the *Batavia*'s stern.

This morning one of the volunteer cooks advances towards the sows' pen holding a sharpened knife before him. Sleek as lard, the piglets nuzzle close to their mothers' bellies, unaware of their fates. Unfastening the catch, the cook slips inside. The sows snuffle the air, expecting to be fed. But the boy grabs a piglet by the scruff of its neck. It squeals in surprise and pain. A sow lumbers to her feet. Quick as a flash the boy is outside the cage. He pins his prize on the deck and lifts the knife. The blade glints in the sun. Kicking and wriggling beneath his foot, the pig begins to shriek, insistent, high-pitched notes, piteous as infant wails. The sows pace back and forth, breathing heavily, knocking their snouts against the wooden bars of the pen. In one swift move, the boy slits the pig's throat from ear to ear and silences its screams. Blood whistles through the gash. The lad collects the hissing stream in a bucket.

I smile. Nice work, I tell him. And he flushes with pride.

For a man of delicate appetite, the roast suckling pigs on the menu today prove tender and well flavored.

Most nights, I watch the north star sink lower and lower in the dimming skies. Already the Plow has lost a second star from its handle and the Great Bear has dipped onto the horizon. Even the moon—this evening a transparent, sulfur-tinged crescent—floats on its back with both points level. We have traveled far.

IT IS OFF THE COAST of Table Bay when I first approach the skipper with my plan. He stands legs apart on the poopdeck, staring moodily into the distance. Every so often he strides to the rail and spits phlegm over the side. Seeing me, he nods.

"She's a good roader and sea-kindly," he mutters. "The merchants puke but she rolls easy enough."

I focus my eyes on the mauve smudge of land rising from the horizon and will the nausea to subside in my throat. How I long to step onto level shores once more. But the skipper tells me the *Batavia* will only pick up stores and not dock at this port.

Just when I am about to confide in him, he marches to the for'ard rail. "Duff," he roars.

A frightened midshipman darts into view.

"Sir?" he stammers.

"Call the leadsman, she's within soundings."

Duff scurries away.

Soundings? There is sounding enough in the creaks and groans of these timbers, the punch and hiss from each wave.

The leadsman is a small, gnarled, nimble man. I watch him scamper along the channels, a precarious platform standing out two feet from the ship. He climbs onto the outer edge, called "the chains" so I'm told, where vast bolted-iron links take the strain of the mast through the rigging. He knots a rope and secures it around his chest and under each arm. From this flimsy cat's cradle, he leans over the surging ocean plains and practices pendulum swings with the lead, an unwieldy, heavy-looking knotted line marked with bunting and leather. Vast spume-flecked waves rear and flounder below him. Still he leans into the wind and flings the lead high over his head.

The deck tilts, sheer as the slope of a roof. I grasp the rail, overwhelmed by a sudden rushing sense of vertigo. The skipper barks orders. Knowing that my scheme will take time to seep through his mind, I see it is useless trying to talk to him here. I'll wait for open seas before seeking an appointment with him again.

Later, in the privacy of his cabin, the skipper is more attentive. Spanish wine singing in his blood, he leans back in his chair and studies me as if reading wind gusts in a sail. "Your alchemy trades in secrets, sir."

I give him a courtly bow and refill his glass. He unfolds an ancient chart before me and lovingly runs a tar-stained finger against its faded lines. "The world is round, sir," he says, "no mistaking it."

Over another jug of wine, he tells me that he too is an alchemist in his secret knowledge of geography and navigation, that he is capable of calculating distances between the moon and the sun or a star, of measuring each second tumbled hourly in a single grain of sand, of computing every roll and pitch of the ocean, the tension tightening a rope, the sudden spring of a spar, the wind in his face, the tunes in the rigging, the shift and rhythms of constellations flying by.

He spreads both hands over the chart and describes how in 1541 his hero, Mercator, projected spheres onto the flat and represented the round globe on all maps of the world; how in 1599 meridional parts were calculated from these projections, which gave straight rhumbs or courses on a plane chart; how in 1594 latitude could be calculated by the angle of the sun; and by 1625 logarithms were applied to all navigational problems.

"We have come far, sir," he says.

I nod in agreement. "Our professions are in many respects similar," I say, "relying as they do on making the most delicate of observations."

"It is a matter of biding our time," he replies.

We shake hands.

"It will be to our advantage," he says. "Now there's so little personal profit to be got in the Indias."

But first, he explains, the *Batavia* must lose the convoy of ships that have been her constant companions since Amsterdam.

"Once we're well into the Southern seas," he whispers, "the monsoon gales will shift them."

I suggest it would be best to give the arsenic to one of the volunteer cooks, who, at a price, could be persuaded to slip it in the coppers.

"It's a fine green powder," I say. "I've been using it for years and it's done me no harm."

He darts me a cunning look.

"And the women?" I ask.

"There's a couple on board who'll be spared."

And we laugh.

I NOTICE LUCRETIA is always late for mealtimes. She arrives in the saloon flushed, hastily repairing her loosened hair with a handful of pins.

Taking her place among the merchants and their argumentative wives, she endures the interminable boredom of the same conversations, same complaints, whenever platters are set before them.

Today, to my amusement, a monstrous, bloated off-white fish is carried to her table.

Such is the confined space of a ship that eavesdropping has become a rarefied art among us all, offering the only entertainment the *Batavia* can afford. So I lean back in my chair and listen.

"Largest cod I've ever seen," a gold trader's wife announces, giving the fish an indignant prod with her fork.

"Correct me if I'm wrong," another spouse cuts in, snapping open a black lace fan, "but surely cod is an Atlantic fish whereas we are in the Indian Ocean."

She glares at her neighbor who is retching into her handkerchief held like a spittoon in cupped hands.

"Cod and no mistaking it," the gold trader's wife says and stabs the bloodless fish with her knife.

Then Lucretia looks at them and smiles. Informs her fellow diners that the dish in question is Portuguese mackerel, a delicacy among the people of St. Jago.

"Nonsense," the gold trader's wife says.

"I only know," Lucretia continues, stung by the undertone of malice in the woman's voice, "because I saw the crew catch a shoal this morning and asked them what it was."

Silence among them all.

"You spoke to the crew?" the gold trader's wife whispers in disbelief.

Lucretia unfolds her napkin.

"Dear child," the wives titter, peering at her with small, beady, inquisitive eyes. "Whatever next."

Zwantie darts her mistress a venomous look of triumph and stifles a giggle behind one hand.

Lucretia must long to escape, stride outside, feel ocean winds lift those heavy tresses from the nape of her neck.

At the head of the table, I see the skipper still can't take his eyes from her, despite Zwantie's simpering smiles directed toward him.

This chaperone-maid has loosened the ribbons around the neckline of her gown and leans provocatively forward to reveal a plump and creamy cleavage.

Her flirtatious strategies are lost on our skipper, who continues to gaze at Lucretia like a lover's fool.

How he would love to subjugate a high-ranking lady to his will, wipe the haughty smile from her face, cuckold her husband, brag of his virile achievements before the crew. Instead he receives the undesired attentions of a maid, who could be bought for a trinket in any port tavern.

By the frown mark on Zwantie's brow, the sullen set of her lips whenever she looks at her rival, she knows it as well.

Much to my satisfaction, Lucretia remains oblivious to the skipper's lecherous stares.

His uncouth, swashbuckling ways, the white scar stamped on his cheek, his ceaseless stream of commands from the poopdeck, merely add nautical color to this exotic floating village she now finds herself in.

I smile. Unrequited love, for a brothel feeder such as him, must be a baffling, unnatural thing.

Pushing back her chair, Lucretia asks her fellow diners to excuse her and leaves the table. Once her back is turned, Zwantie glances sideways at the skipper and giggles. Then she refills her glass and gobbles the untouched fish on her mistress's plate.

I follow Lucretia outside.

Too late. She has crossed the waist and is heading toward the stern, when the Commandeur suddenly appears from the cabin quarters.

Our leader is much reduced. He has a drawn, haggard, sunken look and leans on a carved ebony walking stick. The Commandeur gives Lucretia a stiff, military bow then winces in pain. Instead of curtsying in the correct formal manner befitting her rank, she drops her haughty, disdainful ways and rushes to his side, slipping one arm through his as if they were the best of friends.

Companionably, they promenade back and forth along the waist, she in animated chatter, he nodding gravely, marking each step with his stick. When they pass a group of sailors laying out cables on the starboard side of the main deck, the men nudge one another, exchange winks and conspiratorial glances. One raises his hand in an obscene gesture and the others laugh.

Now this unlikely couple lean against the rail in the shade of the mainyard. Should the skipper clap eyes on this hateful scene, he would not be pleased. Sliding into the shadows, I crouch behind a pile of coiled hessian ropes to listen.

"—not kept a perfect journal," Lucretia is saying. "But an account of the voyage nonetheless."

The Commandeur gazes at her with faithful, fond, spaniel eyes. "I hope there's enough interest on board for a lady to record."

"Oh, indeed, sir," Lucretia replies. "Why, in one month I've experienced more of the world than my entire life put together."

In a breathless rush she describes seeing her first porpoises in flight; albatrosses skimming each wave with the tips of their wings; sharks, their great flat heads closing in on the side of the ship, a sign of death, the sailors told her. Her oak sea chest now contains a collection of gull feathers, shells dredged from the deep in the fishing nets, even a whale tooth pressed into her hand for good luck by the uppersteersman, the Captain's brother no less.

At this, the Commandeur flinches. I notice he has a pinched, defeated look around the eyes.

"For your own safety, madame," he says, turning with effort to face her and lowering his voice, "I beg you not to talk to the men, the Captain and Fitz in particular."

This is the hour when the soldiers not on duty are released from the vile stench of the orlop deck. Watching them scramble through the hatch, the Commandeur breathes a short sigh of relief. So our enfevered leader believes he can rely more on this rag-tag bunch of scurvied mercenaries—the fool.

"As for the crew," he continues, "they're a rough lot, not used to women on board."

Lucretia laughs in disbelief. The Commandeur steadies both hands on his walking stick to conceal their tremor.

"Surely, sir, you would not deny me my freedom," she says. "Or I'd have nothing to write in my journal, except an account of the weather or the dull progress of the ladies' *petit point*."

The Commandeur shakes his weary head and sighs, tells Lucretia he promised her husband he would act as her protector throughout the voyage and, depend on it, he will.

He coughs gray phlegm into a handkerchief. Sweat beads his brow, wilts the coiffed curls of his peruke.

The Commandeur says the Governor-General speaks highly of this husband of hers, has even informed him it will not be long before his election to the executive board, that Lucretia has married a good man and that he will personally see she reaches safe haven.

Brave words. But by the sallow, withered look of him, I don't see our Commandeur lasting the voyage out. They say there is some wonderful mortality on board these ships and in the first season many are carried off by the malarial fever.

"It would give me immense pleasure," he says, taking her small hand in his, "if you will dine with me tonight in the Great Cabin. Your company would lift my spirits."

Surely she, who rejected my modest request for a *rendez-vous*—decorous, above board, to be witnessed by all in the public space of the *Batavia*'s waist—will refuse such a proposition. What can the man be thinking of—promising protection to this slip of a girl, naive young bride, then enticing her to his private quarters without even a chaperone? For that lascivious maid hardly counts.

Why, from aft to fore, the *Batavia* will seethe with a whispered roar of gossip. Already on the quarterdeck I see a brace of wives staring at Lucretia, mouthing hushed words of malice from behind their fans.

Yet, Lucretia lifts her pretty head and smiles. Those dimples appearing on both cheeks give me a fleeting, poignant image of this woman as a child. Trusting, vulnerable, kind, accepting paper twists of bonbons from strangers. She does not realize the danger she is in.

Like the Commandeur, I too wait for her answer.

"I accept gladly, sir," she says. "But I beg you to allow me to return the favor. Something in exchange. After all we're a nation of traders."

My, you are bold, Lucretia. I will not tolerate your impudence. Fitz hurries past and, seeing me in this ignominious position, kneeling behind a pile of cordage, gives an amused gap-toothed grin and waves. I pretend to adjust the buckle on one shoe.

Sunlight flickers through Lucretia's hair. A smile plays about her lips. I am sickened by this scene. Dread what she may say next. The Commandeur leans toward her, entranced.

"Perhaps, sir"—she begins, glancing at him shyly and twisting the signet ring around her finger—"perhaps you will allow me to nurse you, sir."

So this physician's daughter siphons clients from my trade, graces this palsied wreck of a man with favors denied to me. I've misjudged her. See how animated she is in his presence, how she sparkles. No evidence of frigid disdain in that light affectionate banter. This bold-faced whore has the Commandeur purring like a tomcat. Yet with me—and let's face the facts plain—she shrank from my touch and snatched away her hand.

"If only to keep you out of harm's way, I accept your kind offer," he simpers. "But rest assured, my condition is by no means mortal."

He should let me be the judge of that.

NEWS TRAVELS FAST on board ship. Lucretia now receives regular invitations to dine in the Commandeur's Great Cabin.

Rumor has it she is courting favors with the Commandeur in order to secure her husband's promotion to the Governor-General's executive board, that already he has written several letters of recommendation, even promised them state rooms in the Castle of Batavia; some believe this husband of hers is no more than a bold-faced sham, that she's now the Commandeur's courtesan hoping to profit from the private trade of precious artifacts stashed in the hold; others maintain Lucretia is a witch, marked with Satan's touch, who killed that sick woman's baby, for, when she took him in her arms, he went off his mother's milk and died, poor mite.

Whenever Lucretia appears in the saloon, the traders and their wives nudge one another and fall silent.

Learning of her defection to the Commandeur's cabin, the skipper has switched his attention to the maid and eyes her mistress coldly, with unconcealed contempt.

Ambitious, driven Lucretia, the physician's daughter, determined on a man's trade, don't you see the danger you are in, alone on the *Batavia*, surrounded by strangers?

Yet still you treat us all to the same casual indifference, have not even noticed the sea-change in Zwantie, who perceives herself your superior now she's the Captain's whore.

Lucretia must have illusions above her station, forging an alliance with the most hated man on board, making a mockery of my profession. I can just imagine her bathing his brow, feeding him marshmallow oil by the spoonful.

Such arrogance in believing herself superior to the others. Once we lose the convoy and set the mutiny in motion, Lucretia will thank me for saving her from a fate similar to that of those harpies at her table.

Imagine, Lucretia, I will say to her, the typical, tropical lives of these wives, bored to distraction, emaciated by the heat, learning patois from slant-eyed slaves, daily dealing with their sly, sullen ways, a ring pinched here, a pewter platter there.

Imagine those interminable languid afternoons when the air prickles your skin and a palm-leaf fan offers no relief each time a dozing retainer jerks the rope with his toe.

Reclining on a rattan chair, you would lace your

mint juleps with cheap brandy and your head would throb with the palpitating roar of crickets on the veranda outside, the flick of a foreman's whip, the hack and hew of slaves working the indigo plantations. It would drive you mad, Lucretia, and I've saved you.

MOST NIGHTS, I seek solace in those corporate boys, the pampered elite from Amsterdam—Wouter and his privileged retinue of friends, who continue to carouse in the saloon, ordering jugs of wine. Sometimes they chase the stewards around and around the bottle room.

"Out, cats and dogs," De Beere cries. "You've been masters here long enough, now us for a while."

Then good-natured Pelgrom hands the bewildered head steward a chit and orders more wine.

These boys love to sing vulgar tavern songs, the national anthem, and sometimes but not often the Honourable Company's somber signature tune.

I enjoy their company, their youthful faunlike grace. Although I have not entrusted them with my plan, I intend to keep these knights alive for the *Batavia*'s final voyage. A life on the high seas will suit them well.

—✦—

On my way to the privy, I hear furtive giggles from the heads. Scrambling through the forecastle hatch, I see our skipper, breeches around his ankles, embracing his inamorata the maid, one roving hand in her petticoats, the other planted firmly on her breast. Now he has her on her knees, skirts about her waist, and with one thrust takes her from behind in the Viking position, every so often giving her buttocks a good, hard slap. Even I am impressed by the way he rides her, and sweat begins to prickle the nape of my neck. I also admire the finger marks branding that white milky skin each time the skipper brings down the flat of his hand.

When Zwantie utters the lost, ululating cry which I've heard before on other occasions, the skipper convulses and, with one final shudder, is done. Panting, they sprawl in a heap.

Having enjoyed the spectacle, I consider stealing away, but opening her thick-lashed, brown, bovine eyes, Zwantie glances at her lover and begins to speak.

"My mistress berated me today for not dousing the cabin floor with chloride of lime." She sighs and absently strokes her nipples with the tips of her fingers.

Strange this female desire for discourse, when the frenzied hour is spent.

Although a faithful admirer of the fairer sex, my friend Torrentius used to say he preferred the company of those young brothel boys who, lean and famished as stray cats, stalked the shadowed streets of

Amsterdam and, once the love act was done, disappeared into the night.

Propped on one dimpled arm, Zwantie warms to her theme.

"The cabin swarms with bugs, Lucretia said, and would you believe, threw a hairbrush my way, calling me a filthy, lazy slut."

Our contented captain lies supine, sleepy, gazing at the stars.

Zwantie darts him an impatient, sly look. "Why, she's a fine one to talk, when I know for a fact she's besotted with the Commandeur. Lusts after him, no mistaking it."

At this, the skipper frowns. "Besotted?" he inquires.

With unconcealed glee, Zwantie tells him she sometimes takes a peek at Lucretia's journal, for she's no fool of a maid, but learned to read at the village school, and is better educated than many of those fine fancy ladies ordering her about from dawn to dusk with a list of chores that must be seen to immediately.

"Cut to the point, girl," the skipper growls.

Zwantie eyes him carefully before revealing she read it plain that Lucretia wonders whether the Commandeur is married—on the very next page asks if there is someone to love and hold him at night from time to time—and if not, yearns to be the one.

The skipper broods on this information. Then he spits in disgust. "I always knew she was nothing more than a bold-faced whore," he roars. "Yet the bitch even had me fooled for a while."

Zwantie laughs in delight. At last, she has ensnared her lover, poisoned his mind against her fair rival.

I am determined to lay my hands on Lucretia's journal and read this madness for myself, for I don't trust her maid.

Now the skipper appraises voluptuous Zwantie, who lies warm and yielding beside him. Lifting her rumpled skirts, he inspects the scarlet weals on plump buttocks and thighs.

"Your whoring mistress has deceived us all," he whispers, exploring Zwantie with busy hands. "And must be taught a lesson."

She squirms beneath his touch and giggles.

"How, sir?"

"Leave it to me," he replies between caresses. "But rest assured, my poppet, your mistress will never laugh in the sun again."

I wonder if Lucretia should be warned of her fate or left to destiny's capricious devices. Call me cruel if you like, but I'm more inclined toward the latter.

Once again, the skipper makes his paramour kneel before him. Although I am tempted to watch, it is late and I leave them to their games. By Zwantie's shrilling squeals, I would say that second time around, our skipper has forsaken the Viking for a more maritime entry.

FINALLY, in a stiffening brine-soaked breeze, the monsoon storms creep upon us, drubbing the skies indigo, rinsing each dawn with mauve light. The strain of waiting for the most propitious time to lose the convoy begins to oppress the skipper and his men. Even the most hard-fisted of boatswains has become jumpy, over-imaginative of late, sighting unaccountable apparitions over the ocean, sea nymphs circling the ship, lizard-tongued monsters, serpent tails entwined.

In the boredom of waiting, I keep to my cabin. This morning I light my opium pipe and send tremulous blue smoke rings soaring in the hot, still air. A streak of iridescence shimmies through the open porthole. Wings outstretched, a flying fish dives onto my lap. I push it off with a shudder. The fish slithers to the floor, where it leaps and thrashes. I crunch one dragonfly wing beneath the heel of my boot. The fish twitches, the colors of the rainbow flashing in its flanks. I fling the still flailing creature out the cabin door.

How I loathe the ocean and its fecund womb of fish scale and slime.

Once again days slide. Then the gods deal me a trump card in the Commandeur's decision to court-martial Fitz, our birdstuffer, this time caught sodomizing a netmender in the heads. Had the Commandeur been more vigilant, less distracted, he would have thought twice before ordering the skipper's brother to be publicly flogged. Anger brews among the men. They go silently at their work. The Commandeur senses their rage. Inhales it through flared nostrils like a bad smell. On the rare occasions when he has to address the crew on administrative matters—reductions in rations, the stocks in the hold being tainted—a pulse beats at his brow, a nervous tic flickers beneath one eyelid, and imperceptibly at first he begins to stammer.

Once again, he takes to his cabin. Malaria, the official line runs, although it has become obvious to us all that he is losing control.

By late afternoon, the sea is boiling, heat-blistered, waiting for rain. Great packed whorls of clouds, opaque as mother-of-pearl, press down on the ship. The skipper gives orders to bring in the sails. The wind has dropped and the heat still rises. Heavy with artillery, weighed by the cannon on her gun deck, the *Buren* wallows in these new calms and gradually loses ground.

I see the skipper on the main deck. He shoots me a conspiratorial smile and points at the three retour-ships floundering in our wake.

"The *Galiasse* should haul in," he says. "Look at her, slapping about in full sail."

He snorts with contempt. "As for the *Dordrecht* and the *Gravenhage*, such stupid seamanship I've never seen since the invention of the mariner's compass."

He rummages in a leather pouch tied to his belt and produces a whale-tooth carving of the *Batavia*'s bow.

"A talisman from Fitz, sir," he says, offering the carving on the flat of his palm.

"Take it," he whispers. Although loath to touch the brine-stained thing, I extend one gloved hand and accept the trinket.

"Stay inside," the skipper warns. "There'll be a storm tonight. We'll soon lose those bastards and the real work can begin."

Later, as I take my evening promenade, a drop of rain large as a hailstone splashes the deck. Another falls. Slow warm oily rain. Drop after drop pockmark the sun-scorched timber planks. Then faster flurries hammer the ship like musket fire. All around the stealthy momentum of the sea slides backward and forward. I take shelter on the upper decks. Sheets of rain drive against the ship. The convoy is nowhere to be seen. The skipper works his crew hard. Already the merchants have scurried to their quarters. I rejoice in the rain. When I return to my cabin, I celebrate our assured victory with an opium pipe.

I imagine the Commandeur steeling himself to each pitch and roll of the swell, holding a spittoon close to his lips. I can even hear the gasp of his prayers between dry retches. Why, our leader, our corporate man, must be pissing in his pants. And there's good reason. For tomorrow when he wakes, the storm will have abated and the convoy, his sole protection, will be lost without trace.

STRANGE HOW EASY it was, in the end, to lose the flotilla. The skipper simply allowed the *Batavia* to blow off course.

The Commandeur is distraught, has even promised a handsome reward to anyone sighting the convoy.

So at last our plans are in place. Tomorrow, the fourth of June, *Anno* 1629, Canot the volunteer cook has agreed to spike the water supplies with my powder.

The skipper will take night watch, has given orders for the Great Stern Lantern to be lit with fresh tallow. He tells me the *Batavia* is approaching the tail of the Unknown Southland.

"The trade winds are in our favor," he confides. "There's not a moment to lose."

He takes a deep swig of brandy. "At least I've saved my fool of a brother a flogging," he says. "Tomorrow the bastard Commandeur would've tied him to the mainmast."

I remind him that of everyone on board, the Commandeur will be the first to receive the morning water supplies.

He laughs and shakes my hand.

Returning to my cabin in the descending darkness, the *Batavia* seems unnaturally quiet, strangely empty of its scurrying barefooted crew, the shouts and curses from the men in the rigging.

I glance over my shoulder. This is the twilight hour when the soldiers have returned to their unspeakable, rancid coop belowdecks, the Commandeur tosses and sweats on his bed, the skipper takes his place beneath the great stern window in the saloon.

Even so, there is something sinister in this silence, as if the *Batavia* were a ghost ship, cut adrift, trawling drowned stars in its wake.

Then I see her, leaning against the rail, friendless and alone. What can Lucretia be thinking of? I must insist she keeps to the cabin quarters until the voyage is out. Who knows what the skipper has in store for her—having pledged to avenge his inamorata, the maid.

Still Lucretia gazes out to sea, watches gray-green clouds trail across darkening skies.

I hurry toward her. For your own safety, madame, I will say, please allow me to escort you below.

All at once there's a shout. Lucretia turns and looks up, startled.

Five masked men, knives between their teeth, spring from the rigging and, with supple bounds, surround her. No time even to scream.

One has Lucretia by the throat and claps his hand over her mouth. She thrashes in his grasp and kicks out with her feet. Another slips a blindfold around her eyes, a third stoppers her pretty mouth with a roll of hessian which, by the rough way he ties it, will bruise her lips.

Forming a circle around her, the men jeer and push Lucretia from one to the other. They slash her gown with their knives, cut the ribbons of her stays, rip her skirts and petticoats to shreds.

All the while Lucretia struggles until it takes three to hold her down. Helpless, she flails in loveless arms, her elegant clothes torn and in rags.

I must stop these games.

But if I rush to Lucretia's aid, how can I be sure these masked thugs will not whip out their knives and slit my throat? For the skipper would not be pleased to see Jeronimus, his partner in crime, sabotage this attack on Lucretia instigated under his command as the first stage of the mutiny.

Even if I ring the ship's bell to raise an alarm, my fellow mutineers will count me among the enemy to be tossed over the *Batavia*'s side tomorrow at the appointed time.

Whichever way I look, my hands are tied.

From somewhere, I hear a familiar, smirking giggle —the skipper's whore. What would I give to mash that smug, bovine face.

Throwing down a coil of rope, one of the men stands astride Lucretia and begins to unbutton his breeches with a deliberate, insolent slowness.

They would not dare.

The others fall silent, shifting among themselves, uncertain and waiting. Then one grabs Lucretia by the ankles and nods at his comrade to follow suit with both wrists. Together they pin her to the deck. It sears my soul to hear her muffled cries, those vain struggles.

The men clap their hands and break into an obscene sea shanty, all eyes on the masked sailor who drops his breeches with a careless, indifferent gesture.

The sight of his cruel, curved yard makes me catch my breath.

"No," a voice bellows. Not one I recognize. A sixth man, carrying a bucket, steps from the shadows and advances toward them.

"Follow orders." He pushes Lucretia's assailant aside. "Or there'll be trouble."

Setting the bucket on the deck, he distributes filthy rags to the men. "Be quick about it, there's not much time."

Lucretia lies still as a corpse. He prods her with the tip of one toe. "If anyone's been fiddling with her, you'll all pay for it."

He watches the men crowd around Lucretia. One by one, they dip the rags in the bucket and turn to her again.

"Enough," the man says. "Cover her with this blanket and be gone."

He swings the bucket over the side, rinses it and fills it with seawater. The skipper's henchmen fade into the night. The deck thuds beneath the calloused soles of bare feet.

Except for one, still belting his breeches. The sixth man marches up to him and cuffs him hard about the face. Blood seeps through his canvas mask in damp patches.

The man deals a last, final blow which sends him reeling across the deck.

"Mutiny or no mutiny, you could have had us all killed," he says, hauling the wretch to his feet. "In Batavia, they'd smash you on the wheel to the marrow of your bones for less than that."

I wait for them to disappear through the gloom of the forecastle hatch.

Now it is safe. I creep to Lucretia's side.

The huddle beneath the blanket twitches. Not a sound or a murmur. There's a vile stench in the air. What have they done to her?

Lifting a corner of the blanket, I peer at the still shape beneath and my throat contracts at the unmistakable reek of excrement. Her arms, legs, feet, even strands of her lovely hair are besmirched in shit. I drop the blanket and clamp a handkerchief to my nose.

Fighting the nausea curdling beneath my tongue, I put on my gloves, untie the blindfold, the gag at her mouth, and throw these vile instruments of bondage as far away from us as I can. Her eyelids flutter, she murmurs, but her senses drown in deep, merciful sleep.

Steeling myself, I plunge my handkerchief into the bucket and wipe her with seawater, raising one waif-like limb then another. Unpeeling the blanket from her limp form, I also soak the coarse woolen cloth in the brine and somehow manage to scrub the stinking filth from her face, every part of her smeared and be-fouled by it.

Whatever the outcome of the mutiny, I will tell the skipper he has gone too far.

At last I am done. I toss my soiled pigskin gloves, the blanket, my ruined handkerchief, over the side.

Reluctantly I remove my cloak—not my favorite lined with astrakhan, but expensive nonetheless, embroidered with silver and gold silk braid, cut in the French court fashion from the finest damask.

Lifting Lucretia, I wrap the cloak about her. Tomorrow the Commandeur will pay for betraying his fair lady to dangers such as this.

With difficulty, I carry Lucretia across the waist to the cabin quarters. For one so slender, she lies heavy in my arms. From behind the main mast, I hear a pitterpat of slippered feet, followed by that same suppressed laughter.

"Zwantie," I whisper. Silence.

"Attend to your mistress," I call louder this time. "Or—I'll personally see to it—*you* will never laugh in the sun again."

Soundlessly the maid appears at my side and gives me an alarmed look with large, frightened eyes.

Without a word, she helps me half-carry, half-drag Lucretia along the deck and down the steps on the other side to the women's makeshift cabins.

Still wrapped in my cloak, Lucretia lies back in her flimsy cot, very pale. She moans beneath her breath.

Tears streaming her face, Zwantie stares at her mistress, afraid. She draws the sheet over her gently, as if covering a corpse. The whore thinks her lover's henchmen have killed her mistress and that she'll be hanged for this.

"Tell Tonks to fetch hot water from the galley and be quick about it."

With a frightened roll of her eyes, the slut darts through the canvas flap and is gone.

I kneel beside Lucretia. Because of my part in the mutiny, because this time I could not save my lady, I give Lucretia an apothecary's gift. I remove a small phial from a leather pouch in my pocket and anoint those bruised lips with drops from a sleeping draught, which will make her sleep to the journey's end, spare her the butchery of tomorrow's dawn killings, until at last, she is awakened by a prince's kiss.

Although tempted, I am too much of a gentleman to ransack the cabin now for her journal like a common thief. Instead I'll order Zwantie to fetch it when the mutiny is over.

Farewell, sweet lady, good night.

Tomorrow, when all is done, when the corpses have been slung one by one into the waves, I will take my rightful place in the Commandeur's Great Cabin.

The Commandeur's undergarments will be soft, seductive, yielding to the touch. The cloth of the finest spun linen. The shirt light as gossamer. I will fasten the silk stockings with garters lined in gold lace. Slip on the Commandeur's tunic. Admire the mother-of-pearl buttons, the crimson brocaded sleeves, embroidered with gold fleur-de-lis. I will tie the starched lace ruff around my neck. Reach for the Commandeur's plumed hat. How it will fit, and how fitting to become a corporate man at last. Captain-General of this Company vessel.

TWO HOURS BEFORE DAWN, the *Batavia*'s bell tolls. It clangs fast with a harsh, clamorous sound. I hear wild voices, strange cries, punctuated at intervals by sharp twangs like bow-strings.

A sudden violent lurch on the *Batavia*'s starboard side throws me from my bunk. There is a crack loud as a thunderclap. The cabin tilts at a sickening angle and flings me against the door.

I lie stunned in the darkness listening to a cacophony of shouts, whistles, screams. A shrieking rent of torn wood. The entire ship judders in a thunderous uproar—then once again lurches on her side.

The cabin walls begin to quiver with a loud hammering beat.

I find myself observing their undulations in a state of detached reason. As if these horrors before my eyes were strange strands from dreams. Now the door buckles, then bursts apart in flurries of timber and dust.

I scramble through the splintered hole and rush to

the deck. A sobbing cabin boy tries to tell me the ship has struck a reef.

"I've seen waves breaking," he says. The wretch is sick or drunk or both. A jet of vomit splashes against my feet. What is there to say? Spare me the details. They're of no use to us now.

How can these seas have ransacked our plans? Rage beats in my throat. I fairly retch on it.

The soldiers pour through the hatch, desperate to flee the death trap below. "One at a time and quick about it," a voice shouts from the orlop deck. I have never seen them move so fast before.

By fuck, what has the skipper done to put this noose around our necks?

I see the Commandeur. He cowers on the poopdeck in stockinged feet, wig askew, nightgown flapping beneath his tunic. Above, the spars shiver, and several snap from their lines. The mainsail whips against the rigging. The skipper pushes the Commandeur aside.

"Out of my way," he shouts. He rushes to his men, who heave on the pumps in a desperate attempt to discharge the *Batavia*'s watery ballast.

"Set more sails," he calls. "This gale will turn her about." Wave after wave washes over him. But the skipper shakes his head like an otter and battles through the spray.

"Let go of both anchors," he screams. Fitz scurries across the flooded, wind-lashed forecastle. Deft as monkeys, the men scale the rigging, blindly obedient to the skipper's commands, each reaching for his companion's toehold.

But now the topmast splits and careens sideways, swinging raveled mats of ropes, ripped canvas, and shattered yards across the deck. Entangled in the flapping, knitted cordage, the men struggle to free themselves before the mast crashes down. Several are flipped into the air by flailing lines and strike the foredeck like soft, ripe fruit.

I run toward the officers' cabins which vibrate with a cannon-shot thud.

Pinned beneath the mast's fall Tonks the galley servant lies squirming and helpless. I press my hands against my ears to block out the sound of his screams. My entrails knot with a premonition of dread.

I can taste this fear of mine. It is strangely sour and metallic. My heart hammers against my chest and my mind is racing.

The passengers begin to scramble onto the main deck. Lucretia is not among them.

"Get back," the skipper cries. "Keep them back."

Still the mob spills through the companionway. I see Zwantie kicking and clawing her way through the crowd, calling for her Captain. I fight my way toward her.

"Where's your mistress?"

I grab her by the shoulders. She flings out her arms and almost hits me across the face.

"You must go down and fetch her," I cry.

All the while the passengers push past, desperate,

uncaring, each one for himself. I can smell the murderous fear on their breaths. Bleating in terror, the Predikant clings to his wife, swept in the crush surging toward the *Batavia*'s waist.

"Do you think I'd risk my life for her?" Zwantie screams. And with one last struggle, frees herself from my grasp and disappears into the mad jostle.

On the poopdeck, the Commandeur runs around and around in confused circles. "There's not a moment to lose," he cries. "Get to the yawls."

The skipper makes a move as if to strike him. "Are you mad?" he shouts. "I order everyone to remain on board while the ship's above water."

Fitz and the crew attempt to block the passengers' terrified rush toward the longboats secured on the main deck.

I battle against this tide of humanity to Lucretia's quarters. Venturing down the ladder, I see a soldier lurching toward me.

"Help," I cry. "There's a sick woman down here." Together we stumble through the passenger lobby.

To my amazement, Lucretia still sleeps, wrapped in my cloak, pale and still, like a child in her cot. Bathed in dreams, she almost seems to smile.

Water is seeping through the cabin floor and swirling beneath the bed.

"I can't lift her alone," I say. "Help me."

Without a word the soldier swings Lucretia in his arms.

"Take her on deck."

With a curt nod, he splashes through the doorway.

I am about to follow when I see it, floating in one corner. A journal of the finest calf vellum, spine down, soaked. I tuck the ruined wad in my cloak pocket. The soles of my boots slipping and sliding on each ladder's rung, I return to the roaring chaos above. Cowering on hands and knees, the Predikant prays. The *krank-besoeker* careens past clutching at anything, anyone to keep his balance. The soldier with Lucretia is nowhere to be seen.

"Keep them back," the skipper bellows.

Then, with a shuddering lurch, the *Batavia* grinds to an abrupt halt. All at once an eerie, unearthly silence falls. A pale sun spills on the horizon, its dim yellow light swelling behind fast-gathering clouds. A slow dawn heat begins to glaze sea mist wrapping the ship's bow.

The Commandeur creeps from beneath a shelter of sodden canvas. The crew lift their faces to the heavens. The wind whistles brittle as glass. Each man gauges every creak of the mizzenmast, the billowing leaps of the sails. The heaving ocean turns ash-gray flecked with green light. To the south of the *Batavia*, an island sprouts from the shadows. Beside it a fainter outline appears. To the north, a high hummock of land rises. All around the islands of the unknown world spring from the seas.

When the skipper gives word to abandon ship, I place no faith in those flimsy longboats and stand back from the crowd.

Hardly is the first, overladen with women, children, provisions, and water casks, lowered into the foaming tides than a wave, tall as a dungeon wall, lifts the boat and swings it against the ship's side. A boy, Canot the volunteer cook, is swept overboard. He bubbles to the surface, beating the air with his hands before gray waters close over him.

Then I catch sight of her, huddled beside the gunner's wife in the yawl's stern. She stares about her with wide, blank, unseeing eyes.

"Lucretia," I scream above the din.

Although she looks up, she does not hear me. The men pull hard on the oars. This time, the boat soars over the crests of precipitous waves and plunges out of sight. Fool that I am, not to have gone with her—

But the thought of placing one boot over the rail, then the other, clutching at nothing but a slippery rope, desperate to find a foothold, with no one to help, the boat rising and falling beneath me, steeling myself for that final jump—no, I could not do it. Not even to save my life.

Fitz and the crew struggle to launch the second long-boat. But the task proves hopeless. The lines and blocks are tangled. A hessian bundle of possessions tied to his back, Fitz tries to cut the thick cords with a knife.

The Commandeur sits, head in his hands, his body convulsed with strangled sobs. He takes no notice of the chaos around him. Does not even look up when the skipper and Fitz shin the mast and with all their strength crawl onto a yardarm to cut down the lines and free the boat. Knife clenched between his teeth, Fitz climbs into the torn rigging. It quivers in the wind. I watch him edge across the wet ropes. For a moment he stands motionless as a spider in a dew-soaked web. Then, knocked by a strong rushing wave, he almost loses his footing and clings to the spar on which he has been working. Another sheet of water rips the hessian from his back. His treasured birds burst from the sack and, uplifted by swift roaring winds, soar into the moving air, their scarlet wings outstretched in a spiraling, spinning flight, their brilliant plumage catching against the sails.

Another fierce wave sweeps across the deck. When I look up again, Fitz is gone. The skipper inches across the rigging and takes his precarious place where his brother had been.

"No," Zwantie screams and has to be restrained by one of the sailors.

The skipper works hard at freeing the yawl.

My hands tremble. I kneel on the gangway, spittle

rising in my throat. I gag and each time I spew, my bile tastes like blood.

I retreat to the saloon. There is looting and brawling. Wouter and his friends open the kegs of brandy. De Beere and Pelgrom haul several money chests from the Commandeur's cabin. They smash the locks with an axe and pilfer through the stash. All that treasure. All that corporate gold. Clawed from the ground, spliced, stamped, and embossed with the stadthouder seal. Forget the velvets, the silks and brocade. Kick aside the gilt mirrors, the silver dishes, and packed pewter. For it is gold they want. Senseless gold weights stuffed into their pockets, fistfuls of gold tossed into the air like rice confetti or tipped from their wide-brimmed felt hats.

All the time, the surf churns around us, curdles brown flecks of froth which the wind sends scattering across the deck. And the waves close in, predatory as sharks.

~∰◐

Finally, the freed yawl is lowered onto the murderous swell. The blank-faced Commandeur is the first on board, Zwantie is helped over the side. I too should join them. The skipper is calling for me.

I, outsider that I am, preferring the solitude of my own company to the rabble of common man, should be counted among those in the yawl. But shivering in a sweat of terror, I remain in the gangway, glued to the spot.

How I envy those navy boys their sure-footed, acrobatic balance, never missing a step, swinging from ropes to the yawl, the waves hissing and lunging at their feet.

Whereas I hide here, fear piercing my heart like a knife.

～❦～

I watch the yawl heel in perilous winds. The Commandeur and the skipper tack south toward a bare bluff island, first seen two miles from the ship, carrying their boatload of some fifty souls to a barren outcrop of dunes stitched with coarse grass tussocks.

Through my glass, this island looks a stark, arid, pitiless place. Coral its root and bone. Stunted scrub straggles a narrow rim of sand strewn with seaweed and white driftwood. In the shallow hills beyond, there are scatterings of sparse, scorched, indeterminate bush where clusters of taller trees rise in a haze of gray-green foliage.

The fat Predikant, first in the scramble, lies beached on the tide line, muttering senseless prayers between blue lips. Children cling to their mothers, those wide-hipped merchant wives. The women weep. I see them lamenting the dead. They must long to bury those drowned in the wreck beneath marble headstones— in fifteenth-generation vaults, graveyard plots marked in cemeteries on the outskirts of Amsterdam, not this wild pagan place where the ocean beats against the shore and offers no explanation.

Drinking brandy in the saloon, I watch the first longboat, which made it ashore, beat its way once again toward the *Batavia* through buffeting waves. Still the drunken rabble continues to carouse, opening kegs in the bottle room. I plug my ears to their crazed hyena laughter, that braying with wine-stained lips, fear only showing in the whites of their bloodshot eyes.

I put down my glass and will myself to stand. The room sways and tilts. A jug of wine careens across the table and smashes in tinkling shards at my feet. The longboat must have reached us by now. I stagger toward the door. This time, I am determined. Nothing will prevent me from reaching those Godforsaken shores. Someone lurches from the shadows and, grabbing me by the arm, forces me into a chair.

"Drink," he hisses, plucking a brandy flask from his pocket. Not a face I recognize. When I take the flask, I notice my hands are shaking.

"We'll all drink," he says. "Before we die."

"No," I cry and try to get up again. But he pushes me back.

"What's the use?" he murmurs and drains a half-filled tumbler which slides before him. Wine trickles down his chin. Cradling his head in his arms, he weeps.

I take a deep swig from the flask. My legs are heavy as lead. My boots weigh me down. Gulping the brandy, I sob like an abandoned child in the darkness.

One by one they go: the butler's mate, the cook, the cabin servants, the chief trumpeter, the carpenters, the gunners, the soldiers, the blacksmith, the cooper, the tailors and sailors.

The Company is reduced to a naked rock, a drying ground for fishing nets.

ON THE SECOND DAY after the wreck, I wake shivering in dawn light, unable to tell whether it is from the chill or an unspeakable sense of desolation. I find myself quite alone on the vessel. The drunken rabble must have fled, tried to float ashore on splintered shards of broken mast.

All about the ship, inexplicable sounds of puppy-dog whines, an incessant roar of bees. The exposed gangway stairs collapse in sudden bursts of timber. The keel hammers against the reefs.

In the hold, the tethered livestock kick against makeshift stalls and bleat in terror. I fear every clomp of their heavy hoofs. The bull pierces my ears with its enraged bellows. I hope they drown unseen down there.

I negotiate the deck. This endless deck. Uphill work. The ship is now higher on one quarter than the other.

Stray gulls hover above the smashed mainmast. Several perch on the torn rigging, preening snow-white breasts with sharp beaks.

Should I remain on board as long as the ship sticks fast to her coral anchorage or this morning attempt to reach the island? But how? Today the currents are fierce and the spars do not look secure enough.

What to do? Best to wait for rescue, for the skipper to return in the yawl. Without the panic-stricken crowd, surely even I will be able to climb aboard. But what if the ship goes down—will I be pressed like a flower beneath cold gray waters? I am tired. If you asked me now, I would say this is the darkest hour.

Hunger drives me to inspect the stores. In the galley of this phantom ship, the ashes are still warm in the cook's stoves. Copper cauldrons and ladles swing at identical angles from the narrow ceiling. A table has slid against the wall, leaving in the center of the room six chairs bolted to their original positions. On the marble workbenches is a brace of plucked geese, no doubt destined for the Commandeur's cabin. On the floor: crystal decanters, smashed dinner services, bent and dented silver platters, butlers' trays, condiment dishes, sugar pots embossed with the Company seal, and, treacherous underfoot, napkins neatly folded through carved ivory rings.

From the hold, still the sound of hoofs banging against loosened planks. The bull bays for blood. I decide not to venture there. Not just yet.

Descending the ladder to the storerooms, I count the barrels of victuals still secured by ropes and ranged in neat rows. Salt beef, vinegar, herring, anchovies, olives. Dismal briny fare. With the Commandeur's sword I prize open the wooden crates stacked in one corner—tubers from the Americas sprouting moist green stems; coconuts traded for lace fans at Table Bay and piled in their hundreds; yams, of course. I peel back the skin from one. The exposed flesh crawls with pale brown maggots. Each one the same. The coconuts not much better. Although I am able to suckle, tentatively at first, the sour green milk from several.

How I long for the simplicity of a pared orchard apple.

In the adjoining storeroom, a detailed inventory of the wines yields an excellent vintage of burgundy. The cured hams seem in tolerable condition, the jars of sauerkraut have survived intact, even the eggs rattle in their baskets uncracked. The question now is how to salvage them.

The castaway's method would be to study the ocean currents, learn their deceptive wind shadows, identify the exact set of the ebb tides, noting the time taken for each to reach the island between dawn and dusk. Endless calculations in brass cleats and lengths of hessian rope. Then when the tides turn, the singularly laborious task of lowering the barrels into the waves, using an intricate system of pulleys and weights discovered in the wardroom.

But I'm no deck swabber, rope hauler, barrel roller with a thousand sums in my head. When the skipper comes to fetch me, we'll devise another way.

I tire with the waiting. The incessant beat of the waves.

Again and again I return to the storerooms, carrying as much as I can to the poopdeck, being the highest part of the ship, and stow this futile hoard— it would not feed fifty between breakfast and supper —among coils of rope.

 SEEKING REFUGE in the Comman-
deur's cabin, I remember with a start
Lucretia's journal. It seems an eternity since I stuffed the calf vellum in
my pocket. I take out the sea-warped
folio, its smooth, creamy parchment quite ruined, the
pages glued together. I attempt to prize them apart.
Lilac ink has run in rivulets, staining her neat, sloping
hand.

I can just see Lucretia seated in her cabin, journal
propped on the writing flap, setting her quill into a
silver inkwell, meticulously drying each page with a
sander.

I imagine her saying, "I write this down because it is
important to remember."

In one margin, I decipher a date, *2nd April, Anno
1629.* At the top of a page, the words *cabin orderly,
everything fastened, bolted.* Farther down: *sadness about
him* and scrawled beneath: *as if someone close had died.*
On the next: *Never considered myself fearless before.* I
split open the stiff middle section of the journal, where
the brine seems to have wreaked the least damage.

Between ink blotches and splatters, I make out *dulled and alone*, and *sense of dread*. In the last entry—surely the night before the wreck, before the attack under the skipper's orders, when I could do nothing to save her—I read: *Never forget a face*.

Lower down, I decode, *Beardless as a boy, eyebrows plucked in thin arched lines, an expression of surprised innocence*.

At the bottom of the page: *unblinking, absent of*—.

After that the pages are blank. Who is she alluding to? Surely not the Commandeur—one of the skipper's men perhaps, or one of those corporate boys.

Tossing the journal aside, for there is nothing to be learned from those smudged, blotted pages, I stare into the Commandeur's glass. I smile and turn my head this way and that.

I parade before the glass wearing the Commandeur's ermine-lined cloak, embroidered with opals and pearls threaded through gold braid. I try on his plumed velvet hats, his calfskin boots. Opening his sea chest, I unfold the silk shirts, lace undergarments, stockings woven from the finest cotton, satin breeches buttoned with mother-of-pearl. I attire myself in this finery and admire the purple sash around my waist, the stiff white ruff ruched at the rim, just as I always knew I would.

Then I prepare myself for rescue in case there is no time to load my baggage when the yawl arrives.

First, I wrap my medicine phials and my packets of opium in the Commandeur's shirts and stockings. The ribbons, veils, and laces, my cuckold's trade, the buckles, gloves, and garters, all the accessories of jilted love, I parcel in a leather pouch drawn tight.

I slash the cloak's fur lining—although it breaks my heart to do so—and slip these rare commodities within the satin folds, stitching the tear end to end with a needle and coarse sailor's thread discovered in the Commandeur's escritoire.

Lighting a candle, I also take the precaution of sealing my poisons in their usual daytime places, the heavy silver lockets at my breast, the rings on my fingers which spring open at a single touch, the tortoise-shell boxes weighing my breech pockets.

At last I am ready. Once again, I climb onto the poopdeck. The ocean foams crimson at the horizon, but for the moment at least the waves seem to have stilled. Maybe the skipper will hazard a chance in the yawl tonight.

At every shift of the wind, the *Batavia* groans like a shot bear dying. From the foremast, a yard crashes over the bowsprit. The foretop gallants and spritsails bulge the wrong way and with a singing hiss, loose blocks and lines catapult against the rigging.

The splintered shaft of the mainmast still sways in an inextricable tangle of sails and ropes. It is not safe now to venture onto the waist and I don't like to think of the dead down there.

In the gradual darkness, I become aware of a strange, luminous, guttering light, casting ghostly shadows across the deck.

Mouth dry with fear, I turn around and peer into the gloom. Can it be that someone else is approaching my way with a torch or a flare?

"Halloo," I shout. "Is anyone there?"

Silence.

Still a pale light flickers from the stern, evanescent as a glimmer of glowworms.

I clamber onto the topmost part of the poop. Looking up, I see it. Swinging gaily from the stern, the wick still aglow in a worn nub of whale tallow, the Great Stern Lantern winks and blinks through smoky glass. Sinking to my knees I sob with relief then despair, for surely another survivor would be welcome in such a place as this. Wiping away tears with the back of one hand, I resolve to set the lantern ablaze. Like a beacon, it will burn and tonight everyone shall see, skipper included, that one last soul remains on board unclaimed. I, who masterminded the mutiny, a faultless plan—which, mark my words, would have been legendary, chronicled in history books for centuries to come—now demand rescue, damn you.

I rush to the Commandeur's cabin, rummage through his escritoire for a tinderbox, strip his candelabra of wax, and race back to the poopdeck.

There is only one small matter. Climbing onto the poopdeck rail to unlatch the lantern door. In this

gusting wind, alone on a doomed ship, it is mad to attempt it. But madder still not to have joined the others on the yawl. What would that have cost? One boot
over the rail. Then the other. I could have called for
help, had I slipped, or my hands lost their grip, palms
ripping to shreds on rough oakum—someone would
have caught Jeronimus Cornelisz, undermerchant,
former apothecary, and hauled him aboard. Instead,
ignoring the skipper's cries, I cowered in the shadows
and watched them go.

So here I am, still alone. About to embark on something dangerous, desperate. I wish nimble Fitz were
sprinting up the mizzenmast like a monkey, knife between his teeth, mocking the roaring spume below.

I step onto the rail. I close my eyes and gulp lung-
fuls of cold, clear air.

What if I fail?

What if brine spray drenches the tinderbox? What
if I open the lantern and the light blows out? What to
do then? Scream at the heavens.

Hardly daring to breathe, I unlatch the catch and
with one hand shield the glass from the wind. Carefully, I dip new wicks in the smoldering tallow and,
coaxing tender green wisps of flame, fix the candles in
their place. Gently I close the door.

A widening pool of silver light begins to illuminate
the poopdeck. They will see the lantern burnishing
bright and come for me.

AT LAST ON THE THIRD DAY, the sailors drag the yawl into the waves. This morning the seas are high, and with difficulty the men steady the boat for the skipper to scramble into the bow. The Commandeur follows, almost losing his footing in the pounding waters. Then, to my astonishment, I see Zwantie wading ahead, every so often lifted in the curve of glass-green rollers. Instead of ordering his inamorata ashore, the skipper throws Zwantie a rope and pulls her toward the yawl, where she is hoisted over the side. I fail to understand why this maid should take part in my rescue. What use is she but an additional encumbrance on board? And the Commandeur too, who by law is required to remain with the survivors, instead flounders toward the yawl, determined no doubt to salvage the Company's gold, for why else would he count himself a member of this party?

I watch the yawl attempt to clear the surf only to race backward in the swell. How long must I wait here on this nest of brine-soaked timbers ensnared between coral branches in an endless forest of reef?

Once again, the yawl puts out to sea. This time, driven by a flush of wind, she is buoyed beyond the breakers and swings toward the wreck.

I cheer my fearless collaborators, strong men all, who without complaint pull hard on the oars. I even salute the Commandeur, who shivers in the stern.

By the shoreline, the women and children call for water and bread. "*Brood*," they chant like a tedious Greek chorus.

Of the survivors, I have managed to count two hundred men, thirty women, and eighteen children. Two hundred and forty-eight souls. Wouter, De Beere, Pelgrom, those wild, carousing Company boys, are there too. Those who survived, that is. Those who swam and were not dragged down by the gold in their pockets. No sign yet of Lucretia. Or is that her I see wandering the far side of the shore? Why is she not with the others? When the skipper arrives, I will discover what has become of this lady, whom I alone saved.

The yawl dips and then rises. The skipper hauls up the mainsail. Wind shadows scuff the broad backs of fast-scudding waves. The packed plains of the ocean darken, advance.

But one whistling gust whisks the yawl into fiercer currents. Then another rips the topsail to shreds.

The yawl flails in monstrous black swell. Wave after galloping wave threatens to overtake her. Then a stronger squall speeds her toward a fractured sea-washed coral outcrop jutting above the tides one mile between the wreck and the island.

The yawl's bow scrapes against the rocks. Just in time, the skipper drops anchor. Our castaway Commandeur staggers onto this land scrap, exhausted, defeated.

Slamming my fist on the rail, I curse them, but console myself with the fact that the skipper is closer to the wreck than before.

Although I am fearful on this sea-swept vessel which threatens to lose its hold, although in a precarious position myself, it seems that yet again our Commandeur, our devoted Company man, has made a tactical error in trying to save as much of the corporate wealth as he can, for now he is separated from the others, those parched traders who pledged allegiance to his command. And who would volunteer to share that coral plinth with this skipper who scans the seas, no doubt mourning his drowned brother, blaming the Commandeur for the situation they are in?

When the yawl finally reaches the wreck, I will prepare the Commandeur a certain infallible potion of mine. Then, together over a jug of wine, the skipper and I will shake hands on a brave new plan, our former strategy having been scuppered.

In the boredom of waiting, I have observed several larger islands etched on the horizon, and sometimes, much farther still, a faint indigo smudge of land.

Venturing into the skipper's cabin, I find the walls are lined with maps, engravings, detailed illustrations of the East Indies, even a panoramic city plan of Batavia meticulously drawn by the Company's squadron of cartographers. A world map by Houtman, corporate climber that he was, depicts the track of the fleet under his command.

Much as I had expected, the compasses have been prized from their copper stands, the backstaff unscrewed from the table, and the logbook is gone too. Among papers beneath the desk, I find a magnifying glass, a telescope, a pack of dog-eared playing cards, an empty flask of brandy.

Squinting through the magnifying glass like a scholar, I study the finely shaded inkwork sketched by the Company's legions of black-suited clerks. My glass roams the charted oceans, only to return to the Dutch East India fleet anchored in Batavia on quaintly quilled curlicue waves.

Just when I decide to abandon this eye-glazing task, this aimless pursuit of dotted lines—I see it. Houtman's name italicized across a cluster of islets, seeming to share a similar configuration as this same coral shoal. A horseshoe crescent depicts the very island where the survivors are marooned, this speck the Commandeur's perch, the higher island to the north, here the reef on which the ship has run aground.

The Abrolhos. "Open your eyes," the Portuguese mariners warned. "Beware," the gulls called. But we did not listen, placed implicit trust in the *Batavia*'s course.

I even manage to decipher a minute script of meaningless latitudes—sixty leagues from Southland.

Southland—that mythical continent, stuff of navigators' dreams. Southland, who ever believed in such a place? Yet the evidence is plain, these islands nudge the dark side of the world.

Selecting the finest of pens, I delete Houtman's name from the map and inscribe my own.

ON THE FOURTH DAY, the gales cease. The ship rocks on her coral cradle. For the first time, I am able to stand steady on the poopdeck. The ship is strangely silent without the rush of wind through her rigging, the drumbeat of torn sails.

Still marooned on his bare mutton-bird rock, the Commandeur studies the wreck through his glass. Zwantie the treacherous, the deserter, lies curled beneath a blanket, cap pulled down, shielding her face from the sun.

I watch the Captain and his crew repair the yawl.

The men grow testy with the waiting. They are certain they will die here. And they can't help but speculate about who was to blame. Wonder how such a mistake could have been made unless there had been negligence on someone's part. "A straight run," the Commandeur had called it. Agra, Surat, Batavia. Wealth pledged in treaties of cochineal and cloves. They become impatient, willing to accept any explanation, obey any order to move on.

As for the Commandeur, he sits shivering in the sun from some malarial chill, the logbook perched on his knees. Tirelessly his pen travels back and forth across each page, no doubt compiling missives to the Company.

What's the use? And when all is lost, the ship wrecked, the survivors dying, the treasure trashed at the bottom of the sea—what is there to say?

Except of course the obvious: *With a hot sun about two hours before noon, we remain here in order to repair our boat with planks.*

～❦～

At last summoning the Commandeur and his men, the skipper marches back and forth, gesticulating wildly. Now he points in a northerly direction toward the high island. Behind it, a shadowed ridge of land rises barely visible above the swell.

Hypocrites. Deserters all.

The skipper and his men finally clamber aboard the yawl. The Commandeur stands alone on his rock surrounded by the seas.

The skipper begins to hoist the mainsail. The yawl bucks in the wind. The skipper becomes impatient. The winds are propitious, it's time to be off. He calls to the Commandeur. Finally he sends four of his men, my former conspirators, to fetch him. Reluctant, they splash through the waves. Every so often, they cast wary glances over one shoulder as if expecting the yawl to set sail without them. By the time they reach the Commandeur, they are none too gentle. Immediately, he is seized, half-carried, half-dragged to the boat. Were there witnesses to this event, they'd swear he had been kidnapped.

The yawl pulls hard into the wind and struggles toward the wreck. Rescue at last. I knew the Captain would never forsake me. Together we'll leave this hell hole and strike north for Batavia.

Holding on to the spanker boom, I unsheathe the Commandeur's sword so that the blade flashes in the sun.

"Over here," I cry, racing to the leeward side of the poopdeck. I lean over the rail. The time has come. I dare not look at the foaming expanse below, those shifting, hungry waters. Dare not think of the death-defying leap from wreck to boat.

Gathering speed, the yawl is coming closer. I can see the skipper balanced in the bucking bow. I cheer them on. It will not be long before they draw alongside. Now the boat heels on the frisky tail of a windshadow. The sails slam quarter back. All at once the yawl spins around. Ducking beneath the boom, the skipper hauls in the lines. Too late. He turns her about and, changing course, heads in the direction of the island.

"No," I scream. All hope gone. Everything is useless, all chance of escape. My eyes sting with tears. I've been playing games in the darkness too long. When I find some way of reaching the island, these murderers will swing from the gallows for this treachery.

Favorable currents now drive the yawl toward the island. At its approach, a cry goes up among the survivors. The fools cheer. Women and children swarm the shore. The Predikant and his *krank-besoeker* begin waving. Wouter and Pelgrom attempt to rush into the surf. Several soldiers fire their muskets, sending innumerable dun-colored birds into the thin blue air and, from the tide lines, the gulls rise shrieking.

The yawl runs close to the coast. Then, at the Captain's orders, with a crack sharp as a whip, the mainsail swings the yawl—out to sea!

An angry murmur runs among the crowd. The sails flutter wave above wave until, swept beyond the swell, they are last seen tacking northward.

An incredulous silence on the beach. As if some circus trick had gone wrong.

⁓ℳℴ

Now I know what the skipper and his crew have in mind. Hotfoot it in the yawl to Batavia. Find immediate solace in local girls and cheap brandy. Later at the court inquiry, negotiate triple pay for brave conduct, for navigating by a broken compass, beneath a maze of unfamiliar stars.

And my Commandeur, what then of him? Dispatched posthaste on a rescue ship, equipped with a team of Indian pearl divers, for this hulk will have sunk by then.

⁓ֆֆ◎

Strange to think that all our chances of rescue now depend on the Commandeur's management skills. He will need a politician's rhetoric, a courtier's guile, the persistence of a sycophant, to come out of this in a good light.

Imagine his situation. What would I do if we were to exchange roles? How to explain this disaster to the Company board, for there is no doubt—the Commandeur will be held to account.

Whispers of the scandal will hum through the vestibules, the antechambers, the council rooms, the Governor-General's department. The Governor-General will not be pleased.

Redirecting a cargo vessel on some rescue mission will not come cheap, additional salaries will have to be paid, then there's the question of personnel, recruiting a new skipper, fresh crew, not to mention the paperwork, endless memoranda filed back and forth, estimating the cost of the venture.

There will be drafts, counterdrafts, reports, and detailed studies. Only if the gold is retrieved, will the council lawyers advise rescue at the first board meeting.

Brine-blistered, guts bursting with the flux, the Commandeur nevertheless must present himself as an officer, a gentleman, captain of the indigo industry, promoter of the Dutch seaborne empire to the world.

Houseboys must manicure the Commandeur's broken nails, pomade his wind-tanned skin, smooth wisps of sunbleached hair beneath a powdered wig. The Commandeur must take care for his will not to fail, for his hand to remain steady when signing documents in his name. This time I can't but wonder whether he is up to the job.

I almost wave watching them go, the yawl now a black fleck on the horizon. Assuming that all of us here share a vested interest in their survival, I salute them. For if they fail, this narrative forever will remain untold, the flagship of the East India Fleet lost without trace. World without end.

PART
TWO

BY LATE AFTERNOON, it rains. The island wavers like a mirage dissolved of all color. On the shores, the people rejoice, open slack jaws to the heavens. Water spills from their lips, snakes between their thighs, metamorphoses stern merchant wives into summer-palace fountains. Most of all, I notice that only the soldiers fill the empty barrels with water.

In the Commandeur's cabin, letters, cashmere gloves, playing cards, a varnished globe float beneath the bunk and brush the beamed walls. It is time to leave this sinking nautical realm.

What to take? What to leave behind? A silver cask for which I've found no key, this leather purse filled with gold coins, the Commandeur's clothes wrapped in oilskin?

I stuff these and a flask of brandy in the Commandeur's cloak and, tying each corner, belt it to my shoulders like a sack.

When I return to the deck, blue-backed crabs in their hundreds scuttle sideways across the topsides, lifting and clicking scarlet pincers as if I were their new God.

More so now than at any other time, I'm afraid. Always I imagined that I'd be saved. Fear quickening my blood, I climb onto the poopdeck where waves swell in a gray flood without breaking. I listen to the ram and slam of the keel. Water hisses through the deck and spills into dark corners. I am now ankle deep and the seas are rising.

Will these waters now receive me like amniotic tides? Will I be rocked in the saline ebb and flow of my mother's womb? Submerged in a suffocating death of air, am I to be returned to the beginning again?

With a roar of rupture, this section of the poopdeck begins to break clean away. Carved on the outsides of the rail, the *Batavia*'s *mascorons*, those watchful cedar gargoyles, continue to survey the empty horizons with blind, bulging eyes. The rail buckles and rips apart. Several of the *mascorons* topple among flurries of flying timbers.

I am drawn to the familiar leer of one—my old friend Beelzebub, Lord of the Flies. The rail splinters and judders. My *mascoron* will not hold for long. I decide to fasten my chance on him. Seizing a coil of rope, I harness myself to his waist, his dancing cloven hooves.

Then, with a slow shrieking rent of wood, he plunges into the tumultuous swell.

Black, airless waters close over me, blood thunders

in my ears, something cold and unfathomable slithers against my leg. I cling to my blind and fallen angel, who bears me up—and at last bursts the smooth membrane of the seas.

The light dazzles my vision. I let out my terror in short rasping sobs, weep salt tears like a repentant pilgrim, the cloak still bundled to my back.

I drift for hours measured in fear until on strong running tides I float toward the island.

Blinded by the sun, I arrive, sprawling on hot sands, with a sense of being drowned, rotted like a grain of wheat. I ache to the marrow of my bones.

From everywhere sounds of whispering, snatches only, ceasing, alternating, and starting up again.

"It's a miracle," someone cries. "The apothecary is alive."

The crowd presses against me. I can smell a sour-sweat stench of death. Quick questing hands untie the sodden cloak.

I listen to the clink of the brandy flask being passed from one survivor to the other. There is a murmur of approval.

"Look what he's brought us."

Once more the flask is passed around.

"Brandy for the sick."

"The apothecary will heal us." A woman's voice this time. Not Lucretia's nor one I recognize.

"His arrival is a sign from God." The Predikant's nasal whine. "For it is he the Lord has chosen to deliver us from these dark benighted shores."

They fall silent. A child begins to sob.

"With a trumpet blast the Lord has sent out his angels," the Predikant announces in a tone of rapture. "They have gathered his chosen from the four winds, from the farthest bounds of heaven on every side. Let us kneel."

I open my eyes and smile. Eagerly they carry me along the shore. I see that some attempt has been made to build a series of primitive shelters beneath the thin shade of thorn thickets resembling our own native gorse. Around these huts—mere piles of driftwood pegged in the ground—stones have been stacked against the wind. In these dismal hollows small fires gutter and streams of smoke ripple the hot air. Everywhere sand blows fine as flour.

Strange to observe the wreck from the vantage point of land. The *Batavia* must have lifted from her coral vise, for she seems closer to the island than before, so much so that with the tide far out, I see, the survivors will be able to drag rafts to within a quarter of a mile of her.

Perhaps I should have waited before taking a chance on that cedar gargoyle? Yet the ship lists badly on her starboard side, and from the fractured poopdeck, one last splintered *mascoron* swings from torn rails.

~{{@

I am taken to a narrow enclosure—planks of wood driven into the soft sands—and lowered onto a split damp square of canvas which serves as my bed.

Clasping a sea-stained Bible beneath one arm, the Predikant kneels beside me.

"Where is the lady, Lucretia?" I ask.

He tells me she was found wandering on the far side of the shore, enfevered, delirious, her feet lacerated by the rocks and thorns of this land.

"She is strong, sir," he says. "At least she's safe. The women are guarded by the soldiers day and night. The barber has every hope of her recovery."

I smile. I knew Lucretia would be returned to me before long.

Fondling the crucifix at his neck, the Predikant begins to pray. "Without yesterday's heavy rains, it would already have been murder and cannibalism, and everything most horrible," he says, tears streaming his cheeks. His belly trembles against his scarlet waist sash.

"Even so," he whispers, face close to mine, "the number of people here cannot hope to live on the little water they have."

Nodding in agreement, I instruct him to organize every man, woman, and child to dig for wells.

"Now that the storms have cleared, the remaining longboat must be sent to salvage cargo from the wreck."

The Predikant shakes his head. "The boat was smashed when it came ashore," he says in a tremulous voice. "But all on it at least were saved."

"Then a raft must be built," I continue. "The *Batavia*'s stores remain secured and intact."

Our ravenous Predikant licks his lips. "Ever since your miraculous arrival," he says, "the seas continue smooth as a bolt of raw silk."

I instruct him to make sure that the men sent on the salvage mission also retrieve the treasures, which will demonstrate our loyalty to the Honourable Company should a rescue ship arrive.

"What stocks remain here?" I ask.

Counting on stubby fingers, the Predikant itemizes our meager rations: twelve water kegs—stored on the first longboat—now replenished by the rains but not expected to last more than a week at the most, supplemented by a further catchment of water collected in part of the mainsail washed ashore from the wreck; of the provisions: seven barrels of preserved meats, carried in by some miracle on the tides.

A bleak inventory, I'm the first to admit. Not even a keg of wine or a hogshead of rum.

"There is not a moment to lose," I say. "We must reclaim as much from the *Batavia* as we can."

I hand him a small opium phial. "Take this to the barber attending the sick. Make sure Lucretia receives her share."

"Why, sir, all would have been lost without you," the Predikant gushes. He stoops to kiss the Commandeur's emerald ring, a perfect fit on my left forefinger.

"How so?" I inquire. He darts me a hopeful, yearning look.

"Now that the Commandeur, our highest authority on board—"

"Has betrayed you," I cut in. "Broken the Honourable Company's rules and deceived us all by his desertion in the yawl."

The Predikant glances fretfully over one shoulder.

"I confess that with him and the skipper gone," he says in a whisper, "there's been no order, sir. Everyone runs riot, each man for himself, except of course the soldiers, but even they're losing heart in this place."

He explains that on the third day, a group of survivors, fearful for their lives, elected an island council of twelve, including himself, who pledged to enforce discipline according to the laws of Amsterdam.

"But it has proved difficult, sir," he says, glancing again over one shoulder. "We've no defined leader among us."

I raise one eyebrow. "No leader?" I say. "Not even yourself, my dear Predikant?"

"Too kind, too kind," he murmurs. "But I'm a mere clergyman with a hungry family to protect."

The Predikant eyes me thoughtfully. "Truth be told, I'm counting on you, sir."

He pauses and dabs his brow with a handkerchief.

"In that terrible stampede to leave the wreck, everyone remembers how you stood back from the crowd, kept your head, saw to it the women and children went first. Why, so I'm told, you even returned to the cabin quarters to save the lady Lucretia when her treacherous maid had left her for dead."

I stare at him in astonishment and almost laugh. Now this sentimental blubber of lard weeps.

"Heroic, selfless behavior which puts us all to shame, sir."

So I am hailed their hero. Seizing command of this island might be easier than I first thought, armed as I am with promises of cures from my arsenal of medicine phials. To the common man, the apothecary's art is a curious one, imbued with the same mysterious celestial power as our Predikant's craft, his prescriptions of psalms endlessly recited from that little black book.

Look at the minister now, on his knees, Bible clasped in plump white hands, still droning on about my miraculous arrival.

"Daily, I prayed for your survival. Oh Lord, I said, save the undermerchant who was prepared to sacrifice his life for others. And this morning, the Almighty answered my prayers."

The Predikant looks up. An eager, joyous expression lights up his pale round face. My, how he wearies me.

"You can expect my vote, sir," he says. "You must restore discipline, otherwise people will begin murdering one another in their beds."

I thank him graciously. This man is putty in my hands. It's the merchants I'll need to persuade and the soldiers in particular.

"Do you believe your council of twelve will accept me as governor of this island?"

"There's no doubt of it, sir. The council tried to rule and has failed."

"Keep me informed," I say. "For I'll only act in accordance to the people's wishes."

I extend my hand. With difficulty the Predikant rises to his feet and again kisses the ring on my forefinger.

Bowing, he pushes aside the canvas flap which masquerades as a door.

"One last thing," I call after him. "Please send Lucretia my fondest respects, explain the opium came from me and will hasten her recovery. I'll seek an appointment with her as soon as the barber assures me she is well."

"Consider it done, sir."

Stumbling out, the Predikant shields his eyes from the fierce snow-white glare of the shoreline, the ocean's relentless turquoise dazzle. How I long for the tender muted shades of home, morning fogs rolling in great gray dew-drenched clouds across the canals, winter crocuses pushing through frost-stiffened earth. I would exchange my soul for those early spring months when the hoary damp air is expelled in clean, cold streams from one's lungs, when dawn mists gather in swirls at the hem of your cloak, and the sun swallowed by clouds is nowhere to be seen, except a faint glimmer here and there between the dripping branches of linden trees. I would give anything for the sound of rain splashing through leaves, a sudden shower drumming against the roof. I mourn the color green. Not the harsh emerald mosaic of live coral glinting like cheap jewels beneath each turn of a wave, or the pools of coarse moss among the scrub, but a sweet, sap-scented green like freshly mown meadows or hedgerows of dogrose on the outskirts of Amsterdam.

~❦~

This island is a desolate place: flat-ribbed dunes to the east; rough-packed coral hummocks to the west; a blank monotony of low-lying hills to the north. Extending in a slow long curve, a bleak coral shore rims this southern part of the island. Everywhere, stiff tangled scrub creeps toward the water's edge. All the while, the tireless ocean tosses dark green wreaths of weed on belts of sand. The tide line is littered with a tangle of ropes from the *Batavia*. Bleached white driftwood, knotted and entwined, lies heaped like bones in paupers' graves.

In groups and pairs, the survivors roam this harsh new home of theirs.

I watch the soldiers dig the cracked earth with bare hands, still in search of water. The merchants halloo to one another from the coarse hillocks, terrified of becoming ensnared among the thorns and briars of alien bushland.

These traders of the nation weaken. They are men, not gods, and it seems to me there are too many of them.

Only I, Jeronimus, have a plan. Only I think ahead to the future, to the rescue ship glancing the reef on a low tide. The crew rowing ashore. My new mutineers aiming their muskets. Quick, clean, efficient. When it is over, I will wear another uniform, crisp, starched, virgin white and recruit a skipper to navigate the sliding constellations to the Ivory Coast.

 WOUTER'S VISITS cheer this period of convalescence. He brings oysters and news that the traders now call this place Traitor's Island, it being the one the treacherous Commandeur sailed past. They pray for my recovery.

Often in his descriptions of the crazed brawls which, before the rains, flared over the water rations, Wouter flushes beneath the intensity of my gaze. Such an innocent, yet how corruptible that rosebud mouth of his.

"On the first day," he says, "we kept four barrels of water from the others, which we hid behind the rocks."

"You did well," I tell him. "For otherwise how could you have survived?"

"Then we stole bread and some cheese we were distributing to the women and children. After all we're entitled to privileges over the others."

"Of course," I assure him. "You are noblemen from Amsterdam. Superior by birth and rank."

He takes a pack of playing cards from his pocket and splices them fondly.

"Precious rations," he says, "should not be squandered on the traders."

"That's for me to decide."

Stung, Wouter's cheeks flame crimson. But he does not look me in the eye. He knows: if he were resourceful, if like myself a natural born leader, he would have organized a proper salvage mission, instead of pilfering bread crusts and water from the gullible traders.

These corporate youths lack initiative, which will suit my purpose well.

Although in principle I agree with Wouter that the survivors must be severely rationed, and without question more so than ourselves, it is also imperative that I keep these boys, the pampered elite of Amsterdam, firmly in their place. Already Wouter presumes too much in this kingdom of mine.

"Why, they don't even dig latrines." He changes tack slyly in a voice shrill with outrage. "They'd rather shit like pigs outside their huts."

"Well, under my command," I say, "your first task will be to hand out the shovels."

Now he sulks, arms folded, eyebrows knitted in a scowl. First the wreck, then the skipper's trickery, now this prima donna's petulance.

Watching the sullen set of his jaw, I decide for the moment at least on flattery as the most effective strategy to wipe the sulks from his face.

"Have no doubt," I begin, "that in recognition of your senior position within the Company, you will help me govern this island and I will appoint you to the highest rank."

He darts me a cunning look.

"How much power will I have?"

"More than you can imagine," I reply. "For I've only your best interest at heart."

Perhaps I should confide in Wouter. As water is scarce, the numbers here must be reduced by cunning and stealth, for musket fire alone would not shift this mob. All the easier, later, to overpower the rescue ship when it arrives. Wouter and the boys will get the crew drunk; dispatching them will be a simple job. Then, with the corporate treasures stashed in the hold, my band of faithful followers and I will sail to pirate coasts on distant lands.

Give me one lost empire on a cartographer's map, plotted on hope and chance trade winds. Crown me King, carry me triumphant on your shoulders to a canvas castle, set me down on a throne of straw, hand me a wooden scepter and your signatures in blood, and I will appoint you my chosen ones.

ON THE SIXTH DAY, calm skies and seas meet in an equal line of eggshell blue.

I am well enough to leave this wretched enclosure and inspect the island, barely thirteen miles long and four in width.

My boots crunch shells and broken coral, which shatter underfoot with a tinkling musical sound like crystal. Land crabs the size of rats scuttle across my shadow and shrink into dark damp fissures beneath piles of weed and coral debris. The shore stretches mile after interminable mile before tapering into a weathered limestone point where the ocean flings high spouts of spray. Beyond there is the shimmer of the open sea, where the sinister shadows of sharks splicing the waves have been seen.

The reef runs parallel to the coast about two miles out, hemming us in. Pinned on her sharp-toothed coral spine, the *Batavia* resists each merciless brine-swept assault. The men should be able to reach her in time.

In places by the tide line, needle-thin grass leans into

the wind. In others, luxuriant, tight-budded purple blooms cling to dead coral. There is something almost corrupt about those dark-curled fleshy petals sprouting among broken shards, stark white and brittle.

In intervals between scrub, dunes lie shallow as graves, their slack flanks blown and blunted by the winds.

The shore slouches low, almost flat to the water level, as if this sparse atoll were cast adrift on the surface of the seas and we voyage still.

Whichever way I look, the ocean refracts an intense lapis lazuli light. There's no softness or redemption here. Every outline is sharp, chiseled, changeless. The scorched scrub leaves will forever shiver in the wind, sand and grit will always scatter in flurries across the shore, these lizards basking on rocks will whisk endless clouds of kelp flies with their tongues and, motionless in the shallows, cormorants will spread their wings to the sun, day after day, year after year for all eternity beyond the compass of time measured by man. My flesh creeps at the thought.

This island unnerves me. Such desolation I have never seen. I've not even the heart to explore beyond the point. I'd be more at home on the moon than this barren wind-strummed place.

Once again I look at the wreck glued to its sea-washed anchorage. Imagine the Company's prized vessel reduced to this: unpeopled, a ghostship with cattle lowing in her hold.

I hear a shout. At last, I see the soldiers hauling a raft to a sandspit in the shallows. They heave and strain at the ropes. Crafted from two spars lashed together, laid over with scraps of ship decking and boards prized off the broken longboat, the raft is a fine one at that, narrow, almost as long as a barge. The carpenter and his son did well. They will be rewarded for their diligence. The men stand waist deep, sluiced by the swell. With difficulty, they steady the raft. One of the soldiers heaves himself aboard. I hurry toward them.

"Let nothing go to waste," I call out. "From these salvages, the island shall be furnished befitting our ranks."

All aboard their unwieldy vessel, the men nod in agreement. Somehow they manage to pole and punt in the shallows, making slow progress to windward before paddling in frantic, urgent rhythms across deeper channels.

I watch the raft nudge the *Batavia*'s stern. As most of her starboard side is now submerged, I am amazed that the soldiers are still able to scramble into the flooding holds. So determined are they to lay their hands on the stores that this first venture lasts for hours.

Eventually even the bull, flailing in midair, is lowered by ropes into the sea and, urged by the fierce shouts of the men, it manages to plunge through the waves, rolling the whites of its eyes, spraying spume through its nostrils. The goats are delivered the same fate and, finally, one by one they scramble ashore, miserable as half-drowned cats, shaking saltwater from heavy coats. Now the pens of hens are tied fast to the raft. Sadly our tender piglets and sows are nowhere to be found.

Wouter and his friends disperse in groups to tow barrels drifting in the currents. I must keep a watch on them.

Tucking his prayer book in the fold of one sleeve, the Predikant too waddles toward those jubilant shouts from the reef. Sleek as ducks, his wife and daughters follow him in single file.

All day the exhausted men journey from wreck to island in the raft, bringing stocks of sails, ropes, tents, bedding, carpets, cookpots, barrels of beef, salt pork, herring, wine, brandy, the water supplies of course.

With infinite care, the money chests, the Company's gold and priceless artifacts, are secured and ferried ashore. I am pleased with their efforts. For only I, Captain-General of this island, will take possession of the Company's cash, the Commandeur's clothes, and all the national treasures once destined for private trade.

~⚬⚬

For my lodgings, I have in mind an enclosure overlooking the main encampment on a knoll shaded by sturdy clusters of foliage and refreshed by sea breezes.

Of all the positions on the island, the situation I have chosen seems the most fertile. Gaudy painted butterflies flicker between vines adorned with flowers not unlike our own native columbine. In the scrub beyond, yellow-breasted birds the size of wrens carol songs in a pitch pure as nightingales.

ON THE SEVENTH DAY, the men continue their trips to the wreck, loading the remainder of the stores onto the raft, managing this time to bring furnishings ashore, curtains, blankets, rugs, chairs, even the Commandeur's escritoire and the Captain's table prized from the saloon, as well as chests of damask, braid, gold epaulettes to smarten the uniforms of Company men, bolts of silk, cambric, and satin to be worn by their wives at seasonal balls. Emboldened by their frequent missions, the men retrieve cutlery, plates, all manner of cooking utensils from the galley, tools of their own trades, tar, rope, buckets, saws, tacks, nails, hammers, adzes, marlinspikes, shovels, sail needles, thread, all weaponry, boxes of gunpowder, muskets, sabers, and cutlasses.

I exult in their work. Back and forth they go. Tonight I will ensure triple rations of ale are allocated to all those who risked their lives in the salvage mission.

As the gods, mine that is, have cast me here, now it is foretold. For do not imagine that the voices, those siren songs stalking the narratives of my dreams, have ceased. On the contrary, they insist more, and it would be foolish not to listen.

Descending the hill to the main encampment, I find the women sitting in sullen idleness. They don't even fish although this afternoon the reefs lie exposed at low tide. Instead they squat by those dismal, guttering fires on the sands, lost in blind thought, their gaze forever seaward as if expecting something to happen, for the rescue ship, for any ship to arrive.

The squalor of the camp is unspeakable. Children play languid games in the dust. A stench of excrement rises in clouds of flies everywhere. I must set the carpenter to work. One sudden squall and this place will be blown to shreds. Despite the stunted quality of the vegetation surrounding the shore, land must be cleared for the construction of dormitories, council headquarters, not forgetting latrines, of course.

I find Lucretia huddled beneath canvas shade outside a miserable driftwood hutch near the Predikant's lopsided shack, roofed with ripped sails. The barber must have released her from the sick tent. Musket loaded, a soldier dozes in the sun.

Someone has given Lucretia a change of clothes. She wears a simple blue cotton shift; her luxuriant hair is swept beneath a snood, revealing the grace of her long swanlike neck. She stares ahead with the same blank expression as the other women and rocks back and forth on my cloak—the one I wrapped her in that last fateful night. Although the sleeping draught I administered was strong, I wonder if she remembers any details of the attack?

At my approach, Lucretia looks up, startled. Her lovely face is drawn and pale, slender wrists and arms inflamed with bruises and scratches. I will give her some ointment before these cuts ulcerate in the heat.

Kneeling, I kiss the ring on her finger. This time I notice she does not snatch away her hand.

"I'm told you saved my life when the *Batavia* hit the reef. And for that, sir, I am indebted," Lucretia says in a flat, toneless voice.

"I don't recall the precise events of the wreck," she continues, in an inaudible murmur so that I have to lean close to listen. "I only remember that I slept as if drugged, tormented by nightmares, ghoulish, morbid dreams which I tried to fight, but no matter how hard I struggled, sleep refused to release me."

She draws a thin cotton shawl around her shoulders and shudders.

I take her hand in mine. It feels limp, lifeless. She shuts her eyes.

"And when at last I woke, I found myself here."

This is uttered with such bitterness and finality that it wrenches my heart.

But, as I had hoped, my sleeping potion did work its magic. Lucretia's memories of the assault remain embalmed, wreathed in strange, vivid opium visions of a hallucinatory kind: battles between the horned and the haloed, a thunder of cloven hooves, the ceaseless beat of angel wings, voices calling, calling in the saloon of a sinking ship, sinking endlessly down into gray, green waters. Yes, I know the dream well.

"The treacherous Commandeur has forsaken us," I say. "In his absence, I beseech you to consider Jeronimus Cornelisz your protector."

Lucretia stares at me, then turns her gaze to the soldier slumbering beneath scrub shadows, the Predikant's wife shooing fractious children playing in the sand at her feet.

"Thank you, but I do not see the need, sir."

I look at her and she meets my eyes undaunted. Lucretia is a fighter all right.

"My only hope is to die with dignity and grace," she says. "Should a rescue ship not arrive."

Suddenly Lucretia throws back her head and laughs. There is something defiant, blasphemous, shocking in her laughter, as if she were taunting the gods to strike us down. Then she cradles her head in her arms and sobs like an abandoned child.

I am at a loss as to how to comfort this lady. Another dose of opium perhaps. She wipes her face against the sleeve of her gown. Again, I am shocked by this gesture and search my pockets for a handkerchief.

"My maid has betrayed me, but not the Commandeur," she says. "The Commandeur is an honorable man. He will return. We must be strong."

Although tempted to disabuse Lucretia of this opinion—the Commandeur is nothing but a coward and traitor, what more can be said of him?—I observe her ghostly pallor, the suffering etched in her brow, and remain silent. If the Commandeur represents her only hope, then let it be. Above all, I will do everything in my power to ensure Lucretia survives.

She takes the handkerchief I offer and crumples it in the fist of one hand. "But if I decide to accept your protection, will you consider doing something for me in return?"

I, who am destined to rule here, find myself baffled, disarmed by this lady, robbed of my tongue. Any of the other women flung on these dismal shores would exult in the undermerchant's promise of safe haven, but not so Lucretia, who insists on barters and exchanges.

She points to one old crone clutching a half-dead child on her lap, another woman wailing as if possessed, two children shivering in the full glare of the sun.

"The people believe your survival a miracle, they pray daily that you, the apothecary, will be their healer and savior."

She lifts her face to me, beguiling.

"Well you must prove it to them, sir," she says. "And

in exchange, I promise to obey your every command with regards to my safety."

So, clever Lucretia hopes to strike a deal. But I am impressed by the way that on every count, the conditions of her proposal lie in my favor. Although loath to waste precious opiates on this ragged mob, whose numbers I plan to reduce in any case, a few droplets from my medicine phials will surely win their trust and ensure my election as governor of this isle.

And Lucretia, the physician's daughter, will admire my knowledge of the apothecary's art, defer to her leader, even learn to love or at the very least like him in the end.

But she's no fool. See how she protects herself in that last cunning clause—"with regards to my safety" —a small-print codicil allowing her to disobey my wishes if it suits.

I tell Lucretia that as I was able to bring ashore most of my supplies, the very purpose of this visit is to ascertain the needs of the sick. I also remind her the barber has already received one of my opium phials, which surely must have speeded her recovery.

Lucretia graces me with a smile and, to my amusement, blushes. I think it would be easy to make her my accomplice, for she has a will to live despite that genteel desire to die with dignity and grace.

I instruct her to tell the women they must gather outside my enclosure at noon tomorrow, where all will receive medical dispensations as I think fit.

She studies my face with large, watchful eyes.

"Good," she says simply.

Why be disappointed in this reaction? Lucretia has never been one to give much away.

I hand her a small jar of ointment.

"This balm will heal the cuts on your arms."

Lucretia holds it to the light. "Who ever thought we'd be reduced to this?" she says.

I pour a small measure from my brandy flask. She takes a sip and then another.

"We must be strong," she whispers again and again like a mantra. The brandy seems to calm her.

"I owe you an apology, sir," she says at last.

"How so, dear lady?" I ask.

"I fear I may have misjudged you on the *Batavia*, and I apologize for my coldness."

Slowly, slowly, like coaxing a wild songbird to alight on my finger, I am taming my pretty thrush, crumb by crumb.

"Why, think nothing of it, we have time in plenty to renew our acquaintance."

I take her hand and bring it to my lips. I study her carefully but she does not flinch. I would kiss every part of her if I could, but I must move gently.

Instead I describe the verdant hillock overlooking the shore, cooled by sea breezes, where flocks of birds chirrup among the vines and butterflies the size of wrens flit like jewels from leaf to leaf.

I ask if she will join me there in a separate lodging next to the one I intend to have built.

"The soldiers are encamped below. You'll be safe."

Lucretia casts me a steady, thoughtful look.

"Thank you, kind sir," she says. My heart stirs with hope. "But I cannot."

She glances at the Predikant's wife shaking coral grit from her slippers, a brace of wives crouched disconsolate around a fire, murmuring among themselves and every so often peering our way.

"Please understand, the women could not tolerate it if I were seen to be given privileges over the others," she whispers. "I must stay here."

Grudgingly, I concede she has a point. It is a matter of biding my time for I, Jeronimus Cornelisz, future Captain-General of this island, am toying with the notion of taking this fine lady as my wife. Mark my words, she will be led like an empress to my quarters.

ON THE EIGHTH DAY, hot, dry winds gust, sending matted weed tumbling across the shore.

Under the carpenter's supervision, the men are working hard to clear land behind the encampment. From dawn to dusk, the island resounds with the crack of axes splitting wood.

It is most fortunate that most of the victuals and the Company's treasures have now been brought ashore from the hold, as high seas begin to wash away the central sections of the *Batavia*, leaving only the shattered remains of the poopdeck hinged to the reef.

This morning's tides delivered one drowned sow, her pink hairy belly brine-swollen, but edible enough, a sea chest crammed with bonnets, slippers, snoods, gloves, pearl buttons, lace ruffs, the usual haberdasher's stuff in the way of silken threads and needles;

a dented silver soup tureen; a butler's tray, its polished walnut veneer salt-stained, blistered; a child's christening mug initialed with the letters *FC*; and most extraordinary of all, the ship's bell, still attached to the deck beam, which the soldiers dragged ashore like a leviathan from the deep. It now hangs from a timber pole outside the council tent.

All morning how our childish Predikant loved pulling the bell rope. It reminded him of the carillons of home, he said, swinging back and forth, until eyeing him sternly I made him agree to my proposal that the bell should only be rung to summon island and council meetings or in matters of great emergency.

Of our salvages, brought in on the raft or washed ashore by the currents, I have inventoried one hundred biscuit and bread casks; sixty barrels of cured provisions, mainly herring, salt beef and pork; fifty sacks of rice, thirty of corn; nineteen egg boxes; sixteen brandy kegs; most of the Commandeur's fine wines packed in cases, which I've not yet had time to open and count.

Tethered to a post in a clearing of scrub, the bull pines and wastes in this heat, won't even nibble a leaf, let alone the piles of kelp brought daily for his nourishment. Soon it will be time to bring out the knives. Water cannot be squandered on this beast which before us all loses meat from its muscles. Besides, I long for the taste of roast beef.

The goats seem happy enough scampering from

rock to rock, fossicking among the weeds, but before long they too shall be dealt the same fate.

Of our water rations, fifty-two barrels now supplement the stocks already here, allowing each man, woman, and child three cups a day for the next few weeks, without of course taking into account the likely chances of squalls replenishing these stores.

But with a number of survivors relocated to the neighboring islands—let us say half if all goes according to my plan—these supplies would sustain those who remained for another month at the most, by which time a rescue ship might arrive.

The *Batavia*'s bell tolls. I am summoned by the island council, the twelve wise men elected before my arrival.

"The first question," the Predikant begins, "is how to distribute the rations."

The council members stare at him sadly. These stern, decent, upright folk, distinguished burghers, merchants, bankers, the kind that preside with pride over dull banquets in guildhalls, appear uneasy, uncomfortable with their newly appointed roles. They fidget on rough-hewn benches in this broiling makeshift tent. One gray-haired veteran responds by clearing his throat. Beside him, a moustached comrade inquires if all the barrels have been retrieved.

"Have we ascertained the precise value of the stocks?" asks another.

Yet another makes the point that all monies and valuables from the wreck should be guarded day and night, for they remain the Company's legal property.

"But what about the food?" the Predikant says in a plaintive voice. "As council members elect, surely we should be allocated double rations."

They continue this dismal discourse for a while, bickering over cups of wine, until I interrupt by saying that before his desertion, the Commandeur had given me to understand—by shouting orders when the yawl approached the wreck—that the number of people who were here together on this island had to be reduced to a very few.

Much to my amazement, they nod in agreement. Except for one plump burgher who gives me a startled, puzzled look.

"Given the scarcity of fresh water," I continue, "search parties must be sent to the neighboring islands—the high island to the north of the wreck and the one south of here. And should water be found then many of the survivors will choose to camp there. Others, of course, will remain here to guard the Company's goods."

The Predikant holds up one hand like a child in a schoolroom. "But would those who decide to go be sent regular supplies of provisions?"

"Perhaps," I reply. "Yet for obvious reasons they must be encouraged to subsist on the native flora and fauna already there."

At that the Predikant visibly brightens. He pats his slack belly. "My, it's an excellent plan."

But our portly burgher frowns and shakes his head.

"We should all stick together," he says. "There's safety in numbers."

"I agree," another veteran opines. "Besides, no one would volunteer to risk their lives in the search for water."

I smile, reassure him, them all, that several of the survivors, young, brave, hardy men, were already known to me from Amsterdam.

"Leave it entirely in my hands," I say, "and I assure you, gentlemen, these brave lads will be privileged to embark on such a mission."

The Predikant claps his hands.

Our burgher rises stiffly to his feet.

"We have been elected to govern this isle until the Commandeur's return," he says in a grave, pompous voice. "And you, sir, have not."

"We must take a vote," mutters his ancient companion, "in order to decide whether an expedition should explore these islands."

His fellow councillors whisper among themselves.

"With so many gone," one dewlapped elder begins, "I will certainly vote against the risk of losing more young lives."

So the slippery council divides and sides against me. I, who have watched them steal the water rations from their own wives and daughters. Why, these traders did not even think to build a raft in order to salvage stores from the wreck. At least not until I arrived.

The Predikant calls for order.

"I place my faith in the apothecary," he cries, raising his right hand.

In the end, there are nine votes against three. A clear victory.

At the meeting's close, the council members who voted my way thank me.

"We would certainly have died here without you," the Predikant confides.

I return to the solitude of my new enclosure, situated on the hill commanding views of the ocean and shoreline. Held together with rope and sail, it is still a flimsy shack, awaiting stronger planking, a door, maybe a plaited-leaf roof, but once my quarters are ready I will furnish them with the Commandeur's personal effects, now guarded with the stocks by the main encampment. His Persian rugs will cover the bare earth floor, I will adorn my primitive bed—a rough kapok mattress supported on wooden crates—with satin quilts, silk pillows emblazoned with peacock wings. In the center of the room I will position the Commandeur's writing desk, its green baize surface spotted only in places. For a table, I intend to use the Company's money chests.

So now I relax, taking care to dilute my medicine

phials, every so often fanning flies from a tumbler of brandy.

There *must* be fresh springs on this island. I'm prepared to take a wager on it.

A sudden thud outside makes me start. Lifting the canvas flap, I surprise a wild ratlike creature, larger than a March hare, sitting on its haunches. She stares at me full in the face, quite unconcerned, quivering her nostrils with a watchful curiosity. When I unsheathe my saber and steal toward her, she stands on her hind legs, small gray paws clasped against her chest as if in prayer.

I lift my sword. Darting me a look of mild reproachfulness, she hops a small distance away then skitters into the bushes. So—yes—there must be fresh water then. How else would these creatures survive?

I follow her into the brittle, palpitant scrub. At some distance, I can hear the thump of her tail, the thud of her hind legs.

Using my sword, I thresh a dusty track through the tangled undergrowth. All around I can hear the scratch and rustle of countless unseen creatures. My heart leaps at the sound of their chirrups and whispers. There's water on this island. No mistaking it.

Sun filters through the leaves in shafts of pale yellow light. Clouds of midges descend on me. Still I hack and hew a wide swathe through dense briar thickets. I pause for breath in a clearing which opens onto the shore near the point where a vast network of rocks are twice daily rinsed by the tides. Then I see a great hopping herd of these same creatures, loping toward the beach. The most peculiar mammals I have ever set eyes on. They pause by pools of thick green spongy moss. I watch them graze the matted turf, staring all around and starting at each roar of a wave.

I creep toward these rats. One raises its head, ears cocked and nostrils flared. At the sound of a snapped twig, they rear on their hind legs and in a single bound, veer into the scrub.

However these creatures have adapted to the privations of this primitive land, they will nevertheless extend our stocks. Best not to inform the traders. Best to select my own hunters. Wouter will lead the twilight expeditions.

Approaching the verdant patch where the rats had been, flattened and trampled by their paws, I notice in one place the moss appears softer, greener. Kneeling, I examine it closely and to my amazement find this vegetation not grass at all but a carpet of succulent leaves resembling wild cress, which means those creatures were not grazing as I had surmised. I tear at the weeds and almost weep for joy when I plunge my hands in dark, brackish water brimming a shallow hole no larger than a hip bath. Cautiously, I lick the droplets from my fingers, trying not to think of the beasts snouting this same source before me. Lukewarm, brown as boiled tea, it has a rusty, acrid aftertaste but is in many ways fresher, sweeter on the palate than the *Batavia*'s stores. I top up my brandy flask. Half and half, just as I like it.

Glancing over my shoulder to make sure no one is about, I mark the spot with a twisted net of fallen branches. Then as best I can, cover the weeds with leaves. Should any of the survivors chance on this watering hole I will feign surprise, suggest they be rewarded for their initiative; otherwise I will keep this secret to myself, not to be shared with Wouter and the boys, nor even Lucretia, I am sad to confess. I know mankind. If supplies run low, it will be every one for himself. This discovery will save my life.

Shame to think of those wretched hopping animals reducing these springs, but armed with muskets we will soon eliminate all such vermin from this place and have roast meat in plenty.

~⊶⦵

At noon, one by one a ragtag crowd of women and children begin to appear outside my enclosure. Passive, obedient, they wilt beneath a burnished sun. Lucretia too climbs the hill, carrying a toddler on one hip. She takes great supple, swinging strides, oblivious to the heat, flies alighting at the corners of her eyes and lips. Now she stops to help a woman who has snagged her skirt on gorse thorns.

I am glad to see Lucretia has regained her strength, recovered from her ordeal. Once again she lifts the child and picks her way through the track, calling out words of encouragement and caution to others stumbling behind, not so nimble or fleet of foot.

Seeing me, Lucretia nods. Her face is radiant, shining. My strong lady has willed herself to be brave.

Watching the women, I am amused by the sea-change in those matrons, who, parasols atwirl, parading the *Batavia*'s waist, sneered and gossiped cruel malice behind Lucretia's back.

Piteous and forsaken, exposed to the harshness of this barren land, these women are now grateful that Lucretia takes the lead, guides them step by faltering step from rock to boulder, through stiff grass tussocks where they whimper, lifting petticoats in fear of insects or snakes.

"Wait, my dear," they breathlessly call, slipping and sliding in torn soft-heeled slippers. And ever patient, Lucretia takes yet another mewling brat in her arms or goes to the aid of some old dowager scaling a slope in the hillside no steeper than the footbridges of Amsterdam, over which not so long ago this same withered dame would have scampered without a thought between invitations to card parties.

Scrutinizing these people with my shrewd apothecary's eye, I discern no one truly mortally sick or dying among them. Not even that child, now riding Lucretia's shoulders, waving a stick in one chubby hand, chuckling at the shimmer of innumerable leaves set afire by sea breezes in the sun.

I greet Lucretia with a courteous smile and escort her to a place in the shade.

Taking off my hat with a flourish, I bow before the crowd. I am ready. It is time for this charade, this monstrous circus act to begin.

Like a saint, I go from one to the other, anointing swollen tongues with droplets of aniseed and water. It seems to do the trick. Jesus too must have exploited this simple phenomenon of mind over matter.

"He lives. His fever has abated," one mother cries.

"It's a miracle," shouts another.

Such exultation I have never seen. How they savor each inhalation of breath and peer about this desolation in wonder.

See, Jesus, you charlatan rogue, cheap miracle monger, I know all your fancy tricks. I can cure the sick, resurrect the dead from their graves. Can't you hear their dry bones rattle? And although unable to swim, lately I have found that I too can walk on water. Now there's just the small matter of turning it to wine.

With a start, I find Lucretia's green eyes fixed on mine.

"You're a good, Christian man," she says. "I thank you."

Despite my entreaties to stay with me awhile, she shakes her head and joins the cavalcade beginning the descent to the encampment. Almost with relief, I let her go. Although it is only midafternoon, the day has been long and I'm weary, in need of an opium pipe.

LATER, taking a stroll along the beach, I find my boys dozing like a pack of dogs beneath a clump of low-lying trees.

Instantly they wake at the sound of my footfall. Wouter rubs sleep from his eyes.

"You appear before us as if in a dream," he says.

Gracious De Beere spreads his cloak on the sand and invites me to join them. Wouter scowls at the encampment. He wrinkles his aquiline Roman nose at sour drifts of smoke from those infernal campfires.

"The traders stink," he says finally.

De Beere looks up from manicuring his nails. "There are too many of them."

Pelgrom spits in disgust. "Water rations are pilfered and wasted."

So I tell them of my plan to search the neighboring islands for fresh sources. "Whatever the outcome," I say, "it's imperative to reduce the numbers here if we're all to survive. A reconnoiter trip will determine whether a separate colony of evacuees can be established."

De Beere fans the still air with his hat. "Maybe we

should head the search party," he says, "in order to examine these islands for ourselves." He slides Wouter a stealthy grin. "There might be more to gain from them."

Shielding the sun from his face with one hand, Wouter nods in agreement. "If so, it would be best not to tell the others," he says in a low voice.

Throughout this discourse, the younger boys, Carp in particular, hang back, awkward and shy in my presence. I beckon them forward. Through matted curls, Carp and Hans peer at me fearfully. I notice they are the only ones who have neglected their appearance and not bothered to wash. De Beere, on the other hand, looks as if he has just stepped from a piazza ale shop. Wouter much the same.

"Please, sir," Carp ventures, digging his toes in the sand. "Please, sir, when will the rescue ship arrive?"

What to tell this skinny shrimp of a boy? The others remain silent. Not wishing to be reminded of their predicament, this hiccup in their fates. They are young. They are boys. This an adventure. A treasure isle. Already they've stashed the gold they had hoarded in their pockets.

Taking Carp's small hand in mine, I suggest we take a bet on it. At this Andries perks up. So we while away the hours, working out various hypotheses, the speed of the trades, the seasonal currents, the navigational skills of the Captain and his men. At last Andries places his sovereign on forty days.

Then I unpack a basket of cheese, bread, a fine flagon of French wine.

Wouter and De Beere fall on this simple repast, gulping the wine. Only the youngsters take cautious sips from the vessel. For, unlike the others, they have not yet acquired a taste for it.

How pleasant this is, reclining in dappled shade with my boys. We talk of the past, of our lives, of Amsterdam. It comforts them I think to hear about the old world, the known world, its familiar ancient contours mapped on varnished globes. So I speak of that place, that land we used to call home.

~☙~

When I have won the trust of my brave castaways, my future disciples sprawled on hot sands, I will explain that in his teachings Torrentius described how he had wandered through the deserts of Egypt and communed in silent tongues with the wisest sheiks of Syria.

"Sin is only what a man imagines to be within himself," he would say, pursing his mouth in a patrician smile. His lower lip was fleshy, protuberant, curled like a pink worm against the gray fringe of his moustache. Although he was forty-eight years old, he still wore his hair coiffed on all sides, immaculately powdered. Whenever I kneeled and kissed the ruby ring enclosing his right forefinger, I noticed his hands were surprisingly smooth and unfreckled by age. His skin smelled of attar of roses and something else, a sharp, musky scent which I could not define.

In his teachings, Torrentius explained that the words of Christ and the Apostles had died with them centuries ago. He scorned all scriptures and denounced the resurrection.

Sitting at his feet, we, his disciples, were hungry for answers, impatient for solutions, giddy with a sense of unlimited freedom. We had turned our backs on the smug smiles of plain Mary and her plump heaven-pointing child. We laughed at baby Jesus, mocked the overwrought rhetoric of prayers.

In the beginning, Torrentius exacted rules and regulations, all of which we observed with monastic precision. I have always enjoyed the asceticism, purity if you like, of an ordered routine and I fitted in well with this way of life. All prayers, indeed any suggestion of religion, were strictly forbidden. Few crimes would be more severely punished than these. Again and again my friend warned us against the ludicrous fables invented by charlatans and impostors. He even appointed spies to inspect the bedrooms at night. They were also to inform him as to any alliances, those ridiculous friendships that can flare among young boys.

Although accounts of these were more for his amusement and always went unpunished.

At that time Amsterdam brewed with religious ferment, insatiable and ravenous as lust. The wars against Philip II of Spain and his retinue of hooded inquisitors had made our city the fairground, the marketplace of all religions vending toys, ribbons, and fanatical rattles.

Heretics fleeing neighboring nations poured through our gates. Portuguese Jews, French Calvinists, German Lutherans, and a multitude of sects swarmed from inquisitorial cages. These refugees soon discovered that silver in the palm could blunt the sharpest differences, and they paid high fees for assemblies where some might receive sacraments naked, others indulge in promiscuous couplings or decree themselves the true children of God.

Every barn, attic, and cellar in town howled with the Bacchanalians' drunken cries, the Brownist cobblers' verse, the Panonians bleating to their shepherd God Pan, the naked Adamites, and that drear Family of Love who thought fucking your neighbor's wife an original idea.

"Let us see how shining and durable they are," Torrentius said. "Let us see if they can push the State with their horns."

I agreed these sects were more to be laughed at than considered. But we were proud too of our libertine city, its lax, indifferent laws where no questions were asked and burgomasters turned a blind eye.

Even the Catholics, our Popish Roman enemies,

transformed front parlors into chapels which reeked of incense and tallow. Nuns and monks continued to count rosary beads behind cloistered walls. Portuguese rabbis raised mighty synagogues, galleried replicas of the temple of Solomon. Anabaptists thronged the marketplace without exciting offense or comment in their ridiculous black garb of fringed breeches and round velvet hats.

Torrentius reveled in this absurd babel of tongues. For they suited his purposes well and drew a veil over his own designs to teach us to despise Christ's bland slogans, particularly the one about loving thy neighbor as thyself.

"In Amsterdam, men are free," he said, "to practice their beliefs without censure or restraint."

He even read the pamphlets handed hot off the press by fast-talking zealots on street corners.

We agreed with the Adamites that Christ was a mere man and denied his divinity. We even toyed with the idea of meeting naked in the manner of the firstborn, but by then Torrentius had issued us new scarlet uniforms which we liked. We shared the Bacchanalians' pleasure in paganism and good French wines. And although we mocked the Family of Love, we respected their belief that women were mere cattle and chattels to be communally shared. We found nothing new in the Antinomians' doctrine to break all laws and dismissed the Panonians as primitive hill men.

We were exultant then, siphoning from other sects

eager followers to our creed. In the beginning we never thought we'd strum such a common chord in man. Our ranks swelled with endless supplies of fresh young recruits. But looking back, we had spawned a monster when we should have kept the organization lean, sworn our disciples to secrecy in all their hot-blooded pursuits. However, they were harmless pleasures compared to the full repertoire of sin that can be had.

Yet these vain lawless children of ours brought my messiah down with their indiscretions, carnal acts in churchyards, puerile obsessions with masked flagellants, sniggering schoolboy desires to arouse brothel flesh with stolen crucifixes and altar candles. It was only a matter of time before Torrentius was forced to control his unruly rabble with locks and keys, before rumors and vile gossip began to circulate among the stern stolid traders of the town and the magistrates closed in.

~᚛᚜~

Now I gaze at the boys fondly, Wouter boasting of exploits in port brothels and taverns, De Beere doing his best to match him with conquests of his own, Pelgrom and Jacop cutting in with obscene jokes, Andries shuffling cards with a casual croupier's hand, little Carp and his friend Hans, sitting shyly side by side, staring at the others with wide, innocent, uncomprehending eyes.

It is they who will become Torrentius's new disciples. I vow to teach them all I know, corrupt each and every one of them to the very marrow of their souls.

ON THE NINTH DAY, the skies remain rainless and clear. Trenches dug three feet below the dunes' surface have exposed several springs and rivulets. But no collective body of fresh water has been discovered. Clearly these sources will not sustain all.

My enclosure is almost completed, fan-shaped leaves line the walls, the roof is thatched with woven reed. All I now need is a door, instead of this wretched canvas sheet which flaps in the wind and keeps me awake at night.

Much to my astonishment, the foolish council agreed to my suggestion that the *Batavia*'s stores be housed outside my quarters in a simple shed of slatted driftwood, some distance from the pilfering survivors but close to the soldiers bivouacked below in a hollow of the hillock. No theft will escape unnoticed, as this position commands uninterrupted views of the encampment and all activities along the shoreline. I was asked to keep a daily inventory of the supplies and calculate a fair method of distributing the rations. When they voted on this matter, it was once again a case of nine against three.

Everything is going according to plan, just as I knew it would.

The carpenter and his skilled team of recruits have been most resourceful in building the new campsite. I admire their efforts.

Among a chaos of trodden tracks and shorn stumps of bush, the squalid tents and huts remain huddled between poles cut from the *Batavia*'s main mast and flimsy timber scaffolding which sways and creaks in the wind. The soldiers scour every inch of shoreline for pieces of spar and decking.

Nails held between ruddy lips, hammer clasped in nimble hands, the carpenter rushes to and fro, relieved to be at work and of use once more. Sweat soaks his bare back. His freckled face glistens in the sun. Damp sea winds have curled his tawny hair tight as astrakhan. I've never really noticed before but there is something of the Viking in his frame, the blue glint of his eyes. Every so often he shouts instructions to his devoted young son who lashes cedar planking, torn from the *Batavia*'s poopdeck, with thick hessian cords. The tailor joins him, sitting cross-legged, splicing rope, deft as an elf. When not tending those injured by the wreck, the barber, a steady, good-natured, shambling soul, works indefatigably at building a sick-hut set apart from the main encampment in a rough clearing of scrub. He whittles poles with the end of his lancet. Strange to see his sharpened blade put to such a use, that familiar instrument which at home inspires terror in everyone. They whistle while they work, swap jokes and banter. Even Stoffel, the dour-faced caulker, laughs at some jest, then concentrates once again on planing planks from washed-up timber. Judith, the Predikant's buxom eldest daughter, sits among them plaiting leaves. Such a tableau of industry, a picture of camaraderie. Sometimes, outsider that I am, I wonder what it must be like to join the common lot of man.

I find these traders banter in a language which I can never understand. Sometimes (but not often) I'm surprised by a sudden rush of envy for their simple lives, their loving wives, whereas I stand outside the fence of their smug, snug domesticity, shut out, lean and hungry as a wolf.

I scan the shore for Lucretia and discover her squatting with the women at the tide-line, prizing oysters from rock clefts and fissures, a stern, determined look on her face. Every so often she pauses to wipe sweat from her brow or smooth wisps of hair flying loose from a crimson bandeau.

What can she be thinking of? My lady must not toil with the others, harvest these seas like a common fishwife. Now I see she scrabbles the wet sands for cockles and whelks, digs furiously with bare hands, tossing each find in a bucket. She will ruin her nails. I must stop Lucretia from this vile, demeaning labor.

I stride across the sun-baked coral. The beach trembles in the shimmering haze of the heat.

Strange that with each passing day on this desolate isle, I seem busier than ever before, more so even than my past life in Amsterdam. Somehow the interminable march from dawn to dusk, yesterday for example, never offers a moment's respite. You would think boredom would be the castaway's fate. Not so here for the time at least.

Head bent, Lucretia prods the blade of her knife beneath a bearded, barnacled mollusk clamped firm to a rock. With a quick turn of her wrist she uproots it from an ancient web of weed pip and root suckers. She weighs her prey in one palm, then, taking the knife, lays it on the sand and splits open the shell. Tucked and cushioned on a bed of mother-of-pearl, a pale fleshy knotted tendon spasms. With a furtive, guilty gesture, Lucretia looks about her, does not espy me watching in the shadows and, lifting the shell to her lips, swallows the live creature whole.

I turn away in disgust, frightened almost by Lucretia's determination to survive despite even herself.

"Madam," I call. She looks up and, flushing with shame, flings the empty shell in the waves.

"You must not work like this," I say. "It's unbefitting to your rank."

Leaning back on her heels, Lucretia wipes the knife against the hem of her skirt and smiles.

"If I don't work I think, and when I think I am sad."

She jabs the blade beneath another oyster with an angry, violent motion which makes me wince.

"Besides, there's no such thing as rank in this place," she says, dropping it into her bucket. "Although we have stores from the wreck, sir, we must do everything in our power to keep ourselves alive until the rescue ship arrives."

Lucretia puts down her knife and stares at the dazzling beach and the ocean. Streaks of spume foam from the reef. I shield my eyes from those bright fierce peacock waters, swirling and swilling among endless scribbled scrolls of coral until they are flooded by the dark blue of the open sea. The heat presses down, almost visible.

Lucretia is not even wearing a hat.

"You must not expose yourself to this pitiless sun," I say.

She picks up a strand of tawny speckled seaweed and watches it flutter in the wind.

"If boiled, sir, I'm sure this is edible."

I notice a slight, mocking expression on her face. Is Lucretia teasing me, rebuking me for not joining the others in their backbreaking chores?

"It would give me great pleasure," I say, holding out my hand, "if you allowed me to escort you to your quarters."

"Quarters," she says. "Don't make me laugh. This is not some parlor, sir. We are shipwrecked."

Stung by the anger in her voice, I'm at a loss as to how to reply. Now Lucretia turns her attention to a cluster of limpets half submerged beneath the waterline. Green fronds of weed hang over them.

"I apologize," she murmurs, brushing a strand of hair from her cheek. "I'm not myself and best left alone."

Once again dismissed like a kitchen servant. But I decide to take my leave, for this morning Lucretia seems moody, out of sorts. Like us all, she bereaves the subtle nuances, the vaporous sliding seasons of Amsterdam.

Returning to the encampment, I kick the vile clods of coral and they shatter with a tinkling, rattling sound at my feet. I stamp on the splintered shards and grind bone-white dust to the ground. I hurl a stone at a seagull hovering above the tide line and it wheels, screaming at me, then sideslips away. I curse this wretched island, its ceaseless sea noise, the grinding roar of waves pounding the reef, the wind chasing flurries of grit across the beach, the heat beating down, drumming down, so that every sun-scorched leaf trembles and crackles in the scrub, and the tremulous haze casts strange patterns on the sands so you can never be sure whether these clumps of weed, the bleached tangles of driftwood, the ridged dune hummocks are what they seem or the mischief of mirages. I despise this landscape of coral and dust, for it will steal my fair green-eyed girl from me.

I take a swig of brandy. My hands are trembling. I must steady myself. I must watch my mind. It would be easy for madness to creep up and take you by surprise in this place. I drain the flask. I am calm now. Strong.

⁓∰☉

Later I find those corporate boys, my new disciples, engaged in games of tag and dare by the water's edge, oblivious to the activity before them, the shouts from the soldiers to help drag part of the ship's bow from the waves, the carpenter's curses, the frowns from the merchant wives fossicking the tides.

Why should my boys heed those cries when, like Lucretia, they outshine the others by birth and rank?

Wouter so clearly the leader. See how he strides ahead, taking quick, delicate steps, like a gazelle, a faun. He has peeled off his shirt. Already his shoulder blades freckle in the sun.

Wielding a sharpened stick, De Beere tries hard to emulate him. In vain alas. Yet, with his immaculate moustached courtier's smile, he plays an obedient second-in-command.

Pelgrom clowns and cheats. He squints through the blindfold and darts toward the first flit of a shadow across his path. Dreamy Jacop writes his name again and again in the sand. Bored with Pelgrom's antics,

Andries finds a flat rock in scrub shade where, dealing a flushed hand, he invites Jacop to join him in a game of whist. Frowning like Greek usurers, they squat on their heels playing for cowrie shells.

Poor Carp is homesick. He stares at the horizon, sealing him from the known world. Carp must miss his mama, his satin-frilled siblings. He dreams of his playroom, the wooden dolls, the coarse mane of his rocking horse stationed by the window like an old friend. Forlorn at his side, Hans too shares his misery. Arms linked, the two try to wander from the whoops of the others. But De Beere snaps at their heels like a sheepdog and hurries them along the shore with his sharp stick.

If I were playing chess and these boys my knights, I'd set Wouter first on the board.

~

At noon, I watch my party of explorers set off to search the neighboring islands for fresh water. My expedition leaders, Wouter and De Beere, attempt to clamber onto the raft but it rushes back on strong tidal waves. Andries tries to bellyflop aboard. Pelgrom glues root-white fingers to the raft edges. Carp seems to be drowning. He spews spume through his nose.

I forget they are city boys, inept and unnerved by the shifting equilibriums of the ocean. Used to firm

soil, polished oak parquetries, black-and-white checkered tiles. Floors you could lick with the tip of your
tongue.

Watching my boys flounder in the waves, I wonder
whether they are up to this job. Maybe there should be
more of them. Pondering my moves, I see they are all
aboard their precarious vessel. Carp vomits bile into
the swell.

⁓∰◦

At dusk, when the sun weaves gold threads in these
inky tropical skies, Wouter reports to my quarters. He
tells me they searched far and wide, scrambled
through dry scrub and in the end despaired, for there
was no water to be found on either island. Both places
proved a hard hour's punt and paddle through
labyrinthine shallows and channels from here. But
once the raft was worked to windward, it was possible
to reach both shores. In low tidewaters, my valiant
boys had to push the raft, wading and slipping on nee-
dle-sharp corals. In deeper currents, they were followed by sharks, some nudging the raft with their
broad, dark snouts, others encircling the vessel, their
murderous fins slicing the waves.

On the first island, they discovered only stagnant
pools fringed with pale green moss, on the other, several depressions where brackish sludge had collected.

Concluding his breathless narrative, Wouter begins to weep. "It's hopeless, we'll all die," he sobs.

I cradle him in my arms. "Not us," I say. "That is, not if some attempt is made to reduce the number of people here."

I dab witch hazel on his ulcerated, bruised feet.

"If anyone inquires about the expedition, you'll know what to say, won't you?"

Wouter raises his head and casts me a speculative look.

"That we've found water?" he whispers.

"There's no choice," I reply. "It's either them or us."

Poor brooding Wouter frowns, unable to resolve the matter.

"Suppose," I suggest, "you were wrong in your survey. Maybe your excavations were not thorough enough. Were more people sent across—let's say fifty at the most—then surely a second search would succeed whereas your small party did not."

Wouter's green eyes brighten. He takes my hand and kisses the Commandeur's ring.

"Sometimes," he offers, "one has to be cruel to be kind."

ON THE TENTH DAY, I tell my water dowsers to while away the sunshine hours tickling for coral trout in lagoon shadows, and as a special treat for their courage, I prepare each one a strong opium pipe.

Then, ringing the ship's bell, I summon the island councillors. Unable to endure the noise of the construction work outside their stuffy council tent, I invite them to my quarters. The council now comprises nine members. The strain of the last few days must have proved too much for our three dissenters who voted against sending a search party to the neighboring islands. Aged councillors all, they passed away peacefully in their sleep.

The traders, the barber included, have concluded that a bucket of shellfish which, against all rules, this greedy trio stole, must have been left standing in the sun for too long. And I agree, food poisoning seems the most likely explanation.

I motion the councillors to take their place in the shade around a rough wooden table which I commissioned the carpenter to make from warped salt-beef barrels no longer of any use.

"The mission to find water on the islands has proved an unparalleled success," I announce. "On the thin spit of land immediately to our left, such is the profusion of deep wells and the number of seal colonies on the shore, that I have named it Seal Island."

The council members applaud.

I tell them of pools so clear that you can see the rippled wreaths of weeds rising one above the other on a single stem, the round pebbles on the ribbed sand floor. Between mauve shadows, I say, fish flit iridescent as mother-of-pearl and, caught in the pool's reflection, trees swing heavy with plump, moist fruit, some so ripe the flesh is fit to bursting. In this place, grapes weigh the vine larger than a man's fist and pomegranates the size of dinner plates split their skins.

"The first priority," I explain, "is to send some fifty evacuees to this place. Meanwhile, the soldiers will reconnoiter for water on High Island, so named after its steep limestone escarpments."

One councillor begins to wring his soft white hands.

"There will be a riot," he says. "All will volunteer for Seal Island."

The Predikant rises to his feet. "But surely we should be first?"

I silence them. "Gentlemen," I begin, "all your names are on the list."

I spread a parchment on the table. The fools stare at me bewildered. "You were elected by the people and as such have rights to certain privileges over them."

"Hear, hear," one gold trader cheers. "Seal Island it is." Seizing the vellum, he signs beneath his name with a flourish.

"As to quelling the crowd," I add, "straws shall be distributed to everyone." Then I suggest the meeting be adjourned. "All I need," I say, "are your names on the list."

My noble tradesmen murmur among themselves. I listen to their argumentative drone—all determined to be the first to colonize my mythical Garden of Eden, which exists only in fancy, in a cartographer's dream. Now I wonder whether I overdid it.

All signatures are now on the list. Except the Predikant's.

He keeps apart from the others and loiters by the stock barrels outside my quarters. I can see he is finding it difficult to make up his mind. Should he join the evacuees on their journey, or stay here where, for the time being at least, the rations are plenty. He twists the chain of his crucifix around in one hand. Now he counts the kegs of wine, inspects the egg baskets, snuffles among racks of reef fish left to dry in the sun.

I go up to him softly. Back turned, he rummages through the tuber crates. I tap him lightly on one shoulder.

He jumps and drops his crucifix on the ground. With difficulty, he stoops to pick it up.

"Forgive me for startling you," I say. "But you have not signed the list."

His cheeks are flushed, sweat beads his upper lip. He mops his brow with a soiled lace handkerchief.

"My word, the heat," he sighs. "It will be the death of me, I'm sure."

I tell him that straws will be distributed among the people. There is not much time. His pale brown eyes slide away from mine. They are fair-lashed, slanted, like a pig's.

"It's a matter of knowing where I'll be most useful," he says quietly, glancing again at the stock barrels. "In terms of spiritual needs. Bringing comfort to the sick, the dying."

Useful, I almost say. Don't make me laugh. All voyage long I've watched you, my fat friend, reading aloud from that little black book. How the sick longed to be released from your lisping prayers.

"What about the souls on Seal Island?" I ask. "Are they to be abandoned?"

"Oh, no, sir, most definitely not."

Screwing the handkerchief into a damp ball, he returns it to his pocket.

"The council has agreed to let my sick-visitor accompany them," he says.

So he sends his illiterate *krank-besoeker,* that sallow youth, to take his place among the others. So be it.

"I hope you will not find cause to regret your decision."

He darts me a suspicious look. "It has not been easy," he murmurs.

I must watch him, for he may be cleverer than I first thought.

 ON THE ELEVENTH DAY, low gray clouds pile on the horizon, bringing a promise of rain.

The *Batavia* has broken up; the flagship of the East India Fleet disappeared without trace.

In numerous trips on the raft, the men have scavenged every part and plank from the wreckage, flensed her like a whale to the bone.

The morning tides remain bountiful. Today's delivered four clasped bedposts, a chamberpot, and a crate containing five oval shaving dishes, all in pure gold and made to order by the Mogul Court. Other items washed ashore comprise a string of twenty walrus teeth, marbled with black stripes, and a betel box. These, of course, will be taken to my quarters once the soldiers and many of the survivors have been relocated to the islands.

I ring the ship's bell to call an island meeting. Laying down tools, wiping sweat from their brows, the men tramp toward me. Muskets at their shoulders, the soldiers appear silently from scrub shade. They are a lean, tough lot and I trust not one among them.

I watch Wouter and my boys cavort on the sands, their shadows dancing in the haze of morning heat. They do not even look up when for the third time I ring the *Batavia*'s bell. Best to leave them to their games, for I have confidence only in Wouter not to give anything away if questioned about the discovery of fresh water on the islands.

Women and children trail along the beach carrying armfuls of weed and driftwood for the cooking fires. Lucretia struggles behind with the largest load.

Of late, I have noticed she has a hunted, haunted look.

When not gathering mollusks or helping the barber attend to the sick—administering palliatives from my medicinal phials, more of which I have readily given—Lucretia spends much of her time in solitude by the rock pools near the point. Sometimes she paces back and forth as if deep in thought, or stands for hours at a stretch gazing at the thunderous crash of wave after wave tirelessly breaking on the reef.

Now that I've obeyed Lucretia's wishes—relinquished no small part of my precious opiates to be squandered on malingerers seeking oblivion in stronger potions than cheap grog—I find myself once again shunned by this lady, who seems to have returned to her cold, haughty ways.

Yet I remember only four days ago, when Lucretia strode up the hill to my enclosure, a chuckling child on her shoulders, and graced me with a radiant smile. Ah, I was happy then, willing to perform any tricks that were expected and desired. I led Lucretia to a cool green pool of shade beneath the vines and spread the Commandeur's cloak on a broad flat rock sending up clouds of sapphire-winged butterflies. From somewhere in the scrub, a bird whistled a long, clear, trilling note. And it struck me then, that at last I had found a patch of paradise where I could rebuild my life. The child gurgled contentedly on Lucretia's lap and she tickled his cheek, which made him laugh the more.

Although the women were waiting, impatient for the promise of cures, shifting like cattle in a pen, I kissed Lucretia's hand. She did not resist and I remember her saying, "You're a good, kind man."

When the gods snatched Marie from me, when she died and was buried in a pauper's grave on the outskirts of town, when I laid a single white rose on that monstrous mound of freshly dug earth, I never thought my heart would be stirred by another mortal soul again.

I watch Lucretia dump her load of wood and take her place among the women.

I must not think of this lady, now I must drive her from my mind. Instead, I must persuade these people to agree to my plan if we are to survive.

A circle of upturned, expectant faces looks at me, all eyes on mine, watchful, speculative, waiting.

So I begin by reminding them that at dawn tomorrow straws will be distributed to determine in the fairest possible way who will depart for Seal Island and who will not. A ripple of excitement runs through the crowd. My description of its abundance has traveled fast. The councillors in particular seem the most eager to be off. A change of air will do them good.

I explain that all council members, excluding myself and the Predikant, have agreed to accompany the evacuees and superintend the establishment of a second camp. Five strong skilled men must volunteer to help in this endeavor.

A row of raised hands shoots up. The worthy councillors, trustees all to this Eden of mine, give one another relieved, congratulatory looks.

"As for spiritual needs"—I motion the *krank-be-soeker* to stand—"the Predikant's sick-visitor will be at your disposal." The pigeon-toed youth clasps a Bible to his chest and swells with pride.

"For those who remain, Traitor's Island will be run as a tight ship," I say. "Roster calls will be instituted for all activities, including fishing expeditions, the distribution of rations, and use of the latrines." I point to a ditch at some distance from the camp and mercifully flushed twice a day by the tides.

"The squalor of uncovered shitting holes will bring disease," I add. "Imagine how rapidly a fever would spread among us. Why, we'd be wiped out within a week."

I am pleased to see that many of the soldiers nod with approval, admire this call of mine for law and order.

The crowd begins to clap. Several of the men cheer. Then, slowly rising to her feet, Lucretia turns to me and curtsies. At the sight of her, the people draw their heads close and whisper.

I glance at the barber. By the smiles wreathing his good-natured face, I can see nothing amiss in Lucretia wanting to address the mob. Maybe, finally, my enigmatic lady will seize this opportunity to thank Jeronimus Cornelisz for curing the sick.

I gaze at these people, future subjects all. In the Commandeur's absence, I will tell them, you may call me Captain-General.

And I should not be too hasty in banning Lucretia from my mind. Perhaps, pacing these shores, the dear girl was simply rehearsing her speech.

Nodding, I signal her to begin.

"Yesterday," she announces, "I was walking by the point when I saw a speck on the horizon which I'm convinced was a ship."

Has Lucretia lost her wits? How dare she talk of matters of no concern to herself or the women and only to be discussed in private by the island council.

An excited buzz spreads through the crowd.

With a queenly gesture, Lucretia holds up one hand for silence. In a loud, clear voice, she suggests we build a fire, a beacon to be kept lit at all times so that it might be espied by a passing vessel, should the rescue ship not arrive.

"Why has no one thought to do so before?" one merchant cries. "This is the trading season, the *Galiasse* and the *Dordrecht* lost in the convoy might be passing as we speak."

"Quick, quick," our fool of a Predikant squeals. "There's not a moment to lose."

I ring the bell for order. How dare Lucretia instill such insurrection in this feeble herd of men.

A watch fire—imagine that—announcing to the world we are shipwrecked, alerting every buccaneer and pirate for miles around to the possibility that one of the Honourable Company's retourships might have floundered on the reef. Not even the soldiers with their tin drums and sea-damp muskets could defend us from savage attacks, looters seizing the *Batavia*'s priceless cargo, my rightful property.

Tomorrow I shall decree to all those who remain that rations must be prepared in a communal cooking house set apart from the shelters. Separate fires will be banned, representing as they do a similar hazard as

Lucretia's brave beacon. A watch fire—who ever heard of such a thing, sabotaging every part of my plan? Best not to alert the crowd to these dangers. The less said about the Company's treasures, which I intend to claim, the better.

"I thank you for your proposal," I say, trying to conceal the rage in my voice. "But this island lacks the resources to fuel a fire day and night."

When I add it would be a waste of timber, particularly as every spare scrap is required to build a sanitary encampment, Lucretia rounds on me.

"Far more important to plan our escape from this place," she says in an indignant tone which I dislike, "than construct a new camp, when the shelters we already have will do fine."

Not convinced by this, many of the wives shake their heads.

"This scrub is a tinderbox," I reply. "One careless spark is enough for the entire island to go up."

By nervous glances all around, I can see they had not thought of that.

"Oh my," the Predikant exclaims. "We'll be burnt alive in our beds."

Some of the women click their tongues and draw their children closer.

"We'll organize watches," Lucretia declares.

"And when all the timber is used up, what do you propose then?" I inquire.

Lucretia stares at me, eyes wide and fierce. Why

does she have to make such a tiresome scene, defy my leadership in public like this?

"I believe it's a risk worth taking," she says quietly. "And another thing, if we put every effort into attracting a passing ship, there'd be no need to leave for the islands."

Several of the soldiers begin muttering querulously among themselves. On whose authority dare she suggest an alternative to my plan?

"No," one of the councillors shouts, leaping to his feet. "On no account, my lady, will we take that gamble."

There is a murmur of assent.

This portly former bank clerk casts me a sly, servile look. "If some foolish act of recklessness sets this island ablaze, then everyone will evacuate to Seal Island, leaving us all in the same position as before."

"Without the water barrels," another councillor cries. He shakes his fist at Lucretia. "Sit down, woman, you're wasting our time."

The fickle mob starts booing and hissing.

Again I ring the bell. "We'll vote on it," I say. "All those in favor of lighting a beacon?"

Lucretia raises her hand among such a sparse scattering, there's no need even to count them.

The people break into applause. Without a word, Lucretia curtsies and, turning on her heel, strides from the meeting before it is formally adjourned.

Later I will speak to her, for this arrogance goes too far.

~❦~

I am summoned to the soldiers' encampment. The soldiers are stout, strong, land-loving men, proud, nationalistic, with a pleasure in long marches without missing a beat, complicated war games among the dunes, longing for more serious pursuits: the construction of fortifications, battlements on hills, a clearly defined enemy to pit their wits against and kill.

Maybe that's why I want to get rid of them fast— their leader in particular, Wiebbe Hayes, a hero, with chiseled good looks.

In their circle of straight, taut tents, Hayes and his men polish their boots, the buckles on their belts. At my approach, Hayes relaxes his mouth into an imitation of a smile. Deft as a seamstress, he mends a pair of breeches, each cross-stitch identical to the last. He rethreads his needle and bites the skein at one end. His teeth are sharp and white and even.

When I suggest the soldiers investigate in greater detail the exact position of the water wells found on the High Island, he stares at me keenly.

"What proof do you have they are there?"

Hayes is difficult, stubborn, a man with a liking for

hard facts, verging on the pedantic. How I loathe the honesty of his blue-eyed gaze. But soon this preamble will turn tiresome for Hayes, and I know that eventually he'll take the soldiers to High Island. After all, he likes to run his own show. Issue orders from his own hammock and tent.

Whistling between their teeth, the soldiers pretend not to listen, continue to buff their boots. They must hate the situation they're in. Are counting on Hayes to find a way out.

"The civilians will be our undoing," I hear one scarred veteran mutter to his companion, who nods in agreement and smears spittle on the tip of his shoe.

Although the French mercenaries are among them, the soldiers have united in one single group. They are programmed to survive, battle against the odds—it's all part of their training.

Hayes stabs his needle through frayed cloth.

"At the first evidence of wells," he says, "water barrels should've been filled."

I explain it had been a reconnoiter trip only. "But now water is found," I say, "surely the soldiers will undertake this triumphant task."

Ambitious Hayes the fact finder ties a double knot. I calculate his age, height, weight, the probable size of his heart. I think of my medicine phials. Just one prick of a finger would be enough.

Once more I describe High Island. Not lyrically this time. Merely elaborate on the clear streams drip-

ping through rock fissures, the ferns discovered beneath the cliffs, indications of further springs. This is
the long dry hour. The parched hour between water
rations. Several soldiers lick their lips.

When Hayes requests a private interview with
Wouter, who led the first expedition, I know that at
long last I have won. For who could doubt Wouter's
word and not be swayed by the charm, the grace, the
innocence of my green-eyed knight?

~~~

Hayes returns convinced. "He's a brave lad," he says.
"We'd like to take him with us."

I tell him the people intend to elect Wouter council
member. Again Hayes treats me to a piercing stare.

"This young, courageous boy," I say, "represents
their only hope." This is acknowledged with a non-
committal nod.

"If you want one of the boys who went on the expedition to lead you to the streams, I would recommend
young Carp."

Hayes throws back his head and laughs.

"Of what use that sniveling wretch," he says, "cry-
ing for his mother day and night."

I hold out my hand so finally we can shake on it.
But to my irritation, Hayes folds his arms.

"How do you propose we get there?" he asks in an

offhand way, almost as an afterthought. "We'll need to build another raft."

Hayes is becoming a bore. How long must I negotiate here, without even a pipe or a cup of wine? When I point out that constructing a new raft would waste the island's scant resources, particularly as the rest of the timber from the wreck is being used to build the camp, he frowns.

"Pelgrom and De Beere will ferry your men across," I say, "on the one we already have."

Thoughtful now, Hayes rubs a thin white scar puckering the skin across his brow. Beneath his bluff exterior, there's something sharp and watchful which I don't like. Before he can raise another objection, I suggest the soldiers light fires when they discover the springs, to signal that a military encampment can be sustained until the rescue ship arrives.

"And if no water is found?" he says.

"Impossible given Wouter's testimony," I reply, "but should no fires be lit, we'll come for you within five days."

Without a word, Hayes trudges up the hill and summons his men for a meeting. So yet again I, Captain-General of this island, am made to wait for Mr. Hayes to reach a decision. But I know the soldiers will vote my way.

Eventually Hayes beckons me to his bare, spartan quarters, furnished with a rough roll of blanket, his kit, not even a chair to sit on.

"As water supplies are insufficient for us all," he begins, "my men are keen to leave this place. But we must formally agree that the raft will fetch us if no smoke signals are seen."

Doubting, distrustful Hayes. Does it really matter which scrap of land we occupy? I sign my side of the contract on a creased, worn piece of vellum.

At last when all is ready, some of the soldiers even agree to lay down their muskets, in order to load the raft with five days' worth of stocks and water barrels.

"Light fires," I say, "when you discover the springs."

"Hail," they salute, clicking their heels like the painted lead toys from my childhood.

Only Hayes looks distracted. At times doubtful. Watching the soldiers scramble onto the raft, I am struck by the simplicity of my plan to reduce numbers. In one move and two trips, I will have struck forty names from my list.

AT DUSK, I find Lucretia by the point, kneeling, hands clasped, calling to the heavens. For once the winds have stilled. Even the air fanned from the ocean offers no relief. Great, glaring ocher clouds mushroom on the horizon. I fear it will be a hot sleepless night.

Against this pagan backdrop, Lucretia prays. For a ship perhaps, sails set, gliding across pearl-blue seas, the splash of an anchor rippling indigo waters, a crew rowing ashore, the Commandeur leaping from the bow, enfolding Lucretia in his arms, their kiss silhouetted against brassy skies—how any theater audience would cheer at this happy end, our tempest-tossed, castaway lovers reunited at last—but I will not have it.

"I'm disappointed in you, my dear," I say sternly.

With a frightened cry, Lucretia swings round, unaware I am standing close by.

"And so would your God be for inspiring such false, foolish hope in the people, making them believe rescue were possible from a passing vessel when you and I know there's none to be had, when we must be patient and wait for the Commandeur's return."

Lucretia remains silent.

"Why, you nearly incited a riot," I continue, enjoying the hectoring, lecturing tone in my voice, as if admonishing a disobedient child. "Had the survivors heeded your words, the entire island might have been devoured by flames or set upon by buccaneers. And then what would we have done?"

Still not one word from Lucretia. The copper-colored skies dim, tinged with a faint verdigris patina at the horizon.

Spreading my cloak on the darkening sands, I sit beside her.

"My dear lady, I only say these things for your own protection and good."

Lucretia begins to shiver.

"Have the soldiers gone?" she asks, drawing a shawl tight around her shoulders.

"Yes, and tomorrow a further group of evacuees will be dispatched." I smile. "Everything is running smoothly according to plan."

When Lucretia looks at me, her eyes are wide and startled. "But as my lady's protector," I reassure her, "I don't intend you to be a member of that party."

"What is your intention, sir?" she asks in a low tremulous voice.

I stare at Lucretia, quite taken aback. But there's no

reason for her to distrust me, especially as I've obeyed every request for opiates and remedies.

"Why, I've only your best interest at heart," I reply. "Surely you must know that."

There is a long pause. Lucretia scoops a handful of sand in her palm and watches it spill through her fingers.

"And the others?"

Were I not such a gentleman, I'd be tempted to slap her sullen, averted face.

"As water has been found on Seal Island, they'll be safe."

Lucretia frowns. She broods, thinks too much, which I find unnatural, morbid in a woman.

"Forgive me, sir, but sometimes I wonder if your description of its abundance might be mistaken, for surely these islets would all share similar topographies."

So this hussy thinks to outwit me with her outrageous cleverness.

"As neither of us has any knowledge of this diverse region, you are surprised, as indeed I was when Wouter testified to the contrary and discovered water in plenty."

I can feel the anger rising in my voice.

"If that's so," she says, darting me a cunning look, "then why don't we all repair to Seal Island instead of dividing into smaller and perhaps more vulnerable groups?"

Not even hardfisted Hayes interrogated me as sharply. Question and answer. When will it end?

"And leave this camp, which has taken so much effort to build?" I drain my brandy flask. It will need refilling before the evening is out. I offer Lucretia a last sip but she shakes her head with a prim purse of her lips. This evening, she goads me on every count.

Not content with her proposal to reduce this sanctuary to ashes, expose our position to wild, murderous, pirating men, none too tender with axes and sabers—how she would scream for help then— Lucretia now advocates we abandon this camp, lay all our work to waste.

Along with Lucretia's defiant, unruly ways, and like many of the fairer sex—guilders rattling in plump purses, spending freely on all manner of fineries, a pair of satin slippers here, kid gloves there—she demonstrates a complete ignorance of the simplest rules in husbandry, the careful harnessing of resources which are essential to the survival of us all.

"Besides," I add, "I thought it had been made clear that we can't all survive in the same place."

Rising to her feet, Lucretia brushes coral grit from her skirts in a brisk manner as if she had finally made up her mind on some troubling matter.

"Very well, sir," she says. "As I've no reason to doubt your word, at dawn tomorrow I'll take my chance on Seal Island with the others."

She peers around her and shudders. "For it's not possible that anywhere can be as hateful as this place."

Damn Lucretia. Not even I can cheat on chance to ensure she draws a short straw from the fistful bunched in my hand.

Bidding me good night, she refuses my offer to escort her back to the camp and strides into the darkness.

Defeated at every turn, I watch Lucretia go, her shawl floating out like a flag. She is more than clever, no mistaking it, holds me checkmate. If, against her wishes, I order Lucretia to stay on Traitor's Island, her suspicions will become aroused and she might warn the people.

Yet if she wins her game of hazard, it will just be a matter of time before she knows that I've lied. But then, of course, I'd blame Wouter, explain we were all duped by his retinue of Company men.

Weary, I wander the tide line, my boots sinking in soft wet sands. Apart from the cadences of the sea, the island now resounds with a fearful silence, absent even of mewling gulls in hovering winds.

Studying Lucretia's retreating form, head bent, resolute, marching forth, I wonder whether a few days marooned on Seal Island might not be such a bad thing. It would bring this haughty lady down, knock her from that smug, superior perch forever staked on the moral high ground, teach her the true meaning of survival. How she'll weep bitter tears, curse her decision to reject my promise of protection, a safe haven built beside mine, privileges over the others in additional rations, luxuries forbidden to the traders.

When, with a relenting heart, I send a raft to fetch her, let us see how compliant she'll be then. Tamed at last, obeying her Captain-General's every whim.

There the matter is settled. Besides, as governor of this isle, there is much for me to do and best achieved without the distraction of Lucretia taunting and teasing my heart.

 ON THE TWELFTH DAY, no fires have been sighted from the soldiers on High Island.

Beneath a scalding sun, the crowd forms an orderly line on the shore. The barber presses a straw into his wife's eager hands. The caulker curses and grinds a short straw beneath his heel. Putting one arm around him, the tailor commiserates in both their fates.

At last, Lucretia stands before me, hair tied back from her expressionless face. She fixes me with a defiant, piercing stare that sears my heart, and holds out one hand. I notice her fingers are scratched and blistered from gathering oysters among the rocks.

"I beg you to stay here under my protection," I whisper.

She casts me a cool, almost mocking look and shakes her head.

I fight an impulse to slap Lucretia like a foolish, obstinate child, wipe that supercilious smile from her face, anything to make her see sense at last.

When she reaches out for the straws clenched in my fist, I take in every detail, the folds in the bodice of her faded blue cotton shift, the frayed lace hem of one sleeve, freckles dusting forearms and wrists, a coral cut inflaming her thumb, her chipped nails bloodied at the quick, a sudden flash of her wedding ring in the sun.

The tips of Lucretia's fingers brush against mine, my flesh tingles beneath her touch. Slowly, almost tenderly, she draws a long straw from my reluctant grasp.

No, I almost cry out.

⁓⁂☙

It was a long time ago, I remember, when the dawn calls of Marie the hyacinth girl rocked my sweetest dreams.

Those were the dreams in which silent as a cat I padded through the walled labyrinths of Jerusalem. The air was cool, jasmine fragrant. With each step, my sandals seemed to glide across the paved streets as if wings sprouted from my ankles.

In these dreams, I was Jesus and my halo shone brightly. Behind me wove shadows of all the saints, the sinners from worlds elsewhere.

In these dreams, the hyacinth girl was always at my side. Her hair smelled of the sea and the rain. I called her Marie, my disciple, my Magdalen. For I was convinced that only I could change the world. I was destined. Son of God. The chosen one.

Then one morning I woke to the insistency of a cock's crow. The hyacinth girl had fled. And I knew my dreams, my love dreams, were merely the serpent insinuations of false prophets in my head.

The council members scurry back and forth dividing the people into two groups, those destined for Seal Island and those not. The entire process is solemn, ceremonious. There is even one touching moment when some of the men, lucky enough to have drawn long straws, volunteer to exchange this prize with their less fortunate wives.

Strange that chance should play such a cruel trick in this game. For not one single couple among them has won two long straws. The wives plead. But the husbands are resolute, adamant they will stay. Back and forth the straws go. Their currency weighs heavier than gold.

"Hush, Mayken, they've found water there." How the young lover sighs. He gives his lovely wife one last caress and with a gentle push sends her into the group of evacuees. Mayken. That is all I know of her and of all these people. There she goes, thin as a sparrow, to join her fair sisters.

Compassion. Sweet Jesus. I'll give you compassion. Take one hard look at this situation. Were it not for me, these people would die here. Instead I've offered them faith, hope, even conjured a Garden of Eden, for any fool can see they can't all stay in the one place. Put it this way: I've opened the gates to my kingdom. They are free. Free to choose their own destinies, orchestrate their own fates. No one can hold me accountable. And besides, if I were to believe your God, your master chess player, then it's his decision, his will. Let him select one by one the souls who will join him in Heaven. After all, it's predestined, foretold. Why should I care who lives or dies, when this sky God of yours has already tallied the odds? Quite frankly, it's no longer my problem.

Lucretia now gazes at a shimmering white sliver of shoreline, all that can be seen with the naked eye of Seal Island. She twists the straw round and around one finger then tosses it to the winds. A gull soars screaming and with a sideways swoop snatches the twine in its beak.

Now Jesus, what would you have me do, step forward, extend one hand, save her? But why, when her name is already inscribed in tablets of stone on your father's infallible list? Look, she's your type. Her dry lips murmur prayers. Tell me, where is this God of hers, when she needs him most? You would have me play his part with courteous words and a gracious smile. And I am tempted. For today my appetite is fierce.

Tirelessly the Predikant shuffles the two groups like a pack of cards. "This way," he says, marshaling the women into a line.

Skipping among them, young Carp does violence to the Jewish harp. Such a child. No one has informed him where these women are going. Pelgrom and De Beere know the score. As Wouter said, it's a simple matter—them or us. Most peculiar of all, Jacop still insists he discovered the water springs. I did well to increase their daily dosage of opium.

In this carnival atmosphere of hope and expectancy, the children become fractious. A blue-eyed cherub of a boy runs to his mother. Several girls, no more than ten years old, hoist fretful siblings to their hips. How the Predikant fusses, turns his handkerchief into a glove puppet, a turtledove, a flower. In the shade of a rock, twirling a parasol, the Predikant's wife grinds her teeth, unable to fathom why their names are not on the list.

Apart from the council members and camp workers, the evacuees now comprise females, young boys, infants, forty-eight in all.

Once the women have signed the council document, I suggest they empty their pockets of valuables, assuring them that it is far better for these souvenirs to remain in safekeeping until their return. Until, that is, the rescue ship arrives.

Some of the merchant wives seem happy to accept this explanation. But many demur at the removal of wedding rings, gold lockets, silver chains, trivia from the old world.

"It's only a temporary measure," one bride announces. She shoots me a winning smile. I notice she still wears her pearl earrings. The sneaky slut.

Lucretia stands by the tide line. Waves foam at her slippered feet. She could be persuaded to change her mind, there is still time, but studying her stern, imperious stance, that fierce, almost angry look on her face, I don't see the point.

With a heavy heart, I turn away, console myself with the fact that Wouter can be sent to fetch her at any time. I'll give her three days.

Cross-legged, De Beere and Wouter watch the women. Wouter even stands to get a better look. First he can't take his eyes from the girl with pearls in her ears, plump and soft as Eve, then he appraises Lucretia. To my surprise, the sudden shamelessness of Wouter's leer stabs at my heart.

When the barber conducts his brief yet thorough medical examinations, a roar of protest runs among the crowd until I explain that no one found sick can be sent to Seal Island.

Childbearers all, used to ignominious handlings by strangers, the wives dutifully submit to the barber's busy fingers. The children and younger women flinch at his touch.

When the barber reaches Lucretia, he kneels, kisses her hand, commends her soul to the heavens for her help, when it is me he should thank.

~❦~

Wine goblets are shared, tears shed, loved ones being left behind hugged. Families cling together distraught. A pathetic sight. All those kisses and sighs. Eventually I have to ask the Predikant to prize them apart.

Without even bidding me farewell, Lucretia is the first to venture toward the raft, her skirts spreading out in the waves. One by one the councillors follow. The Predikant's *krank-besoeker* flounders in their wake, gripping his drenched felt hat with one hand.

With all their strength, Wouter and De Beere lean on the poles. The raft strains to its ropes. The currents are at half tide today. Pelgrom lifts Lucretia onto the rough wooden slats of roped decking, where she crouches in the bow, if such a term can be applied to this singular, primitive vessel. Somehow, the councillors manage to scramble aboard.

"How many can she take?" I cry, running to the shoreline.

"Twenty at the most," De Beere mutters, gritting his teeth, hanging on to his pole against a rising swell. "Tell the women to be quick about it," he shouts. "Two trips should be enough."

Despite the weight, the raft moves swiftly, De Beere and Wouter both punting with the elegance of Venetian gondoliers. My sweet pilgrims cheer *adieu*. I salute them all. Seated like a figurehead at the bow, her red hair streaming behind her, Lucretia still watches the horizon.

PART
THREE

FROM MY CALCULATIONS, the number of people here has been reduced to some one hundred men and boys, not counting my new disciples, Wouter and company, and the sick, that is.

When the last raftload of souls leaves these shores, a mist of melancholy settles on the encampment.

After all the excitement, the activity, those who remain, mainly merchants and the *Batavia*'s craftsmen, seem at a loss as to what to do next.

The carpenter paces the shoreline. Mayken's husband sits hunched on a rock, shoulders heaving. The Predikant wanders aimless among them offering solace and prayers.

Impatient with this idleness, I tell the minister to organize these men into fishing groups. For the people here must still work for their daily bread.

꩜

At the hot, dry siesta hour, I sit outside, in deep shade, on the Commandeur's escritoire chair, my elegant sandalwood throne, placed at the head of the table.

In the blue distance beyond the reef's outer shelf, the fins of sharks continue to slice the waves. I admire their effortless ruthless flight.

Sometimes the ocean lies sullen and still, lead calm, and then, with no warning, a line of waves will march out of the seas and break across the reef in a thrilling rush of white froth at least one fathom wide.

I am happy here, lulled by sea cadences, wind whispers in the herbage around, all the noises of this island. And there are many. The clamorous click of cicadas against powder-soft, paper-white bark, unseen scuttles from claw and tail, the crackling scrub which never seems to shed its leaves.

～◍◎

At last Wouter reports to my quarters. I am shocked by the sight of him, the lacerations on his bruised, swollen feet.

"Did they all arrive safely?" I ask, pouring him a tumbler of brandy.

"The last trip was the worst," Wouter replies, taking a swig from the cup. "The raft proved unmanageable with that many on board. De Beere thought we'd all drown."

I remind him such a crossing need never be repeated. "And the lady, Lucretia?"

"She and the councillors made it easily ashore—for on that first trip, the wind and the tides were right."

I smile. My brave lad did well.

Wouter describes how the currents ebbed and flowed against them during the second voyage, pushed the vessel into deeper channels, forfeiting the small progress they had made, and by the time they reached the shore, low tides had exposed a perilous reef, leaving no choice but to disembark and push the raft across a flooded network of coral shelves which tore and bloodied their feet. Several of the women slipped and suffered severe cuts to their legs and arms.

"Any later and we wouldn't have made it," he says.

"And when finally you reached the island, how did you find the councillors and Lucretia?"

He tells me she was caring for the children and the others were setting up camp in the scrub; already one of the water barrels had been opened and it was decided not to explore the island until the following day as they needed to recover from such an arduous journey.

"How much water do they have?"

"Enough for a week at the most." Wouter holds out his cup for another tot of brandy. "I must say, sir, I thought you were most generous with the supplies."

He looks at me and grins. "The lady, Lucretia, she's a good looker and plucky all right." And he laughs.

A week should be long enough, allowing me to de-

vote my thoughts to matters of a more urgent kind
than the games played with fair Lucretia.

After tending to Wouter's abrasions—my, how this
vile coral rips the skin to shreds—I give him a leather
pouch filled with gold coins to be shared with De
Beere and the others. They must be rewarded for their
efforts.

⁓✿⊙

At the twilight hour, I watch the sun sink lower and
lower in incarnadine skies, bloodstained as fields after
battle. This evening, even the waves seem shot through
with fire and the horizon flames scarlet.

Checking the names of my new island council, I am
proud of my disciples, have every confidence in them
meeting the challenge of their new positions. I have
even taken the trouble of summarizing job descriptions, for each will be required to fulfill a different role.

Wouter, of course, I've elected councillor-general,
for he has definite qualities which I admire. At times
reminding me of my younger self.

⁓✿⊙

When Father died—I became renowned throughout
the district for being the only one to have survived the

plague which visited his house—I was taken in by my two aunts, still fearful for my mother's sanity.

Interpreting my survival as a divine act of their God, my aunts considered me a marvel, a miracle, an idol, whose every whim was indulged. I became a tyrant in their midst and, believing me angelic, a golden-curled Jesus, they refused me nothing.

I whiled away my days in the garden with playmates among the sons of the doctors, merchants, and lawyers of the town. At first they were innocent games. Hopscotch on pathways crossing the lawns, agate marbles sent on winning spins, horse chestnuts jousted from lengths of string. From the parlor my aunts picked at their embroidery like hens and smiled at me fondly through half-opened windows.

Raised in the conviction that I was superior to the others, I became spoiled, impervious, exacting as a Spanish Infanta. I ran my clipped-lawn empire like a despot and gradually our former games began to lose their luster.

As Torrentius used to say, nothing quite encourages as one's first unpunished crimes. There was a fat boy, Jacques the banker's son, whom we'd all tease. Like the parents of the other children daily dispatched to my domain, his father believed he could count on my support throughout his son's life. The boy feared me. I could smell it souring his breath, read it in the sweat beading his brow, the gray flecks of saliva at the corner of his lips, those damp palms reluctantly meeting mine in the routine trysts of our gang.

In blindman's buff or hide-and-seek, he'd run squealing for cover like a stuck pig. We only had to listen for his knocking heart, the asthmatic rasp of his breath, to flush him out. In each game, the loser had to submit to forfeits and punishments which I devised. First I gave orders for my victim to be bound to the paling fence at the garden's end. Even now I can remember the strong plaited cords, the glint of rust dust from hooks nailed to the timbers.

Then always I dressed for the occasion. As Torrentius said, I had discovered from an early age a thrill in delaying my final pleasure.

Dusted in camphor, packed in a trunk, Father's clothes were an education in foppery and fashion. Each night, I'd set the ringlets of his wigs, polish his pigskin boots, the military medals, his swords.

Long since discarded by my aunts, a dressmaker's dummy stood at the foot of my bed. This I attired in various outfits: scarlet tunics, gold-brocaded uniforms, astrakhan evening coats, and always Father's voice would roar in my ears like the noise in a crowd.

Bedecked in my finery—breezes riffling the plume in my hat—I returned to fat boy panting in the sun. The noose around his neck chafing plump folds of tender skin.

—⁂—

Like many of the inhabitants in the district, my aunts indulged a mania for flowers. These they arranged symmetrically in separate beds according to species and color. They planted lilies, hyacinths, and tulips of course, in alternating stripes like a national flag.

One spring, at great expense, they bought thirty tulip bulbs which bloomed crimson at the base, each petal streaked with scarlet flames.

My aunts delighted in this riot of color. At dusk I'd watch them take turns around the garden, watering cans clasped in frail, tremulous hands.

One day my friends arrived to show off a Labrador puppy which chased its tail and tugged the end of its lead.

Distracting them with my new set of painted toy soldiers, I unclipped the dog's ribbon, silly restraint that it was, and threw a stick which landed plumb in the middle of the flower beds. In a single bound the dog followed and, one by one, the slender tulip stems snapped.

Like harpies, my aunts flew from their perches and hauled the unfortunate children by their ears to the parlor. My friends sniveled and pointed accusatory fingers my way. At that, my aunts unhitched the boys' pants—even now I love that sudden snap of garter—and forced them sobbing to their knees.

Giddy with the turn of events, I sank down on a banquette, only to find my aunts beckoning me.

"You are master of this house," they said, handing me a cane. "You exact the punishments."

And I did. Over and over again, I did. And again on numerous other occasions. As for the puppy, I forget. Maybe my aunts drowned it, for like me they were not fond of animals.

AT THE APPOINTED TIME, at the violet hour, when the ocean turns coral-pink streaked with mauve light, my new councillors arrive outside my quarters, some sluggish, a little glazed from opium. I make them kneel before me.

"I have called you here to announce the new council members." I find myself trembling with the excitement of the occasion. "And I welcome you all to these appointments."

Wouter flushes with pride. Carp bites his lower lip.

"But first"—I advance toward them—"I will need your signatures in blood."

Carp begins to snivel.

Slowly I unsheathe the Commandeur's sword from its scabbard—for, like Torrentius, I too have a liking for theatricals. Lifting the sword high in the air, I sense a frisson of fear among my boys, except Wouter of course, who watches my every move.

"As councillor-general," I say, "Wouter will administer the blood rites."

Pelgrom gives a polite clap. Wouter grasps the sword

in a firm, steady hand. Briefly I explain the protocol of the ceremony. At my command, they begin to unbutton their sleeves. Hans and Carp fumble with hooks and eyes. I forget they must miss their light-fingered maids.

The dying sun seeps behind the island like a wound and stains the rim of the horizon crimson. The waves seem bathed in blood, as if some unfathomable leviathan of the deep had been savagely slaughtered. A swollen gibbous moon slowly rises.

At last the ritual can begin. With the flat of the sword, brave unflinching Wouter nicks a thin line on his blue-veined wrist. The blade is sharper than he thought. Blood fills the cut to the brim and, before he can take the quill, begins to trickle down one arm. De Beere rushes to his aid and dips the nib. I am impressed by the elaborate, aristocratic Gothic script with which Wouter signs his name.

Keen to be next, De Beere rolls his sleeves like a laborer. Showing off now, Wouter swings the sword military-style, making Andries step back at each swish of the blade.

"Go in deep," De Beere cries. "I'm not afraid." And Wouter does. He slices a translucent sliver of skin clean from his wrist. Jacop gasps like a spectator at a firework show. Pale, solemn De Beere inscribes a careful cross to his name.

"When healed," I tell him, "the scar will testify not only to your courage but your new position as the council's second-in-command."

It is then that Carp tries to tiptoe into the scrub. Wouter reels him in and quick as a flash flicks the sword tip across Carp's cheek. Blood slowly stitches the gash end-to-end. Silent in astonishment and pain, Carp clamps one hand to his face.

"When healed," Wouter says, "that scar will testify to your cowardice."

"You won't last long here." De Beere cuffs him about the ears. "For people are peckish. One day, our fat Predikant will roast you for breakfast."

Supervising Wouter's delivery of the ritual, I explain that the new council must be sharp, vigilant —people are indeed treacherous and, most dangerous of all, hungry.

"How do we know they won't murder us in our beds?"

Spoiled, silly Carp shits his pants. Jacop has to take the wretch to the shoreline and make him clean himself up.

Once the brandy cups are filled, I ring the bell for silence, for a speech. Every occasion, even this, requires a final ceremony of sorts. So I begin.

"You have pledged your honor to assist me in governing this island."

Wouter bangs his cup on the table. Pelgrom cheers.

"But anyone discovered reneging on this contract will find themselves under immediate arrest and court-martialed."

"String all traitors from the nearest tree," De Beere shouts.

"Hang 'em by the toes," Pelgrom volunteers.

Wouter calls for order and lifts his cup.

"Hail, Captain-General!"

They drum their feet on the ground.

"Hail!"

Hammer their fists against the table.

"*Hail!*" And like a Roman emperor, I salute them.

This island reminds me of a high-walled city. Kingdoms are clay. Here is my space. Engaged in an elaborate game of chess. My disciples are knights, the traders pawns. The game begins at dusk, at the hour of gulls skimming the waves with the tips of their indigo wings.

 I AM THE FIRST to admit that the soldiers are clever, resourceful. But on the fourteenth day no fires have been lit on High Island, which rises like a hump from its halo of green-tinged waters.

Despite his initial resistance, Hayes proved easier to dupe than I thought. Wouter has also assured me that the scrub on High Island is too brittle and thin to attempt to build a seaworthy escape vessel. It is only a matter of time. *Adieu*, my brave warriors, farewell.

Should any of the gullible traders ask why the soldiers have not sent signals, I will confide in them that it is my belief they were murdered by the treacherous French mercenaries, those loathsome Frenchies who should never have been allowed to board the *Batavia*. If in the next week no smoke is seen, I will tell them a raft will be sent to discover what has become of these men.

At my instructions, the Honourable Company's money chests, all artifacts and treasures, have been brought to my quarters. Sometimes I find it soothes the mind to plunge one's hands in corporate gold, pile the shining bullion on the bare floor, count and hold each piece to the light.

Wouter's hunting expeditions have confirmed that this island is rich in animal life: wildfowl, sandpipers, turnstones, curlews, gulls, several species of spiky-tailed lizard, and those curious hopping animals with a flavor similar to venison, which my hunters have tracked down in dense copses where they take shelter in the hottest part of the day. Seafood too is plentiful. Gold-striped coral fish trapped in reef pools at low tide prove as flavorsome as our own native cod.

Although with such abundance of wildlife all around and no immediate risk of us going hungry, the traders will, of course, be strictly rationed, as it could be months before the rescue ship arrives.

The carpenter and his skilled team of recruits have been most resourceful in completing the new campsite, which now comprises two neat dormitories, one for my councillors, the other for the men. I am pleased with the design of these rustic dwellings, sheltered from harsh winds and the pitiless sun.

The carpenter made good use of the largest pieces of mast and spars washed ashore—for upright beams, which he sunk into the ground to form rectangular frames about twelve feet wide and twenty feet long. The cedar poopdeck boards have been tied together and placed at an angle to make the sides. Each dormitory is roofed with strong sail canvas. Inside they are spacious, the floor covered in dried grasses. The Predikant and his family have been allocated a separate hut of poles and reeds. Set back from the main camp, the hens seem happy enough in the livestock pen, scratching for kelp flies among rotting mounds of weed. Why, I find myself landlord of a veritable village and am proud of every man's efforts.

I ring the *Batavia*'s bell and call an island meeting.

Muskets at their shoulders, Wouter and De Beere appear from the council quarters and take their place as sentinels on either side of their leader. From the reef, knots of men begin to trail across the shore, bringing in the morning's catch: iridescent coral fish flapping from hooked lines. I notice our nimble-fingered tailor has even devised an intricate net woven from flotsam washed in from the wreck.

Another group emerges from the scrub carrying armfuls of twigs and leaves. Watching these traders trudge toward me, I notice there is something lost, defeated almost, about them. The Predikant too seems more withdrawn, silent of late, no longer so eager and obsequious in my presence. One by one, my loyal subjects squat at my feet.

"As Traitor's Island will be run as a tight ship," I say, "rules must be instituted to maintain order here."

The carpenter and his son seem uneasy and exchange glances. They stare at Wouter and De Beere, proudly gripping their muskets, and look at one another again.

First, for the safety of everyone, I suggest a curfew must be observed from dusk to dawn.

The crowd falls silent.

"Have no fear," I say. "I will select a night watch of armed men to guard you."

"From which dangers?" the Predikant bleats.

I smile. "Don't forget, we've voyaged to the dark side of the world," I reply. "No doubt these waters teem with buccaneers or pirates." Now that the treasures are safe in my possession, I can instill fear in these men with the new threat of savage attacks.

"Oh my, I never thought—" the Predikant squeals.

"Unlikely, I'm sure," I cut in. "But you all must agree night watches will not only protect us but safeguard the Honourable Company's precious cargo until a rescue ship arrives."

There is a slow mumble of assent. Any mention of rescue always lifts their spirits.

Second, I tell them, rations from the *Batavia*'s stores—four ounces each—will be distributed daily at noon.

"Four ounces," the Predikant wails, patting his belly.

"Of course, organized hunting and fishing trips will

help augment these supplies," I say, ignoring the minister's whines. "And triple rations will be allocated to the man with the largest catch."

Still the carpenter studies me warily. Strange how there is always one dissenter, a troublemaker in every mob. But he would not dare oppose me. Not when these traders have shown such gratitude for all that I've done.

The people gaze up at me, solemn, waiting. I do believe they welcome the formal ceremony of these public meetings, are reassured by their familiar officialdom recalling the assizes of Amsterdam, have come to regard them as an entertainment of sorts, a way of passing the time.

"A show of hands from all those who agree to obey the proposed council rules," I cry.

Everyone votes in my favor except the carpenter and his son.

Satisfied with this outcome, I call the meeting adjourned.

As I pick my way through the scrub to my quarters, Mayken's husband suddenly appears at my side.

"Sir," he ventures, "many of the men were wondering whether they could take the raft and visit their wives."

I examine this naive gold trader who pines for his love. He is tall, stooped, slight as a girl.

"Are you a nautical man?" I ask, barely able to conceal the scorn in my voice. "Can you swim?"

"Few of us can." He falters.

"Do you realize that Wouter and De Beere almost lost their lives ferrying your women across to safe haven? The raft nearly capsized beneath the load."

He gives me a piteous, beseeching look. "We would not exceed those numbers," he pleads. "We just want to know they're safe and well."

"And widow your loved ones in the process, risk wrecking our lifeline, the only vessel we have? Don't be a fool, man."

Tears start in his eyes. His face is pale and swollen, as if he has not slept for nights.

Something in my heart relents, softens, for this youth brings to mind yet another method of reducing numbers here.

"Listen," I say in a kinder tone, "in the next few days, Wouter and De Beere are leaving for High Island to check on the soldiers. I'll ask them to visit Seal Island and make sure everything is all right."

"Sir, I beg you"—he falls to his knees—"allow me to go with them."

I smile and ask how many men have expressed a similar interest.

"There are ten of us, sir," he says, brightening with hope.

I almost laugh out loud. Such joyous simplicity in this scheme. Pacing up and down, I pretend to think hard on the matter.

"You must love this wife of yours," I say. "Why, it's barely a couple of days since she left."

The callow fool wrings slender, gold-weighing hands, tells me they were childhood sweethearts, sworn to eternal love, why he has pledged his heart, his very soul to his dear, sweet girl, Mayken; recalls as a boy he was bewitched when he first clapped eyes on her dancing around a maypole in a village fair, there were flowers in her hair, kingcups and marigolds, he remembers it well; and when he first kissed his young virgin bride she smelled sweet as a mown meadow.

"I would lay down my life for her, sir," he says.

And so he shall. Like his capricious God who snatched Marie from me, I too will play games with this youth's destiny and ensure he never sees his silly sot of a wife again.

I explain that I am touched by his tale, sympathize with the plight of every gallant here separated from their wives, I even confide in him the tragic death of my one and only love, Marie, buried in an unmarked grave on the outskirts of Amsterdam.

He hangs his head and wipes away a crocodile tear, for what does this boy care, who longs only to caress the soft warm breasts, the tender flesh of Mayken.

On my word, he shall be called to account and learn

to repent all his filthy practices. How dare he taunt my broken, yearning heart with idle talk of love, giddy virgins and their sly giggling siren cries, ribbons twirled about a maypole.

Glancing at him, I notice he has risen to his feet and eyes me strangely.

Once again I treat him to my most courteous smile.

"Tell your comrades to sign their names on a list and Wouter will fetch them at the appointed time."

Throwing his hat in the air, he whoops in delight.

"Thank you, sir," he cries. "I was the first to agree with the minister that you are a good man."

Motioning him to be quiet, I make this gold trader promise not to breathe a word to the others. Ten men only will be taken with Wouter on some other expedition, volunteers all—say, on an organized fishing trip.

"Now that I've agreed to your reckless plan," I whisper, drawing close, "what do you propose in return?"

Kissing the Commandeur's ring on my finger, he says they will do their best to persuade every man, even the doubters—he names the carpenter and his son—to obey the Captain-General and his new council.

He bows, then slips into the shadows of the scrub and is gone.

As this frail, lost, lovelorn boy would not have survived a single bout of fever in the plague-infested cities of the Indias, his soul just flies faster toward

Heaven's Gates, that is all. No need to burden the conscience when his fate is already predestined, foretold.

In the privacy of my quarters, I watch the women on
Seal Island through my glass. Can that be Lucretia I
espy, roaming the brittle shoreline, cloak whipping in
the breeze, her hair scorched into fiery points by an
implacable white noon sun?

That must be her gathering sticks, leaves, shreds of
dried kelp, digging the sand grit with bare hands. Now
she returns to a sparse encampment where the others
sit hunched around a desultory fire. Two men stand
guard over the water barrels. Perhaps more determined than most, she flicks burnt mussel shells from
hissing embers with a charred stick and gorges on the
tough brine gristle. Looking at Lucretia, I wonder if
maybe of us all she is destined to survive.

I put down my glass. Soon I will send Wouter to
fetch her.

ON THE SIXTEENTH DAY, still no sign of fires from the soldiers on High Island. I decide it is time to eliminate all the soldiers' names on my list, beginning with Hayes. I have told the traders that when the tides are propitious, the raft will be sent to quell a possible French uprising or mutiny.

The men seem content with this explanation, for there is scant love between the merchants and these soldiers, who, sequestered below the *Batavia*'s decks, remained a breed unto their own, like the sailors.

⚬─ঞ⊙

Still no rain from the vaporless skies, flat blue desert skies, scorched dry as this island. Day after day, a hot wind whistles in my ears, tangles the ringlets of my wig, blows sand grit in my eyes, sucks moisture from our shallow water holes, forcing us to dig wider channels which we cover with canvas to keep precious supplies from the sun's glare. The water brews bland and brown, the texture of boiled tea.

At the last count of our water stores, thirty-six barrels remain. Twelve were allocated to the women and Hayes and his men. I of course replenish my flask from my own private supply, which to my surprise no one has yet found.

I have been examining other methods of reducing our numbers here. Although we have food rations in plenty, my daily inventory of the stocks shows that vital supplies are being squandered on the sick. Provisions gone to waste on those who might not survive or remain too weak to assist in the daily management of the island. Twenty-seven still on the sick list, mainly children and those injured in the wreck.

Beneath the thatched eaves of the hut, the rancid sick lie slumped, three to a mat.

Silent and in bare feet, the barber flits from one to another. At my approach, he pitterpats toward me.

"Without medicines, there's nothing I can do." He speaks in a hushed whisper as if in a church.

I explain that rations are scarce. A furrow deepens on his brow. The barber is obsessed with the notion of saving this mob. I pity him.

"This child over here—" He directs me to a still, small shape beneath a blanket. "The boy needs opium. And over here."

One of the women, a pretty one at that, delirious with fever. Endlessly she recites recipes to some maid.

"Don't forget," she says, "asparagus are in season."

"She will not last the night," he confides.

And then there are amputees, swaddled in soaked sheets. At the sight of them, he turns his blunt, bald face away. I agree there is nothing to be done against this death tide.

"Unless of course—"

The barber pricks up his ears. This is what he is waiting for. His soft beagle eyes widen with hope.

"Unless of course the council decides to donate precious medicines to this cause. Document what is required and tonight the council will vote on it."

The fool drops to his knees. Tries to please me with "Hail, Captain-General."

~❦~

Hemlock is a gnarled, pale root. Of all the poisons in the known world, this is the most painless, the most subtle. A gentle numbness of the senses. With this root, death begins in the feet and seeps upward. Imperceptible at first, the paralysis charts swift blood currents in its navigation to the heart. It's a noble death. A philosopher's death, offering, as a final gift, time to muse on dragonish clouds. First grate it as you would a carrot. Then pound the flesh to pulp. Press the juices through a muslin sieve. Mix in a jug of sweet dessert wine.

I return to the barber waiting impatiently at the hut's entrance.

"The council has voted in your favor," I say. "The sick will be saved." I place the wine vessel in his great bear paw of a hand and instruct him to give each patient a single sip.

"Or should that fail, soak biscuit wafers in the remedy and place one on each tongue."

The barber is scrupulous in this task. He lifts the potion to everyone's lips. Whispers kind words of comfort and reassurance. Ensuring that all will receive his care, I leave him to it. He follows me outside.

"Captain-General, you are a good man." He bows. "It will never be forgotten."

ON THE SEVENTEENTH DAY, pouring water into my favorite agate vase carved with horned and bearded satyrs lascivious between acanthus leaves, I hear cries from the beach.

"Dead, all dead." On his knees, in the dust, the barber wails and beats his breast like a player in some overblown tragedy.

The sea is gray today, weighed with slate clouds. Barbed words of malice and mischief rush toward me and are swallowed by the wind. As usual the Predikant is nowhere to be seen. Men sprinkle across the shore like ants in a sack of flour and surround the sick-hut. From here, if I held out one hand, I could halt their procession with a flick of my wrist, scoop them in my palm.

The facts are plain. Set them down. *On the seventeenth day, the sick passed away in their sleep.* What's new? They were dying anyway. Remember how they suffered so? Not even the barber nor all the opiates in the world could help. Surely the main expediency was to quicken the process, not slow it down, as you would to a dog or a horse that was lame. In these modern times of surgical skill, when cancers are sliced from flaps of skin, when physicians pillage the morgues and students probe the pumps, the arterial networks of the heart, we tend to forget the mortality of man. Man who has but a breath in his nostrils. Tell me, this man of yours—how much is he worth?

Tight knots of men cluster around the barber, who continues to howl in the doorway of the sick-hut. The main question on everyone's lips is how these deaths occurred.

The Predikant reluctantly joins them, a handkerchief clamped to his mouth. At the sight of him, the mob fearfully draws back and tries to coax the barber to his feet.

The carpenter's son is the last to understand. Then he runs screaming into the waves. "Plague," he cries.

My, how that magical word drives fear into the breast of man until only the barber is left, refusing to leave his charges stiffening beneath cotton shrouds.

Maybe it is time I intervened.

When I reach the dormitory, I see through the doorway that it is the blacksmith who tries to calm the panic-stricken traders. They unanimously vote on taking the raft to Seal Island.

A small stocky barrel of a man, the blacksmith has to stand on a wooden crate to make himself heard.

"I for one will stay here," he shouts over the men. "Would you cowards risk contaminating your wives and daughters?"

The traders fall silent.

"The apothecary was right," Stoffel the caulker offers. "It was only a matter of time before fever visited these benighted shores."

"Plague, pestilence, and everything most horrible," the Predikant wails through his handkerchief.

"First we must at once hold a funeral," the tailor suggests. Perched on his bunk, he looks drawn and pale, his earlier sprightliness quite gone.

The upper trumpeter runs one finger over the dented rim of his sea-tossed instrument. "I'll play the march," he volunteers. "Then we should torch the hut and bury the ashes in the sands."

"Fire." The Predikant quakes. "The apothecary said this island was a tinderbox. If plague doesn't finish us, we'll be burnt alive."

Plague, fire, and brimstone—how their imaginations run wild.

The carpenter bangs his fist against the wall.

"Silence," he calls in a firm voice I've not heard before. "Why have we placed so much trust in the apothecary?" he asks. "What do we know of this man who sprang to these shores like a magician, who marches ahead and commands us to follow?"

So this woodshaver still doubts the Captain-General's word, I, who have led them all from deg- radation and squalor.

"But we can't manage without him," the Predikant whispers, aghast at this mutinous turn of events.

"Yes, we can," the carpenter replies. "Look at him strutting about like a lord giving orders but not once lifting a finger to help."

Stoffel the wary, the fearful, glances over one shoulder. I dart into the shadows. "Quiet," he hisses. "What if he hears?"

The carpenter stares at him scornfully.

"I vote on calling a new election," he says. "We've no need of the apothecary. Besides, there's something queer about him which I don't like."

So this ingrate, this humble tradesman, dares to topple me from my throne.

Not a word from the bewildered traders. They don't know what to think or whom to trust. They long for home, their safe mercantile lives. What a predicament they're in.

I will placate and reassure them, suggest we hold a funeral. And given the seriousness of the occasion, I will decree the following day a public holiday. For, as their ruler, I am generous, I am kind.

HOW BORED my disciples are. Desperate to please. Forever requesting permission to sharpen my sword, polish my boots, fill my shaving dish with hot water, or take it in turns to boil gull eggs for my breakfast. When I ask them to dig long ditches on the shore, they are exultant to be given something to do.

I keep my boys shackled to an ordered routine. Knives, axes are sharpened, although any instrument would do. I have forbidden the use of muskets. These will be needed for the rescue ship glancing the reef on a low tide.

For the last three nights, we have been blessed with a sulphur-yellow moon rising full on the horizon. It is always an unpardonable crime for my crepuscular strolls along the shore—gull wings humming the night air, phosphorescence gilding the waves, all these unexpected pleasures of the tropics—to be interrupted. Tonight it is by the carpenter and his son, both tipsy on a tapped keg of wine siphoned from the storeroom.

The carpenter has to lean on his son in order to walk. At my approach, the fool draws up his fists.

"I know your game," he says. "I know what's going on."

"You are drunk," I reply. "You've broken the rules and stolen liquor from the Honourable Company."

"And you've betrayed us," he cries.

I strike him hard across the face. With a roar of rage, he lunges at me, but his frightened son holds him back.

~*~

I summon the council and give immediate commands for both to be drowned in punishment. But my council of idle thugs demurs. Refuses to meet my eye. De Beere says punish the father but not the boy. Pelgrom remembers it was they who helped fashion the raft. Both should go free, Carp cries. But, throwing down a coil of rope, Wouter begins to bind their legs and arms.

The carpenter wrestles. The son tries to make a run for it but De Beere grabs him by the ear. Patches of sweat begin to mottle the carpenter's shirt. Wouter clamps one hand over the carpenter's mouth.

"All is over with them," I say.

Carp hangs back.

"Come here, boy," I shout. Angry now. "As council members elect, you will show neither pity nor mercy."

Carp trembles before me. I point out a round, flat stone with the tip of my sword.

"Pick that up, boy, and call these wretches to account for all their filthy practices."

The others remain silent, watching. Arms tied behind his back, the carpenter still struggles. De Beere tightens his grip on the boy. Carp takes aim at the whimpering son, who screams. The stone falls with a thud at his feet.

"Come now," I say softly. "Let the council show Carp how justice is done."

In the end it was a botched job. Messy business. De Beere heaved the stone at the carpenter's head. He fell backward onto the sand. The son shrieked and, fearing he would be heard, Wouter slit his throat. They dragged the bodies by their feet into the waves. The water revived the father, who began to thrash like a hooked fish, and De Beere had to hit him again.

It was then I returned to my quarters, for there is nothing I hate more than the sight of blood.

ON THE EIGHTEENTH DAY, fine dawn rain shrouds the island oyster-gray. Barely enough to fill the water barrels and distill the hot, brine-coated air. Now a fierce sun burns through the mist, sucks rain-dews pooled in curled spines of bush leaf.

My disciples seem subdued. They moon by the shore. Even Wouter abstains from his spectacular dolphin dives, which without a ripple can puncture the blue shallows. What can be the matter? Surely not the incident of last night? Come rally, my boys. For justice was done. I've rung the bell twice this morning and still no sign of Carp.

Although the boys relish the extra rations, the fine wines at my table, all the privileges of authority, they don't want the responsibility that goes with it. I ring the bell again. Of what use my council if at the final hour I can't count on them to weigh the scales of justice? Of what use, if they turn squeamish at the scaffold? They pledged their honor to help govern this isle. And that they will. Or I shall strip them of their badges, their fancy lapels, and send them to fish with the traders, and two ounces of biscuit in their pockets.

Of all, Wouter disappoints. His hands shook when finally he buried the bloodstained stone in the sand. On reflection, perhaps it was the manner of the executions. Even I admit it is hard to kill a man. Next time, I'll suggest it's done fast, with the points of their sabers.

Ah—at last I hear a splash. Wouter swims strong effortless strokes. Shoals of sapphire fish shimmer across his shadow. With a shout, De Beere plunges in. Now Pelgrom smacks the waves. In no time, all of them splash and paddle without a care in the world. As it should be on this paradise isle.

All except Carp. Anxious, fretful Carp. Now I see him, hunched on a limestone ledge, chin resting on bony knees. Carp, the problem boy, who still wakes from untold terrors of ghouls and phantoms in the night. I wonder why Carp takes life so hard. He was only a member of the jury, a witness at the trial. Why can't he be more like the others?

Besides, it was the carpenter's fault. He and his son stole the Company's property. They broke the rules, disobeyed the twilight-to-dawn curfew, all instituted for their own safety and good. Had they kept to the dormitory, none of this would have happened. Certainly we regret the outcome, wish circumstances were different, for it has to be said the carpenter excelled at his profession.

Carp must pull himself together. He unsettles my boys, giggling and whispering to himself in the sun.

Joining me at breakfast, Wouter and De Beere fall on the bread, the cheese, the wine.

I ask Wouter why Carp is not with us. All at once a silence. Wouter pauses between mouthfuls.

"Carp is not well," he says. "Carp is troubled by last night."

The boys fidget on their chairs, the ones the carpenter made. De Beere flicks flies from the rim of his cup. Pelgrom chews nails already bitten to the quick. Jacop shreds bread crusts to crumbs. Hans's lower lip trembles. For young Carp is his special friend.

What can be the matter, one minute good cheer and now this sudden melancholy?

Wouter puts down his knife. "Carp kept us awake. He talked and sang and cried all night."

De Beere knits his brow and struggles with the illumination of a thought. "Wouter, I mean the councillor-general, believes Carp has lost his wits."

The others remain quiet, serious. Waiting for an answer.

"Well," I reply, "we must help Carp find them again."

Although De Beere sniggers at the joke, Wouter seems uneasy.

"We must eradicate Carp's doubts," I say. "Make him overcome this affliction." Studying the worried, expectant faces of my boys, I smile. Carp's behavior seems to disturb them more than the carpenter's squeals.

"Today, we'll appoint him chief executioner."

Much to my disappointment, Wouter flinches.

"But no one has committed a crime," he says.

I refill my glass. This morning the boys are slow, sluggish on the uptake.

"The barber blabs," I say. "The barber is convinced the sick were poisoned." I explain that the barber is a treacherous, plot-hatching man, leader of his own secret cabal. Unfolding a parchment from my sleeve, I tell them that the barber's henchmen include the cooper, the upper trumpeter, the blacksmith, and the gold trader.

"Keep a watch on them."

Wouter holds up his hand.

"Will there be a trial?"

I laugh. Wouter flushes with shame. "I think not. Already the men are mutinous. Would not do to incite a riot."

At the word *riot*, Pelgrom and Jacop stir restlessly. I believe my council is scared. Even Wouter.

"How will it be done?" he asks in hushed tones.

"You will invite the barber and his men on a fishing trip."

"And then?"

"Bind the usurpers with ropes, weigh their feet with stones, and Carp the executioner will tip them overboard."

"And should Carp refuse?"

"He won't, for his life depends on it."

Wouter frowns. A pulse beats at his temple. He looks sideways at De Beere's open-mouthed admiration of the plan and the other way to Andries, who smirks, showing that he is not afraid. Hans bursts into tears. Still Wouter says nothing. His mouth is tight and pale. The silence becomes oppressive. I drop the parchment on his plate. Wouter, who has pledged his soul to deliver justice on this isle of misrule, stares at the scroll of names, which slowly unfurls in the heat. Finally De Beere picks up the document and tucks it in his pocket. Hans continues to snivel.

All eyes on him, Wouter pushes back his chair and slowly rises to his feet.

"One last matter." My tone is kinder this time. "Take Hans as well, for Carp might not be strong enough to do it."

Hans tries to wriggle between Jacop's legs. De Beere grabs him by the collar.

When Wouter turns to me, there is something in him changed, hardened. As if the old Wouter—the gifted golden boy from Amsterdam on whose slender shoulders untold fortunes sat, whose careless laughter rang from quadrangles and city brothels, whose gaze turned virgins giddy and made nuns blush beneath their wimples—has been sloughed clean. The old Wouter is no more. A husk blown to the winds. Instead, my own creation stands, beating fierce angel wings. My son of man reborn. Vengeance trills in his veins. In time, all the boys will be the same and I won't tell one from the other. Nor even need to bother with their names.

~⚭~

At sunset Carp, Wouter, and De Beere return on the raft. Wouter paddles fast. Carp screws his wizened monkey face into the blinding violet sun. Every so often he covers that strange lopsided smile of his with the back of one hand. I notice too that Hans must have failed in his mission. I never liked the runt. So my disciples are now five.

ON THE NINETEENTH DAY, I study the women on Seal Island through my glass. I see they are down to their last two water barrels, over which several of the councillors stand guard. And there is Lucretia, squatting by the tide line, tickling the rippled surface of a wide rock pool with a flimsy hook and line, an intense look of concentration on her face. Already she seems thinner, more haggard. When I send Wouter to fetch her, my lady will dine in my quarters on the most sumptuous fare this island can offer.

With a deft flick of her wrist, she pulls up her line. I laugh in delight, for my clever girl has landed a fish!—not much larger than a minnow but a catch nonetheless. Carefully she pockets her prize in a pouch she has rigged at her waist and, rising to her feet, wades in deeper, casting the line across still emerald waters.

Hatless, beneath the sun's glare, Lucretia is the only soul toiling on the beach. She has tied a kerchief around her exposed shoulders and throat. Her fair complexion is now freckled as a peasant's.

I scan the scrub through my glass. Here among the bushes, a few women shelter listless and lethargic in pitiful shade, there, playing on powder-white coral, a group of ragamuffin children half-naked, begrimed with dust.

Crouched by a guttering fire, the girl with pearls in her ears winces in pain and bandages an ulcerous wound on her ankle with a strip of cotton torn from her petticoat. Why, I even espy Mayken, the gold trader's wife, lips burnt and swollen, murmuring prayers to an uncaring, heedless God.

And sobbing by the shadows of the water barrels, the Predikant's pallid *krank-besoeker*, the wide felt brim of his hat crinkling in the heat.

I focus the lens on Lucretia again. She gazes out to sea, examining the horizon. Then, with a sudden sideways glance, it seems she stares straight at me. With a start, I lower the glass. See how she stands there, hands on hips, bold as brass, silent and accusing.

I reach for my brandy tumbler. Taking a swig, I laugh. I must have imagined it. In this place, it is important not to lose hold, vital to remember the exact sequence of each passing day, no matter how swiftly they fold back on themselves, replicate moment after moment like the ceaseless shift of the waves.

A pale pink crab crawls across the tip of my boot, pincers open at the ready to fend adversaries from this new wrinkled leathered landscape it now journeys across, exiled from the sand and coral boulders of home, the cool moist caverns excavated between roots and tendrils of rotting weed.

Flicking the crab on its back, I feel a twinge of sympathy for the predicament this lone, banished creature now finds itself in. Struggling, spider legs flailing, the crab rocks back and forth. I could be kind, benevolent as a god, drop this scuttling shell into the dank, dark hole of his birthplace. Instead I crunch it beneath my heel.

The sight of Lucretia on distant shores has unsettled me. I lay down my glass.

How time weighs. Not a ripple on the ocean. Not a breath of wind. Nor a cloud in the flat papier-mâché sky. I'm tired of this vista, this blue void.

Even a Roman cameo fails to please. The costly jewel said by Gasper the Amsterdam jeweler to be the rarest carving in the known world and which the cunning Commandeur smuggled aboard for his own private profits, his secret negotiations with sultans at the Mogul Court.

Although the Commandeur pretends to be a corporate man, a man of honor, good as his word, incorruptible, with impeccable credentials, I discovered among papers in his desk that he is Rubens's agent, that aged voluptuary, who wants his antiquities collection sold to buy himself a younger, creamier, more corpulent wife. When the Company uncovers the Commandeur's ruse, the Governor-General will not be pleased.

I place the ancient agate aside. Yet on most occasions its theme thrills my blood—a Roman emperor, his chariot drawn by two centaurs, their feathered hooves grinding fallen enemies to the dust, while, above, winged Victory carries a wreath in strong, athletic arms. I like to think it was this same Roman who nailed our false prophet to the cross.

Endlessly I have traced the outlines of this treasure, marveled over the folds in the emperor's gown, each vine leaf twined through Victory's wreath, the fine whorls in the centaurs' horns. There is speed and breadth and depth in it.

But today I put it back in the box with the gold and silver, coined and uncoined, the trinkets and other valuables once destined for private sales in the Indias. Instead I stun flies with my fan, capture them in my hand, tear gauzy wings from dry frail hinges.

~*~

The Predikant toils up the hill. He seems agitated, in an unusual hurry. Strange that after such a strict regime the minister remains fat. So tremblingly huge. Unless—could it be—our psalm-singing magpie is thieving the rations. Seeing me, he waves.

"Captain-General," he calls, scrambling up the track. He pauses and wipes sweat from his face. Then plunges on, gasping for breath. When he arrives, I wait for him to recover.

"Bad news to report," he manages to say at last. "Men have gone missing."

First he names the barber and his cabal, as I knew he would. His small piggy eyes are round with fear.

"There must have been an accident," he says.

"When were they last seen?"

He hesitates. Cautious as a diplomat. For it would not do to accuse my boys outright.

"With Messieurs Wouter, De Beere, Hans, and Carp on a fishing trip."

"And they did not return?"

He shakes his head.

"And for the last two days, sir, I mean Captain-General, the carpenter and his son, such able souls I'm sure you'd agree, have disappeared."

He strokes the crucifix at his throat.

I ponder my moves. How to take this bishop.

"Minister," I say, "I've something to confess."

At the word *confess*, he darts me a hopeful, expectant look and, folding both hands in his lap, presents a perfect bedside-manner smile. So I begin.

"Secretly those same men came to me and begged permission to join their wives on Seal Island—said otherwise their hearts would crack."

The Predikant peers at the ocean, the faint smudges of land wrapped in mist, the sharks swifter than wind shadows closing in on a scent beyond the reef.

"They must not give way to despair," he says, alarmed.

"Quite the opposite," I reassure him. "As your God preaches love and compassion, I took a leaf from his little black book and granted their wish, but first swore them to secrecy, for if everyone went, we'd be in the same predicament as before."

He nods gravely. "One island will not sustain all."

"Exactly," I say.

I am in my stride now, almost moved by this narrative which springs with such ease to my lips.

"Why, you might ask, were these men rewarded over the others?"

The gullible fool hangs on my every word.

"Why, for their fortitude, their skills, without which we would not have the chair you sit in, the clogs on your feet, these timber pikes which the ingenious barber fashioned."

The Predikant eyes the pikes.

"But would your tyrannical sky God have reprieved them in the same way as I?" I ask. "Adamant as he is that we suffer this vale of tears?"

Flustered by the question, the Predikant breathes deeply. I draw my face close to his.

"Minister, tell me that I'm a good man."

"You've not finished your confession, sir," he ventures in a low voice. His crucifix flashes in the sun.

Confession, don't make me laugh.

"I've nothing further to confess," I say. "For, perfect in virtue and goodness, your God is not able to send into my heart anything bad because there is no evil within himself."

Checkmate. The Predikant sighs. Maybe it's the heat, but he appears older, wearier than I've seen him in a long time.

"Even though our provisions must be rationed," I say, "trust should be placed in the council which acts as a *de facto* caretaker to you all."

But I spare him the dismal news that further petty pilferings were discovered, namely a nub of cheese hidden in a cabin servant's hammock. There will be reprisals. This time I'll appoint De Beere executioner. For I want all my boys to grow accustomed to the smell of blood.

ON THE TWENTIETH DAY, I decide to call an island meeting. At the first ring of the *Batavia*'s bell, Wouter and De Beere take their places on either side of me, muskets at the ready. The traders trickle across the shore and one by one gather in a crowd, squatting and crouching at my feet. Their faces are watchful and intent. Wild rumor and gossip have spread since the mysterious disappearance of the barber's cabal, the carpenter and his son, and the other men.

Some believe they were attacked by sharks while fishing in the reef, others maintain they were kidnapped by savages or dragged into the waves by leviathans from the deep. Several claim they lost their way in the scrub and a search party should be sent.

I give the Predikant a sharp glance and, although he flushes, he manages to remain silent.

I hold up my hand. "Despite these strange vanishings, which the council is investigating, I've good news to report."

All eyes are now fixed on mine.

"Yesterday a perilous crossing was made to High Island and the soldiers were found alive and well."

A cheer rises among them.

"Why didn't they send signals?" someone shouts.

I smile. "Hayes decided to wait for the raft to arrive because he had an important message to impart."

I tell them Hayes wants all to know his new colony is flourishing and can sustain twenty extra evacuees at the most.

The crowd roars.

"He also says that those married among you can collect your wives from Seal Island and bring them to his haven."

Wouter shoots me a sly, surreptitious grin and steps forward. "Be quick about it," he shouts. "First show of hands are the first to go."

I am amused by the sight of our poor, baffled Predikant, his wife tugging the hem of his sleeve, trying to raise his hand in the air. He peers at me fearfully, almost apologetically, then waves at Wouter with the others—but too late. Twenty are already chosen. Sobbing with relief, they rush to the dormitory and collect their meager belongings.

This time I will make De Beere and Carp navigate the raft, armed with sabers and muskets; one trip should suffice.

 ON THE TWENTY-FIRST DAY, I am wakened by a sound of singing from outside my quarters. Vile, biblical verse. The Predikant and his genuflecting mob of psalm singers are beginning to grate on my nerves. How many times do I have to explain there is neither Heaven nor Hell and that these are only fables?

"Come now, devils with all sacraments, where are you?" I shout through the canvas flap. The chorus falls silent.

But later at breakfast, it pleases me to see how easily my disciples are persuaded by my belief that, perfect in every virtue and goodness, their God is unable to send into the hearts of men anything bad, because there is no evil or badness within himself.

I also make them understand that for us there is neither good nor evil. The vulgar polarities between saints and sinners, Heaven and Hell, God and the Devil, those primitive instruments of repression should be used only on the common man.

My wide-eyed disciples remain silent, except Pelgrom, who raises one hand.

"What is there, then?" he asks in a small voice like a frightened child.

I laugh.

"Why, freedom of course."

So. I now command that anyone found praying on the island, including the Predikant, must be reported to the Captain-General. For all religions restrict pleasure. How Wouter smacks his lips at that plump, moist word, *pleasure*.

───✺───

Each morning through my glass I watch the women on Seal Island, those castaways wandering their coral shores. They root for mollusks among the seaweed, search beneath shingles for brackish waters.

It is time I retrieved Lucretia from her exile. As for the others, I sum up the situation.

How desperate these women will become, weak as newborn kittens, slaking thirst from rank puddles. The children in particular. Why, they won't even have the strength to bury their dead.

By the last count, the number of men here has been reduced to sixty-five, not including my disciples, that is.

───✺───

Most nights, at the still point of the eastern skies, Orion cartwheels against a luminous massed haze of unknown, random stars. Man has never countenanced such confusion in these castaway con- stellations. Without the constancy of the pole star, the scurrying heavens have lost their compass. The planets spin on their sides, tipped from their axle, and the known world tilts upside down.

—❦◉

Wouter and De Beere have taken to creeping outside the dormitory in the encampment.

"Jesus was a man without age in child's garments," Wouter cries. "And the Father of Lies."

Not knowing that I am watching from the shadows, he mimics my words to perfection. He darts De Beere a proud, daring, defiant look and sniggers.

De Beere stares at him, admiring, aghast.

"There is no God," Wouter whispers. Arms outstretched, he whirls around and around in a mad capering dance, head flung back, gazing at the stars. "There is no God," he shouts, exultant and triumphant.

A fearful expression steals across De Beere's face. His shoulders tense, he almost flinches, expecting to be struck by some fiery celestial blow. With an involuntary shudder, he glances about him into the darkness.

Wouter laughs, gleeful as a schoolboy who believes he can outwit his stern master with nicknames or ink pellets flicked from a quill.

De Beere giggles and, determined to match his friend's bravado, cries, "God is dead."

His words are swallowed by the night.

"I declare all prayers and sacraments void," Wouter rejoins.

The tailor and the caulker are the first to peep bewildered from the dormitory. Unlike the tailor, who offers his fists, the caulker looks at Wouter with an expression of reproachfulness.

"Child," he says, "prayers are all we have."

Wouter laughs in his face.

"This is blasphemous talk," the tailor cries. "The work of the Devil himself." He makes to rush at Wouter but, with a firm hand, the caulker holds him back.

Disturbed by the commotion, the cook and his apprentice step outside. The apprentice, a fearful youth, slides behind the cook's shadow. De Beere repeats my recent instructions.

"Anyone found praying on the island"—he glares at the tailor—"will be reported to the Captain-General."

There is an astonished silence.

"The Captain-General has given orders," Wouter says. "He will not be disobeyed."

Outraged and whispering among themselves, they retreat to the dormitory. I listen to Wouter's laughter ring in the darkness.

 ON THE TWENTY-SECOND DAY, it rains, hard, slanting rain which brims the water barrels, dimples the serried sludge of our yawning caskets. Fat, sweet goblets of rain pucker the slack-bellied ocean, which sends panting waves pacing the shore, sniffing and raiding the damp air for more.

In the shelter of my quarters, I watch spouts of rain bounce off the leaves and course into deep rivulets between tracks where the land has been cleared.

Already this merciful squall has replenished our supplies, some thirty barrels filled, as well as an additional catchment in empty salt-pork and beef casks. The level of the water holes has also risen.

I have to confess a growing impatience with the idle traders who, between fishing trips, squat among the rocks, picking lice from tangled hair. So by my orders, my disciples will now have them quarrying the coral for the construction of a lookout, as it is better for them, for us all, to keep to a strict routine. Lazy seawatchers all, they degenerate fast, have lost every sense of themselves, and the filth, the vermin on them—an intolerable sight.

This morning, I have given Wouter instructions too for these traders to have their heads shaved. After all, it's a matter of hygiene, not to mention decency. Should they resist . . . well, the council will persuade them the procedure is for their own good.

I have also suggested the men be numbered according to the alphabetical order of their names. All the easier for the council to keep control. And it will be a relief not having to remember those names, all those Hanses and Jans.

Carp is now responsible for my toilette, the laundering of the Commandeur's white silk stockings, the soft linen shirts, so appropriate for this heat of the tropics, and I'm pleased to see him serious at the task. Each day he scrubs—rub-a-dub-dub—in the shallows, and by now understands that one single speck of dust is enough to cause my displeasure.

Despite the primitive conditions we now find ourselves in, I am fastidious, exacting. Each morning, I admire my reflection in a pewter hand mirror once inventoried as trade. I trim my moustache, rub my lips with cochineal and, on pain of death, insist the council does likewise.

Appearance, I tell them, is everything. Not on this deserted isle, nor anywhere on the known globe, will we be reduced to barbarians. We are not baboons but noblemen from Amsterdam. By birth and rank different from the others, those wretches sent to work on the reef.

~∯⊙

By noon, the rains cease. The sun pierces a blanched sky. The island steams. A hot, still mist smears the gray-green scrubland, clings to every fern frond and leaf tip. On the shore, my boys march back and forth, sabers glinting at their shoulders. How proud they are of their new scarlet uniforms, cut and stitched from velvet curtains salvaged from the wreck, each sleeve and epaulette embroidered with gold brocade.

By late afternoon, Wouter appears through a canopy of creepers, like a nymph, like my very own Ariel on Prospero's isle. I put down my opium pipe.

"At first the traders refused to be shaved," he says, pushing back his thick fair hair and dropping on his haunches beside me.

Sunlight spills through the foliage, beads sweat on Wouter's lean shoulders. Once again, my councillor-general has disobeyed and taken off his shirt. I must remind him not to do that anymore.

I ask whether the council had explained that in the interest of hygiene the men must be shaved and their names were no longer required to maintain order.

Wouter slaps a fly at his elbow.

"The cook, a stubborn man, said that if the council took from the people their prayers, their hair, their names—what should then not be spared?"

I clap my hands in delight. For it cannot be denied, this cook speaks the truth.

Now Wouter begins to enact the scene.

"'Shame on them,' I said. 'How could you doubt the Captain-General's word who has only your best interest at heart?'"

Proudly my boy paces his imaginary stage. He tells me De Beere had to remind them of who and what they once were—Company men. He even gave them a mirror so they could see for themselves. He laughs.

"Finally the tailor was persuaded to clip each man close as spring lambs with his scissors."

But as to taking away their names, Wouter shakes his head. "Pelgrom was convinced there'd be a riot," he says. "He almost shot a grape of musket in the air."

At this I frown, for the use of muskets has been strictly forbidden. Registering my disapproval, Wouter treats me to his most seductive courtier's smile.

"The sly merchants only agreed to sew numbers on their lapels if the prohibition on prayers was waived."

"And your answer?"

"I said this last council rule was the most important and must never be disobeyed."

I raise my cup of wine. Strange how easy it is to demoralize and disarm these traders.

"You did well."

〜✹〜

Each night, through slats in the dormitory's crude planked walls, I watch the traders light wicks in the worn nubs of pilfered candles. They shall be held to account. The Honourable Company would abominate such petty theft as this. Wouter will be informed of it. The men lie on their bunks, breathless and awake, like barnyard roosters in the slow silent slide of hours governed by adders and rats. I inhale their fear in the staleness of their sweat, the sour piss-stained corners beneath each bunk. I hear it in their sly whispers of escape. "We'll steal the raft," they murmur, "and make for High Island."

Insomniac that I am, impatient for the rise of Sirius, my sun, I relish their terror. I prowl outside the dormitory on my haunches like a wolf. I laugh at the teeming skies, ferrying westward their senseless ballast of stars.

ON THE TWENTY-THIRD DAY, my boys are not as efficient as I would have wished in their foray to Seal Island.

Instead of obeying my instructions to seize Lucretia, Wouter said the boys lost their nerve when they saw the castaways running toward them. Some of the women rushed into the waves and almost capsized the raft trying to climb aboard. Others attempted to pull Wouter and De Beere from the vessel. Poling in the shallows, Jacop slipped and lost his footing. One of the councillors lunged at him and, grabbing him by the throat, held him thrashing and flailing under water. In this chaos, Lucretia was at first nowhere to be seen; fearing for their lives, my lads had no choice but to open fire.

Somehow many Seal Islanders managed to escape. Unknown numbers fled into the bush or flung themselves beneath the waves. The councillors and four women were seen drifting beyond the swell on planks of wood. My boys will have to be sent again. But several of the escapees have at least saved extra work: for who could hope to navigate and survive these shark-infested seas?

At night and in stealth, Wouter and my lads returned, navigating the raft around the other side of the point. Summoning me, Carp led the way across the rocks, leaping ahead in great splashing strides, I following the flickering light of his taper.

Scrambling from boulder to boulder, slipping on weed slime, spray mist threatening to drench us, I cursed this madness, this unfathomable secrecy, until at last I espied the raft looming through opalescent wreaths of mist.

With all his might, De Beere drove his pole into clefts between the coral. And then I understood.

Six women clambered from the raft. Seeing *her*, I smiled—my fair lady returned to me at last, not alone as I would have liked, but safe nonetheless.

But—without consulting me, my lustful councillor-general could not resist these five other women, key witnesses all to the shooting, which means they will have to be kept under lock and key and constant surveillance. And who does Wouter propose will do that? Guiding his herd of young brides onto the shore, my boy was right to give me a wary look and a rueful grin. But I concede these women are modest maids and, could one persuade them to smile, they'd even be fair.

Then Wouter moved the women forward with the bull-hide handle of his whip. Afraid, they huddled together ankle-deep in soft gray waters, nostrils flared like cattle when, made to take an unexpected turn through abattoir gates, they catch the scent of their own blood for the first time.

I did not step from the shadows, extend one hand to greet her, escort Lucretia to my quarters, for to my surprise I found I enjoyed seeing her treated like the others, a concubine to be shared communally among us.

Without a moment to lose, I told Carp, these women must to be taken to the storeroom beside my quarters, where the nuptials would begin. I also gave Pelgrom orders to keep an armed vigil outside the dormitory.

And then, unobserved, I stole into the fading darkness of the night.

When a dawn sun burst like egg yolk on the seam of the horizon, my brave councillors arrived one by one. Dapper and uniformed, they were silent, solemn.

Wouter was first inside the storeroom when at last I slid the timber bolt from the door.

Trussed like turkeys, cowering in the center of the room, the women blinked in shafts of dim dawn light. Earlier, De Beere had taken the wise precaution of stoppering their mouths with rags. At our approach they moaned from the backs of their throats.

Wouter made the women stand against the salt-pork barrels stacked by the wall. Quite a catch. Even I admired them, ranged side by side, manacled by hands and feet. The councillors strutted back and forth, valuing their future wives. They untied the gags, forced fingers into soft mouths and prodded pearl-white teeth. They measured ankles and wrists and encircled their arms around slender waists.

Finally, Wouter chose a raven-haired girl, somewhat sallow in the cheek for my liking but pretty enough. De Beere was tense and undecided. He marched from one woman to another. Carp skipped around the room chattering nonsense to himself.

The women flinched from their touch and shivered in silence. Their wan posture and passive endurance reminded me of plaster-of-Paris saints.

Later, I gave Wouter orders to build a concubine pen in dense scrub some distance away from the main encampment.

~ఘ్లీ~

I've accepted my bride graciously of course. Pale and expressionless, she sits like a doll in my quarters. She is lean. Has lost those Rubens breasts and thighs, those dimpled cherub buttocks I despise.

She will do. I will brush her long red hair. Dress and

undress her in council uniform. Make her parade naked before me wearing only the Commandeur's hat.

ON THE TWENTY-FOURTH DAY, much to my astonishment I sight a plume of smoke rising in the thin blue air from High Island. Against every expectation, the toy soldiers must have found water. For surely otherwise they would not have survived this length of time. Another puff billows in the wind.

The question now is what to do with them. Damn Wouter. First he assures me there was no water on High Island, then botches the Seal Island venture by allowing several witnesses to flee.

If there's water on the island, why didn't Hayes light fires within the time frame we'd agreed? If, on the other hand, distrustful Hayes smelled a rat—there was always something brooding about his look which I did not like—if he wanted to see whether I'd hold true to our contract and send a raft to fetch them, then why light fires now? Unless, of course, those who escaped into the sea from Seal Island have somehow managed to join his mob. In which case these signals are none other than a declaration of war.

Ever the professional, how Hayes must regret leaving many of the muskets behind. What hope do these fools have against our artillery? Had they a tyrant in their midst, they'd be court-martialed and strung from every tree. But I, a benevolent ruler in this far-flung empire of mine, will buy the soldiers out, win their trust. For a skirmish between us will sabotage my plan. They might be the first to alert the rescue ship when it arrives. I'll send Wouter across with triple salaries, corporate cash. I know the way to their hearts, the French mercenaries in particular, who switch sides according to the weight of gold in their pockets.

ON THE TWENTY-FIFTH DAY, blue smoke hangs like a gauze above High Island. They are still lighting fires.

This morning, my emissary of fools returned from the soldiers' island—defeated. Wouter says the raft scraped the reef and they had to continue on foot, slipping and sliding on seaweed mudflats. Then they were ambushed by stones hurled from the soldiers' primitive catapults. As I had surmised, several of the escapees from Seal Island are also among them. They've even built a rudimentary fortress on the hill. Without meat or wine, their uniforms in shreds, how *could* Hayes and his men have put up this resistance? But my boys must not have had the right manner, and in this place even gold has lost its currency. I will woo them instead with blankets and bread.

❧

Dipping my pen in the last of the ink, I am careful in the composition of my letter.

Beloved Wiebbe Hayes, beloved brothers and friends, I begin. *The more we consider amongst ourselves your previous faithfulness and brotherly friendship, the more we wonder that you—who left willingly at my request to survey High Island—did not first bring us word.*

More, I continue, *we think it strange that you seemed to give hearing to the tale-bearing of some evildoers who here had deserved death on account of mutiny but came to you without our knowledge. Now then, beloved brothers, let us sign a truce to help us maintain justice. After you receive this, Wouter will return on the raft for your answer within five days.*

I sign with a flourish.

 THIS ENDLESS HEAT becomes oppressive. Daily the pirating winds raid clouds from smooth unruffled spinster skies which mock us with their barrenness. How I long for fecund, frisky consummations between air and vapors, the first splats of fragrant summer rain, splashing dust from linden leaves, pockmarking the paved and cobbled streets of Amsterdam.

I am finding my wife's silence a bore. She sits so still on the bed, beneath the only mosquito net saved from the wreck. I, gallant that I am, now spend the nights swinging from a hammock hooked to crossbeams on either side of the bolted door.

My wife has a fancy noblewoman's name. Lucretia. Like the tragic heroines in romantic melodramas. And she is tragic, sitting there so pale. A damsel in distress. For whom jousting knights would slay dragons, decapitate giants, neglect their holy grail.

Imagine the joyous roars from any theater audience, sucking bonbons in cheap stalls, to see you, Lucretia, plucked from the jaws of death by my naughty savage boys, at times themselves none too tender with axes and sabers. Saved for the grand finale by the hero, striding center stage, handsome in his scarlet gold-brocaded uniform. Listen to their rapturous ovation.

Lucretia is a fine name but too dramatic for my taste, for this gentle idyll, this prelapsarian pastoral. I should call her Marie. Marie the marionette. What does it matter? She would answer to neither and turn her proud patrician profile to the wall.

⁓⟊☙

This morning, Carp bathes my bride in rosewater, paints her lips into cupid bows, brushes her streaming hair until it crackles and flickers like flames.

Still not one single word. Carp sweats at his work. He should be rewarded for his devotions. Be allowed to kiss the lady. Eager Carp pastes his gargoyle grin against her fingers. Ah—a reaction. She flinches and snatches away her hand.

Cruel lady, you should be kinder to this love-struck fool. See how you affect him. Spittle drools from one side of his lopsided mouth. A kiss, my dear, just one single kiss. But no.

"Dress her, Carp," I say.

Obedient Carp lifts her arms. Slips silken petticoats over her obstinate head. Buttons my pretty puppet's chemise until she is attired in the garments of the dead.

Dismissing Carp, I watch him trot down the hill to his own child-wife tethered with the others in the concubine pen. For, as I explained, the council must have equal share of the rations, the goods, the chattels.

~~~

I should take my leave. Let her listen to the song birds outside and learn from them how to trill and squeak.

But it's time my wife and I had a talk. I pour two glasses of vintage burgundy and draw a chair beside the bed. Lucretia averts her face. Gently I lift the mosquito net. She crouches against the wall. I want to watch her speak, watch her lips. I am worn out with desire for this lost green-eyed girl.

She begins to shiver. Maybe my poor darling is afraid. Yes, it's time we had a talk and there is much to say. Gently I drape my cloak about her shoulders. She stiffens but does not resist. I place the wine glass in one cold hand and urge her, gently, gently, to take a sip, which she does, and then another.

First I apologize for the primitive conditions of her first night's accommodation here.

"The harshness of this place has turned the men

wild," I say. "You were kept in the storehouse solely for your protection."

She crouches there but I know she is listening. She remains silent, eyes fixed on the bolted door.

"Don't be afraid," I whisper. "For I've pledged my soul to protect you and I assure you there can be no stronger bastion of defense than these quarters."

She slides a glance toward me and away again.

I study her. She has drawn her thin, childlike body tight against the wall and clasps the wineglass as if she'd never held one before. I watch her take another sip.

I look at her. I go on looking at her. There is something illusory about her. I want to inhale her every breath. But her silence shuts me out, makes me want to close my hands on her delicate blue-veined throat.

If only she would allow me into her mind. If only she would speak. But not a word. There is nothing to read in that blank, averted face, no emotions reflected in those large, vacant eyes. My lady is a mask. I long to strip away the mask and see her face plain. But how? If only she would speak, for these are strange games we are playing in the darkness.

Wouter said he found her on the far side of Seal Island cradling a dead child in her arms.

I ponder my moves. How to take this queen? As rightful emperor, it would be easy to have her. Gently part those slender thighs, stroke her childish breasts

—but I don't. For where's the joy in forcing it? I might as well use those gaudy sequined mannequins my friend Torrentius once devised, those wooden puppets with frilled hair and padded silk for breasts. No—this wife has become a personal challenge of mine. She will love me in the end.

So. How to win Lucretia's trust? For I would rather crown a queen than hold my wife prisoner, cringing on this leaf-strewn floor. But I've gauged her strength, measured her will. Only by force would she bend to my desires and receive the scepter in her hand.

Thinking on it, it would be easy to make Wouter the enemy, the villain of the piece. I could describe how Wouter and his crazed band of henchmen have run wild. Madness sings in their blood now they've seized control of the island and made me their puppet leader with half-witted Carp my keeper. Taking her in my arms, I would ask whether she understood the mortal danger we were in and the importance in pretending to be one of them, that only by colluding with the enemy could we help ourselves and perhaps others to survive. I would kiss those wordless lips, nuzzle the inexpressible softness of her skin and tell her to be brave for it was only a matter of time before the rescue ship arrived.

An intriguing scenario, I'm the first to admit, and having Wouter play the villain a clever stroke. But my own part does not convince as much. There's something lacking in the texture of it. Try as I might, I can't see myself cast in the role of fate's hapless hero.

No, I want her to love me for who I am, Captain-General of this isle.

I must give Lucretia her liberty, draw the bolt from the door, allow her to exercise her own free will and choose whether to remain with me, her protector, or take a chance with Wouter and his men.

I'll give her the facts and she'll hear them plain.

I inform her that this island is a dangerous place and my position as governor by no means an easy one. Daily, the thieving survivors trick and deceive us. Used to having their way, I say, the hot-blooded councillors take liberties with liquor rations and resolve council disputes with sharpened knives.

I tell Lucretia she is free to seek protection with whomever she chooses. Next I also make the point that should she leave the safety of these quarters, I would not be accountable for any hazard she might meet.

This time she looks at me. Her huge dark eyes sear my heart.

"Do you know why you've been brought here?" I ask.

Again she remains silent. Not a flicker of emotion on her face. She swirls the last of her wine around and around the glass and takes a furtive sip, and another, until only incarnadine dregs are left. She stares at these droplets as if they were the rarest of jewels. She makes them slide from one side of the glass to the other like beads on an abacus.

She is looking at me now. Wants me to watch. And I do, unable to take my eyes from her.

ON THE TWENTY-EIGHTH DAY, marching my councillors up and down the beach in their new scarlet tunics, I notice an unusual number of sharks by the reef sending a blue light each time they rise to the surface.

Terns too are arriving in flocks. They swarm over the waves like bees, unsettling my boys, whose nerves seem frayed, set on edge lately.

At breakfast I offer my wife, still mute and unsmiling, six of the plumpest oysters, which I place on her plate. She stares unseeing at the ocean, stirred with the fins of sharks. All around us a beating of wings. Wouter has taken to eating with one arm over his bowl as if expecting the birds to snatch food from the table. It gives him a furtive expression which I don't like.

A cloud of terns spirals into the sky. They seem to be fighting over fish innards, which stream like pale pink pennants from their beaks. I can't help admiring the ruthless pageantry of their flight. They swoop toward us, pecking and shrieking at one another.

A viscous strand of bloodied membrane drops onto my wife's plate. Her scream makes Wouter jump.

I prod the fleshy gristle with my fork. Remarkable. Pierced with one single pearl, the earlobe remains intact. I remember her well, she was plump and soft as Eve.

My councillors bow their heads. I'm more amused than disappointed by Pelgrom's sly genuflections. Prayers will not help him now.

ON THE TWENTY-NINTH DAY, it strikes me how much of my time on this island is spent waiting.

Waiting for the rescue ship to arrive.

For my wife to speak—so far not one word.

For the council to report on the previous night's activities.

For daily reports of petty thefts and disobediences.

For Wouter to stop fucking the wives. He goes at them like a bull day and night. But I do indulge him in these pleasures. Even though I'd rather he were at my side.

For the lookout to be built. Crawling with sand fleas, the coral festers on the shore like a dung heap. But I never expected much from those gold counters and indigo traders, who don't know the meaning of a hard day's work. More beasts than men. Why, ribs now poke through the caulker's skin.

Each morning they stumble to keep pace with the summoning blasts of De Beere's bugle. I've been watching De Beere. He takes pride in his job. A good guard who enjoys cracking that whip, the blows he inflicts.

He exhibits a keen curiosity in the suffering of man. It is not that he acts in hatred or in anger, but is curious to find out how a certain flick of his whip can snatch skin from a scab.

I would call it a scientific study. He makes an eager student. Adept not only at the whip, but at gauging the exact register of tone to sink a man.

"Is anyone to be boxed on the ear?" he calls. "I will do it for a tot."

If someone, say Stoffel the caulker, complains that his hands are being cut to ribbons by the reef, he is hauled before the others.

"What is your number?" he shouts. "Who are you?"

If a man makes the mistake of describing his profession, he spits in his face.

"Remember you are nothing here."

If he comes across a slacker picking off dainty coral crumbs with his fingers, he'll round on him.

"You pig," he screams. "I've been watching you the whole time. I'll teach you to work yet."

Then fierce as a leopard he is on the man, forcing his head into gritty pools of water.

"I'll make you dig with your teeth."

The man is brought up, choking and retching.

"You'll die like an animal."

Most curious of all, the others continue their monotonous toil, chipping and breaking the coral, and take no notice of their comrade's plight. Past caring.

De Beere is not only an exemplary student but an efficient teacher. It seems a long time ago when I had to placate an angry mob with funerals and twilight prayers. Look at these men now. Meek as pet bunnies. Obedient as sheep in a pen.

Again De Beere pushes the unfortunate's head down then drags him to his feet. The man sways sadly, forlornly, as if dancing to some half-remembered tune. Perhaps he misses his wife. Tied to a post in the concubine tent! For they still don't know of our recent arrivals. Kept under lock and key.

⁓✸℘

By the last count, the number of prisoners here has been reduced to forty-two.

 ON THE THIRTIETH DAY, pouring water into my agate vase, I notice iridescent whorls of grease rising to the surface. Our water stocks turn rancid.

In this heat and with no promise of rain from empty skies, it is imperative we forge an alliance with Hayes on High Island, combine our resources, share our supplies. Today I'll send Wouter across on the raft for Hayes's reply to my letter, which in my mind clarified any misunderstanding we once might have had.

It is to my advantage that Hayes is such a sensible, practical man. He will be the first to dismiss the wild ravings of hysterical women. Whining shrews all, those who together with the ex-councillors escaped from my boys to High Island. Who of right mind would believe their delusions, their insane talk of sabers and killings?

Hayes and I will agree on a deal. He'll send water and I provisions.

Beneath the mosquito net, my wife lies slumped on the bed. Catatonic witch. I have wooed her with fond, flattering words and caresses. Not used harsh words or chastised her. I have acted the perfect gentleman, chivalrous to the end. I have also safeguarded her privacy. She finds solace in solitude and has no reason to believe there are spies among the shadows, spiders waiting in the darkness.

Of all the survivors on this island, she receives the finest delicacies: poached gull breasts, fillets of fish, the *Batavia*'s precious rations, salt beef, cured hams, even eggs from Dutch hens.

And these succulent libations the fair lady eats. No refinement there. She snatches food with her fingers and bolts it like a dog, even though she has been given a wooden spoon. Knives, of course, I have forbidden.

The little gourmand cannot refuse the treats I procure. She belches after each meal like a common brothel hussy. Sometimes I think she acts in this way to provoke me. She knows I don't like it.

Today I set the tray beside her. A ham cooked by Carp to perfection and carved from the haunch of those wild hopping animals which Wouter so artfully ensnares in the scrub; a platter of coral fish, crisp as whitebait; and one dozen oysters.

Always when I arrive with these feasts, my wife creeps across the bed and crouches on her knees. Without looking at me, she extends her hands to grab the tray, then quick as a flash slithers to her usual position by the wall and gorges on her booty. How she gnaws and gulps and crunches. It fairly sets my teeth on edge.

Yet I am certain that in her previous life, taking lunch in the hour between *petit point* and harpsichord practice, between games of lansquenet and visits from the minister's wife, Lucretia would have crumbled bread rolls into small, fastidious pieces and lifted them to her mouth with a languid, lace-gloved hand. She would have sipped her tisane and set the cup on its saucer without a clink or rattle. She would have peeled a grape, deseeded a pomegranate, or pared an apple with a polished silver fruit knife. She would have cut pastries into elegant, wafer-thin slices and left crumbs on her plate in polite tidy piles. When it was time for the frilled and capped maid to pitterpat across the parlor and clear the cherrywood table, when the dishes were set aside and the starched white cloth folded, unstained by one single drop of ale or smear of butter, my wife would have dabbed her immaculate painted lips with an embroidered handkerchief scented with lavender water.

Look at her now. Cross-legged on rumpled sheets, back against the wall. Wide-eyed, predatory as a cat, she watches me pour the wine, which I do slowly, drop by ruby drop. I inhale the pungent blackcurrant bouquet of a rich burgundy, which seems to be her favorite. Sometimes my wife becomes impatient and almost growls in the back of her throat.

When I hand her the wine through the mosquito

net, she pounces on the glass, takes a deep draught, and smacks her lips, watching me all the time.

Usually I give her the tray, but today I have decided to vary our routine.

From my top pocket, I take out a gold knife and fork once commissioned by the Mogul Court.

First, I prepare the ham. My knife sinks into the rare pink-veined flesh which, soft as butter, falls in fragrant slabs from the bone. My wife narrows her eyes and slides her tongue around her lips.

I cut the meat into small cubes and skewer a piece. She crawls across the bed. I dangle the fork before her. With a gull-like swoop she devours the morsel.

Strange, this hunger of hers. Yet, no doubt in Amsterdam, my elegant wife would have attended balls and banquets only to push food around her plate and feel each mouthful press against her whaleboned corset.

Besides, I am sure she was fed yesterday, or if not then the day before. But time shrinks, telescopes, plays cunning games on this island and it becomes more of an effort to flick open the past like a fan.

Again I proffer a succulent portion, again she wrests it from the prong of my fork. Juice dribbles down her chin.

Tenderly, I wipe it with the tip of the Commandeur's handkerchief. Stabbing the meat, I allow her another taste.

I have often wondered at man's brutish fear of

mortality, his determination to survive when surely the choicest blessing of this life is the power to end it.

But perhaps my wife's flesh creeps at the thought of committing a mortal sin.

At the next forkful, the fish this time, I demand a kiss.

"Just one," I say.

Now she stares at me fearfully. Gently, I place one hand on the nape of her neck. She'll eat my food but not look at me—the sneaky slut. Although she trembles, I am able to brush her lips with mine. Her hungry mouth is greased with meat fat. She flinches but allows me to stroke her hair, weigh it in my hand like a burnished skein of silk.

And for these modest yet exquisite pleasures, I reward my lady well. Look at her now, swallowing brine-sweet oysters fresh from their shell.

Because last night I left the door unbolted and my wife made no attempt to flee, because today it seems Lucretia has made a choice to remain with me, because in the exchange of kisses and caresses the hours slide closer to the consummation of our marriage vows—and for that we have time in plenty—I decide to celebrate. I unlock the Commandeur's escritoire and share my joy in his private hoard of jewels.

First I take out the Roman agate cameo and run my fingers over its familiar grooves and curves. I hold it up to the window. A soft early morning light plays over the cameo's honeyed surface and makes it gleam like gold.

Kneeling beside the bed, I show this treasure to Lucretia. But having gorged, she feigns indifference once again.

I tell her the amulet once belonged to Rubens, who consigned it to the Commandeur for private trade. I unclasp the black velvet choker and beckon her to my side. She makes no effort to move. I lean over and, sweeping that heavy hair from her shoulders, I fasten the cameo around her neck.

"Now it's yours." She touches the jewel lightly with the tips of her fingers.

"It will buy you kingdoms," I say. "Imagine the furor such a sale would create among the burghers of Amsterdam."

Do I imagine it, or did she look at me and smile? I study her. But she retreats behind her mask of silence, molds her features to its wooden expression of passive endurance. She brandishes this silence before me like a talisman. It locks the door to her soul, the one possession I am not allowed to have.

Yet I will give her everything as a token of my love. I slip the Commandeur's emerald ring from my finger and enclose it in the palm of her hand. Her small fist tightens beneath my touch.

I am even tempted to offer her the carved agate vase, but decide to wait until our wedding night, when I'll fill the precious artifact with all the perfumes of Arabia, anoint and prepare my bride for a lover's bed.

Afterward, when the rescue ship has delivered us from these shores, I will take Lucretia to a distant land, where I shall reign as emperor, and she as my queen. We will ride through our new kingdom on be-jeweled elephants with retinues of leopards snapping at our heels. I'll resurrect Torrentius's words and teach new disciples to become his children of the sun.

Together my wife and I will explore pleasure in a journey without end. I will build a city of marble palaces, jasmine-scented courtyards, gold minarets and domes. I will give my queen the keys to her own private harem and watch her rule like Cleopatra over eunuchs, dwarves, virgin slaves, bought at a fair price in the marketplace.

It makes my blood quicken to think of it.

How my wife must relish her good fortune in hav-ing found salvation in the Captain-General, who treats her with the utmost courtesy and kindness, at-tends to her every meal like a devoted butler, daily lav-ishes her with gifts and costly jewels. She, who was condemned to a marriage of convenience.

I can just see this husband of hers riding perfectly balanced on a gray mare, heels firm in the stirrups, back straight despite the heat, the flies at the corners of his lips. He urges his horse into a gallop and hurries to the port where no anchor is dropped, no ship docks. I wonder what the smooth corporate custom officials told him from behind neat polished desks. I wonder what they said about the loss of the *Batavia*, their Company ship.

"When I arrive," I imagine Lucretia saying to him, "we'll suck oranges on crescent coves, gather shells on wave-flattened shores."

How naive you were then.

"When I arrive," you said, "I'll unhook mosquito nets, hang washing in the sun, learn patois from slant-eyed maids, scrub indigo trays, and sweep ants from our hearth."

But you have not arrived. And the gods have re-turned my lost, green-eyed girl to me.

AT LAST Wouter brings word from Hayes.

We sit outside in the shade, out of earshot from my wife, who at this languid siesta hour sleeps, lost in dreams. Sometimes her life returns to how it once was, then she wakes, stretches—and with a start remembers. Then, how still she lies, one arm reclined beneath russet curls twining the nape of her neck, the other clasped around both knees. Bunched above slender ankles, her cotton petticoats reveal blue veins pulsing on the arched curve of each instep. I long to kiss those forbidden networks of ink.

This matrimonial bed has become a netted sanctuary for Lucretia. Each night in my hammock, I swing restless as a bat beneath the eaves of this hutch, embalmed in celibate solitude, sleepless in the darkness. But I'll not touch her. Not just yet.

Pouring Wouter a glass of wine, I reflect that it seems a long time ago that I had to comfort an anxious, eager slip of a lad who thought we'd all die here, who lamented the fact there was no water to be found, either on the soldiers' or Seal Island. Regarding the latter, at least, he was right.

Today, Wouter seems restless, ajitter. His hands shake when he gulps the wine. Maybe I should soothe his nerves with an opium pipe.

Blowing fragrant plumes of smoke through his nostrils, Wouter tells me that he and Pelgrom wisely refused Hayes's entreaties to land the raft, on account of the hail of stones they previously received from the soldiers' catapults. Instead they requested that Hayes alone meet them on an outcrop of rock lying on the north side of the island.

Despite the suspicion, the distrust that has grown between both parties since their last *rendez-vous*, it seems that Hayes thought my proposal to share the rations worth considering. But said he must discuss the matter with his men, who would not however be difficult to persuade. Hayes also told Wouter that the escapees from Seal Island were being held in custody until such time as an agreement was reached between us, which he hoped would happen soon enough. So he has instructed Wouter to return unarmed with wine and clothing and he will negotiate a date for us to officially draft a reconciliation pact.

Wine and clothing—I always knew Hayes would be cheap to buy. The French mercenaries will demand more than that.

ON THE THIRTY-FIRST DAY, a citrus dawn floods the horizon. At this hour, the air is pure. Gulls rise in shafts of newborn golden light. I love these first quickening rhythms of the day, before the sun shrinks in the quivering skies.

Allocating rations to be sent to High Island, I decide on a keg of fine vintage brandy for Mr. Hayes and his doughty warriors, Bordeaux for the French mercenaries, and two sides of salt beef, five jars of sauerkraut, three of salt herring.

On reflection, it must be said that Hayes is a good man, maybe somewhat nationalistic for my liking, but he is a battler. There were too many parades in Amsterdam, young men like Hayes marching in step to the trumpeter's call. The civilians came out in droves, threw streamers from chilblained mittened hands, cheered these sons of the nation, who, with heads held high, helmets buckled beneath beardless chins, neither looked to the left nor to the right.

Pondering my moves, I wonder whether I should take a risk and raise the stakes in this game—my final checkmate. Once I gain his trust, why not make Hayes my confidant? Unfold my secret plan, the precise course of action to be taken when the rescue ship arrives.

An alliance forged between us would seal the successful outcome of my strategy, equipped as Hayes is with more knights than I.

Imagine, I will tell him, the rescue ship glancing the reef on a low tide, the jubilant shouts, the oars splashing the waves. After such a long journey, the crew will have had a hard time of it. They'll be cheered by the feast, the roast meats, the speeches, libations and wines.

At this, bon vivant Hayes will smile, conspiratorial in the candlelight.

We'll make the crew drunk, I'll explain, in order to kill them more easily.

And Hayes will grasp my hand like a true friend, like an old friend. Like Torrentius, who bid sad *adieus*, before the English ambassador escorted him to the court of King Charles.

The more I think on it, Hayes is my man. When Wouter delivers the provisions, I will request an appointment. Meet him fair and square on his own home turf, on the shores of High Island.

The Predikant has not graced me with another interview following our last exchange. Strange, for I thought he was eager to hear my confession. Instead he keeps to his hut and forbids his wife and children to venture outside, not even for the daily rations, which only he collects.

I notice too that the Predikant has lost his paunch, those plump folds of skin. His gown is looser, longer, and trails sand and leaves in his wake.

At dawn, at the night-watch change when those next on duty still slumber in their bunks, he steals across to the dormitory and goes from one prisoner to another, offering comfort and prayers, pleading with them to hope against hope, not give way to despair.

In lengthening shadows, in shell-pink pools of light, they kneel. Then my stealthy Predikant brings out a parcel from beneath his belt. Not a Bible this time, but a contraband of rations. These he breaks into crumbs and distributes to the men, who beg for more. Shame he's not learned the old trick with fishes and loaves.

Why should these traders have such a haunted, hunted look when clearly choices are available in this empire of mine? They can take many courses of action in order to survive. They can join my disciples at their game for an extra day of life, to tip the balance their way. Yet they do nothing, except wait, weighed by a sense of submission or defeat. De Beere says it is because they all expect to be executed at any time.

On the *Batavia*, the merchants were so confident of their arrival. How quickly they became bored with the voyage, marking time with dances, games of lansquenet, idle feints at tedium, anything to keep occupied.

Now they'd trade their souls for that endless blue-gauzed monotony. Of course, they heard rumors on board, talk of pirates, whispers of mutiny, malaria among the crew, but they took no notice. After all, the *Batavia* was a Company ship, strictly business, a corporate venture. Then one day an appearance of gulls on a slanting wind. They should have feared that graceful, soundless flight. Instead they cheered when the crew baited them one by one with hooks nailed to bamboo sticks.

I do believe the Predikant has changed. This interlude on the island has made a man of him. A brave one at that, for should De Beere catch him at his charitable work, he'd whip out his sword and chop off his head. This man of God is truer here than at any other time.

In his former sanctuary of marble colonnades and stained-glass images on arched windows, our Predikant was susceptible to the perks of his profession: braces of pheasant, jugs of claret, cakes baked by those tearful, repentant merchant wives, sieving their sins in pastry bowls of flour and water, butter on plump fingers loosening wedding rings.

Sin—what did they know of the word? Sin, round

and juicy as an apple. Red as the cheeks of the tailor's wife, the cooper's youngest sister, the caulker's daughter.

Now the Predikant reminds me of another. The way he strokes his beard, listens to each man's lament. The gliding step, the sandaled feet, the flowing gown, recall an ancient adversary of mine. In the haze of early morning heat a halo even shimmers above his head. Tell me, shriver of souls, is your destiny to become this unmapped hemisphere's first saint?

MY WIFE STILL allows me the privilege of feeding her, has come to expect it. And I enjoy my new role as Lucretia's provider. Indeed, my love for her is brewing from my soul a tenderness which I never knew I had.

Her appetite knows no bounds. Already she has sucked the rockpools dry of lobsters, crayfish, and shrimp. Carp has to scavenge beyond the point and venture farther along the exposed ragged stretches of coral sluiced by fierce tides, which I know he fears and does not like. Wouter has hunted those hopping rats in such numbers that the herd is much reduced. But my wife must eat and has my word she'll dine on the finest fare this island can produce. See how I look after her? Were it not for my love, my tender solicitude, she would starve like the wretched traders. But I will never allow that.

In many ways, I believe my wife and I are alike. Set apart from the common lot of man, the tedious toiling grind of life—gross couplings, bastard births, infirmity, and death—the ceaseless trundle of mortality rolling like plow wheels on a dusty, rutted track.

Still she does not speak, but I allow her this one freedom and have become accustomed to her silence.

Besides, why talk, why should she utter a word, when so vividly I can imagine her former life, almost as if I were there?

Whenever I ask her to describe the house where she was born on the Herenstraat, I already find myself treading the paved paths strewn with winter leaves beneath avenues of limes. I pass the clipped box hedge, click open the gate, and enter the walled garden. I pause to admire espaliered rows of flowering peach, for whenever I think of my wife's life in Amsterdam, it is always early spring, days of mackerel skies tinged green at the horizon. I take the path toward the sundial and there I see her, seated on a carved stone bench in a dappled pool of light. Head bent, she embroiders peacock tails with emerald silk. Her false suitor kneels at her feet, plays the lover's fool, weaves fast-fading wreaths of daisy chains. He is older than I thought. He talks of their new home in Batavia, tells her of silent saffron rivers, earth baked crimson, cobbled streets awash with violet infusions. He entwines the flowers around her dazzling white shoulders and brays in delight like a vulgar goatherd. She can't love this man, who stoops to kiss the gold ring on her hand.

Arms linked, they stroll toward the house, and I

follow just one step behind. A gardener tugs his fore-lock and a greyhound runs squealing at my approach, recalling some other time, the details of which I can no longer remember.

I admire my new family and size up the dowry, a fine merchant's mansion, gabled in the traditional style. There is Mother in the doorway, dewy-eyed at the sight of her first engaged daughter. There is Father in the study, poring over his tithe rents. A young sibling, flaxen ringlets spilling from her cap, drives a hoop along the path. From the parlor, I glimpse another sister tinkling some sad refrain on the harpsichord. An elder brother paces the checkered, polished entrance hall, no doubt yearning for the hour of *bagnios* and stews. Apothecary that I am, it would come as no surprise to learn that his balls are ticklish and will require a physician's prescription soon.

Maybe I, their future son-in-law, should introduce myself. Her family would approve, I am sure. And the dull rival hovering at their side would diminish in my presence.

I look at Lucretia and smile. I tell her there is no need to confide in me when I know all her secrets.

My poor darling sits there so gaunt-faced and pale. You would think she'd enjoy my excursions into the past, at the very least thank me for delivering her from a tedious end, a mere wife consigned to primitive, unpeopled lands.

I must bring the blood to her lips. It is time for my

wife to take her medicine. She does not seem to suspect that the wine which she gulps, the endless libations I offer, even coarse brandy, are laced with the subtlest of brews.

Today, I prepare quintessence of mithridate, calcine vitriols, and opium tinctures. With infinite care, I mix this love potion in a cup of canary wine.

Despite her frail frame, my wife has a remarkable constitution: it takes a while before the aphrodisiac has the desired effect and her legs go limp, her eyes glassy, even though I administer double the dose.

I have always reserved my philters secret from hackney apothecaries by preparing them myself. This particular potion purges from the blood all phlegm and melancholy humors, produces hectic fevers in the breasts and loins of either sex, and operates briskly. I have expanded my range of compounds and witnessed their efficacies from repeated experiments on convicted malefactors in Amsterdam's jails—our city magistrates allowed apothecaries to try new medicines on felons for the good of mankind.

And for the good of mankind they were. Like no others. I was not the garden-physician that the dungeoned and doomed were accustomed to expect, cramming mouths with juleps and syrups, stuffing resistant sphincters with suppositories and pellets. Resigned to swing on dawn scaffolds and dance with death, how gratified the condemned were to see their poor shriveled yards rise for the last time.

Taken in various strengths, my potions brought more solace and joy to those damned souls than any Predikant's prayers. On judgment day, they would rather spit their seed than receive stale wine and wafer sacraments.

I considered my experiments a civic duty, a charitable exercise in philanthropy, for it has to be said that, noose around their necks, my obedient and willing patients died content.

I trialed my medicines too in the women's factory and noted similar effects. Once, to my amusement, the prison warden decreed her inmates possessed by the Devil and summoned the chaplain, a blushing stammering man, who the previous week had been called to exorcise a neighboring convent, afflicted by a similar hysterical condition: violations with candles and crucifixes, bondage and self-flagellation in every cell, a cruel epidemic of lust which strangely our fair wimpled sex seems to enjoy. But cowering behind prison walls, dousing the women with ineffectual sprinkles of holy water, the chaplain shrank behind his Bible, confessed he had never seen quite such a case as this, and fled from the scene.

My wife's cheeks are flushed, her pulse rapid, her parted lips pink and swollen. She responds well to the opium and sleeps, bathed in dreams like a princess from a fairy tale. I want her to sleep, dive in deep, spiraling underwater descents, and not have those blank staring eyes fixed on mine. For today I intend to study my wife. As any anatomist will reveal, a close observation of the human body is crucial to the apothecary's art and provides a competent knowledge of its natural constitution in all parts.

First I remove from my bride a jacket of Indian cotton, presented by the Company to the carpenter's wife, then a sleeveless bodice decorated with crimson vertical bands, belonging to the caulker's spouse. I unbutton a pale green satin dress. How proudly the gold trader's wife paraded its elegant tapered lines, swished the ruched train at the back.

I slip from my wife's shoulders a shift embroidered in forget-me-nots, a pink lace petticoat (with a neat mend at the seam darned by the cooper's daughter), white frilled undergarments. Last, I untie a maroon velvet toque which that shameless hussy, the girl with pearls in her ears, pinned to her snood at fashionable angles.

I am pleased Wouter discovered several of the women's sea chests on Seal Island. For it would not be fitting for the Captain-General's wife to go about in common rags.

My wife reclines naked on the bed, embalmed in the veils of my drugs. She moans and murmurs beneath her breath. Her eyelids flutter. Looking at her, I wonder if perhaps she is feigning sleep, longing for my embrace, playing games in the darkness.

Gently, I unplait her hair and watch those rich burgundy tresses burst from their bondage and stream across her shoulders. I marvel at the contrast between her red hair and her white skin. My Lady Godiva, riding through town with her head held high.

I stroke the soft, sumptuous novelty of her skin. I slip my fingers into her mouth, search for her moist tongue, the sharpness of her teeth.

Strange, but today in this most intimate moment we so far have shared, I feel nothing.

I feel no lust for her, except a thrilling sense of wonder at her flawless beauty, as if she were an emblem of her sex, a precious sculpture into which I've breathed life, and at last has come into my possession to be stored among rare and exquisite artifacts, the most prized acquisition in any connoisseur's private collection. I kiss the cameo at her throat, the emerald ring on her finger.

I want to set her like a statue on a pedestal, on this bed, and watch her pose in every profane attitude of desire. I won't touch her. I only want to look, venerate her body, still innocent and unaware of the fabulous power of its beauty. She has no knowledge of her small childlike breasts, yields them unknowingly in her dreams for hands to caress, for lips to eat, for teeth to bite.

I will catalogue every part of her, the sculpted, high-cheekboned face, the mole on her upper lip, the lines of her spine, each of these vertebrae etched like an engraving along her strong, slender back, the sharp curves of her hips, the porcelain smoothness of her belly.

Watching her, I revel in my absolute power of possession and I am satisfied. That is how I feel for this wife of mine. She drowses lightly, drifts on the cusp of sleep. She will remember these dreams, and when she wakes will yearn for them to return again.

I am worn out by her beauty. It's too much. Something precious to be taken out of a perfumed box, revered, worshiped, then wrapped in gold cloth and put away again.

ON THE THIRTY-THIRD DAY, skies and sea waver in a luminous blue haze. Five prisoners have escaped. They threw themselves into the brimming swell while working on the reef. De Beere fired his musket but they dived underwater and he lost sight of them, although he did observe several sharks swiftly closing in. These predators of the sea have proved a most effective deterrent on this island, more so than any prison wall. But from now on the men will be shackled together to make sure this incident does not happen again.

I despair of the lookout being completed. Terns circle the coral mounds on the beach, snapping at kelp fleas and other indescribable vermin surfacing from the relics of the reef.

Standing there, cracking his whip among beating wings, De Beere has a satanic look. He reminds me of a fallen angel. A watchkeeper at Pandemonium's gates.

This youth has found a way into my affection. More so sometimes than Wouter, my fiery hot-headed ram.

If I'd known, I would have rounded up the wives sooner or saved more to be kept constantly at the task with him.

When not with the women, Wouter prowls the main encampment. Had fate not dispatched him to this graveyard at the world's end, had circumstances been different, Wouter would have cut a fine figure in politics, gifted as he is with subtle rhetorical skills. In his old life, he would have dazzled the nation.

Listen to him now. "Who wants to be stabbed to death?" he calls. "I can do that very beautifully. Who wants to be stabbed?"

Gulls sheer into the wind at my approach. De Beere has to shout commands over their constant shrieking staccato. The birds float like petals over the waves then curve toward the shore again.

De Beere is conducting an experiment of sorts. Gently he strokes his whip across a cabin boy's back. The boy must be insensible to pain. He continues to work with barely a shudder. I watch the men tear the reef with their bare hands. So little for their labors, it makes the bile rise in my throat. Over the shrilling gulls, I call De Beere.

"Slow work," I shout.

De Beere nods, unable to take his eyes from the boy. Gulls swing back and forth on ocean rhythms.

I take out my dagger.

"Stick Stoffel," I say, pointing out the caulker, slipping and sliding in the shallows. "Stick Stoffel," I say louder this time. "The lazy fellow who stands there working as if his back is broken."

De Beere grasps the knife.

"Stick him," I command. "Through the heart."

And De Beere does, again and again he does. It has to be said, out of all my boys De Beere does me proud.

—⁂—

At dusk, I watch trails of shipwrecked clouds drift across burned rust-red skies. This is the silent hour after the gulls have ceased their whirling descent to twig and weed rookeries, when only the wind scratching the island's coral pelt and the creeping rush of the sea can be heard. Filmed in a lunar phosphorescence, the shifting waters seem membranous, muscular, sleek as dolphin backs.

This is the long, languorous hour when I like to return to my quarters, lift Lucretia from her box, spread those precious wares, anatomize the quintessence of female beauty.

I have taken the precaution of again locking the door, not to keep my bride prisoner, but for her protection in these perilous times.

But this evening when I slide the bolt through the catch, she fixes me with such piteous, accusing eyes that I cannot bear to look at her and have to turn away. There is something else about her expression, a defiance which I've seen before and do not trust or like.

Yet I thought I had tamed my wild bird, who feeds so prettily from my hand each time I open the gilt door to her cage; but perhaps I've underestimated the power of that monstrous silence which she flaunts as her one freedom and right.

I light the candelabra. In the lengthening, flickering shadows, I feel her watching me.

Maybe only now am I beginning to understand the implacable strength of this mute, wordless wife, a very portrait of submission, yet who sets her silence on me like a wolf baying for blood.

I pour a glass of wine. My hands tremble. I must be tired tonight.

Her silence lives and breathes. Everywhere I hear its prowling presence. Why, the room roars with the sound of it, pressing against the walls, forcing open the door, sprouting tough briar shoots and stems around my sleeping beauty's bed.

Yes, I am beginning to understand this diabolical silence of hers which she commands to wink and sneer at me, spew obscene torrents of unspoken words, rattle vile vermined batwings at my approach.

She thinks to make a fool of her Captain-General, cuckold him with silence. I've been slow to catch on to her devious games, duped into playing with a puppet —Marie the marionette—which smirks lascivious smiles from a doll face, while the real Lucretia, flesh and blood wife, stands impervious behind the shield of her silence and scorns my loving tenderness.

At last I see her plain. By refusing to speak, my wife safeguards her innocence. I admire her self-control, that constant vigilance. She is stronger than I thought. Not a sentence or a syllable will escape those closed lips. She'll not be condemned by words. She's far too clever for that. In order to survive, my ingenious wife needs to double her bets, have it both ways, bend the truth a bit. This silence makes her invisible, invincible, and, most important of all, innocent. Even offers a refuge without conscience. Why consider the plight of the starving traders, or pray for the drowned, their last breaths blown like glass through the waves, when she too is selected among fate's victims, a castaway, marooned on this island—albeit with considerable privileges over the others?

If asked, my quick-witted wife would explain that her silence seals a contract, represents the only bill of exchange for the unspeakable: shelter, protection, pleasure, my love perhaps—bought fair and square without judgment or hindrance.

Yes, I understand this double-faced silence of hers, which spins in creaking winds like a Grecian mask and denies me all power of possession.

 ON THE THIRTY-FOURTH DAY, Wouter arrives outside my quarters. Preparing the opium, I admire my beauteous boy, with each day grown fairer on this joyous retreat from the known world.

I ask how the council dealt with Hayes and his men. He smiles and takes a deep draught of the pipe.

"Bought easier than we thought," he says. "The French in particular were almost too easy, snatching the rations, chattering like monkeys."

He unfolds a scroll and hands me an invitation from Hayes to formally settle the alliance on High Island.

Courteous Hayes is no letter writer. No embellishments here. Just instructions scrawled in a rough, hurried hand. We are to meet at noon in six days' time.

So Hayes still calls the shots, commands his leader to wait a week. But perhaps he believes a cooling-off period is required before we sign an agreement to end this senseless skirmish between two scraps of land.

How Wouter's eyes shine during his description of

the latest expedition to Seal Island. He says that when they landed the raft, De Beere and Pelgrom chased five boys into the waves, whereupon Andries took out his knife and cut their throats.

All perished except the last, who ran a little way among the rocks. Pelgrom went after him. The child fell to the ground, begged bitterly for his life, that he might be allowed to say his prayers. Pelgrom sat on his chest and stabbed him twice in the neck. But he could not bring him to death, his knife being blunted, so he asked for De Beere's sword.

Then, beating the scrub to flush out the wives, Carp chanced on a pregnant woman who was known to De Beere.

De Beere took her by the hand.

"Mayken, my love," he said, "you must die."

She wriggled like an eel. Pelgrom came to his aid. They made a halter from her snood and with that strangled her.

"Her snood?" I inquire.

Wouter smiles.

"A snood, sir," he says. "They found this woman half-naked, yet her hair was plaited in a snood—a tattered one at that."

We laugh. The vanity of the fairer sex knows no bounds.

Leaning back in my chair, I exhale a stream of smoke. Events are unfolding my way just as I knew they would. Yet I confess to a certain melancholy. After all, I have never felt freer, unleashed from the confines of that ancient chartered continent we used to call home. This is my space. Engaged in an elaborate game of chess. Lately in my dreams the rescue ship never arrives.

The netmender, our uppersteersman's sodomite, has been captured on Seal Island. Tomorrow I will decide what to do with him.

MY WIFE IS BECOMING sneaky, I grant you that. This morning, I leave her alone with Carp for the first time. Crouched by the barred window, I watch her study the boy like a painting. But she does not speak to him yet.

Ever since the council executions began, Carp acts like one in a trance. He hides himself in the bush when not on duty and is constantly smiling. Look at the half-wit now, dressed in all his finery, prancing around my wife like an organ grinder's monkey.

Sitting at the locked escritoire, my wife tries to entice him to come closer, but the fool skips to one side, all the while staring at her with bright, round eyes.

Then she hums a lullaby, some tender refrain from the past which distracts Carp. He stands head to one side and strains to listen. My wife continues her song, her long swan-neck outstretched.

I can just imagine her at the Honourable Company's annual ball, hear the rustle of her fan and chantilly lace, see her dancing in yellow satin shoes, sashaying from suitor to suitor in a giddy succession of quadrilles, while I, cloaked in another's life, sit at a card table with three plump merchants and tap my foot to the band's gay rhythms. I wonder how many suitors led her to the summerhouse by the ornamental lake, where willows trailed green shadows, where they proposed. I like to think of her at the ball and the assurance in her full-lipped virgin smile.

Entranced, Carp tiptoes closer and kneels beside her. Humming softly, she strokes his rat-brown hair then darts him a sharp look.

"Those keys around your waist," she begins, giving them a playful rattle. "Show me, Carp, the locks for each one."

He shakes his head, both afraid and delighted by what she's just said.

So my clever wife thinks she'll win Carp's trust, enough at least for him to slide the bolt from the door. What will she do then? Run away, seize the raft, take a chance with sharks and quickening tides? Escape where?

There's no escape, my pretty one. Not for you or anyone. Your world has shrunk, encompasses this bed, the circumference of a stunted palm.

You can only hope that one day some mariner, traveler, historian, crayfish catcher will sink their boots in these shores, sift sun-bleached bones like grains of sand through their fingers, and try to make sense of it all.

Still my wife persists in this charade with Carp.

"Unlock the door," she continues in the same quiet voice.

At this Carp rubs the scar on his cheek and giggles.

"Please, Carp," she whispers. "Promise I'll never tell."

She does not realize that Carp is too dim-witted to turn the enemy.

 ON THE THIRTY-FIFTH DAY, the Predikant sits motionless on the shore, shivering in the glare of a full noon sun.

"Horror of horrors," he murmurs beneath his breath.

"What are we going to do with this one?" De Beere asks. Wouter wants to cut his throat. Pelgrom would rather poison him. They weary me. Constantly demand my attention, squabble like children. They bait the Predikant with their knives and make him dance like a circus bear on flint-sharp coral.

"Let him live a little longer," I call. "He might be useful in ensuring the soldiers on High Island keep to their word and join forces with us."

Now I need to placate my petulant disciples, angry they cannot have their way with the Predikant. I take wine down to the shore and summon the netmender, the crew's favorite catamite. Although impatient, I allow De Beere to drain a quart of wine before handing him my sword.

"Try that on the netmender," I say, "and see whether it's sharp enough to cut off his head."

The Predikant staggers to his feet.

"For a long time now," he begins in a low, tremulous voice, "I've expected to be murdered at any time. For pity's sake, kill me and spare the child."

Pelgrom throws grit in his eyes. "Save your breath, swine."

Wouter forces the netmender to his knees and blindfolds him.

"Sit still, boy," he says. "They are only joking with you."

De Beere draws the sword. The blade begins its whistle through the air—but Carp steps in front of the boy.

"No," he shouts. Tears stream his cheeks.

There is a silence. The netmender pisses through his breeches.

Carp begins to argue in plaintive tones that De Beere is not strong enough and another should be chosen. I smile. Such tantrums and moodswings. I am finding them difficult to please.

Carp tries to snatch the sword from De Beere. They roll like puppies, scuffling and snapping at my feet. I pick up the sword and tell Wouter to go sharpen it.

The others laugh, except Carp, who weeps like a spoiled child just because he has not been allowed to do it. I leave them to their games.

The Dominie stumbles ankle deep in swirling waters. He rips the crucifix from his throat and throws the chain high in the air. It flashes blue in watery light.

Gulls sail toward the trinket. With a shriek, one snatches the cross in its beak.

"There is no God," the Predikant cries and curses the heavens.

So, at last he denies that cruel sky God of his. In this I commend him, although it took a while.

⁓⁂

Later, at the hour which sets the sky and ocean on fire, fringes the island in yellow-red flames, sends fierce night winds scurrying toward my quarters, I unlock the Commandeur's money chests.

Although I admire my rare collection—these coins by the fistful, the Roman cameo, the agate vase, the medallions, betel boxes, silver bowls, my wife of course—I begin to wonder whether these treasures are enough, whether they satisfy, when there are always more to be found.

I lift the precious vase from its stand and trace the veined spines of the acanthus leaves, the pearled fruits between, the ridged horns on the two heads of Pan, the coiled curls of their beards, all pared and worked to the translucence of honeyed porcelain by some enraptured fifth-century artisan.

Yet its beauty tires me so. I am weighed down, burdened by it. I require a new chase to stimulate the appetite. Something better.

I could auction this vase and watch it pass into a stranger's hands without a qualm. There are so many artifacts. And no single one is that priceless, or important.

Maybe this is how I feel about my wife. Perhaps I've discovered that you can only truly possess even the most exquisite object for just a short time, before finding you want to sell it and move on.

I no longer pamper my hungry wife with delicacies. What's the point when she gives nothing and expects so much? If he remembers, Carp doles out a bowl of rations, the usual fare, perhaps a hunk of bread smeared with meat fat. I've also reduced her wine consumption. Those rich red burgundies tend to discharge melancholic humors in one so slight.

I refill my glass, salute her, and take a long, slow sip.

This evening, in cruel candlelight, Lucretia has a sour, pinched look. I confess to a certain impatience with my wife. A wife in name only. She, who owes me her life. This gallant courtship has gone on long enough.

I lift the mosquito net. She sits cross-legged against the wall, sheets rucked around her ankles. I am shocked by the soiled worn state of those silken coverlets, which once adorned the Commandeur's bunk.

It seems a long time ago that I attired my wife in her fair sisters' finery. Now the elegant green gown appears faded and threadbare, frayed at the hem. The copper gleam in her hair also seems to have coarsened and tarnished. There's a sickly pallor about her face. She looks unwashed, sallow. A stale musty tang rises from the bed. I wonder when Carp last attended to her toilette.

Leaning forward, I stroke the cameo at her throat. She lifts her head and stares at me dully. I prize open the gold clasp. The velvet choker drops in her lap. I must have tied it too tight, for raw, red weals blister the exposed skin on her neck. I slip the emerald ring from her finger and press her hand against my cheek. Scalding tears course between the creases of her palm. Why do I weep? Surely not for this silent wife, who, unmoved and untouched by my grief, sits there so still.

A moth flutters beneath the mosquito net. Lucretia takes no notice. It hovers above the sheets. Alights on her arm, brushes against her lips. Still she tolerates its impudence. Indulges it with intimacies denied to me. This time my lady goes too far. I ring the bell for Wouter.

When he appears, grinning like a satyr, disheveled, unkempt, not even shaven or wearing his hat or his ruff, the gold braid on his tunic splashed with blood, it strikes me that standards are slipping. The councillor-general sets a poor example. He will be reprimanded for his negligence.

But first I get to the heart of the matter. Taking him aside, I confide that I cannot accomplish my ends with either kindness or anger. Wouter takes stock of my wife with a shrewd mercantile eye. She shrinks against the wall.

"Don't you know how to manage that?" he says. "I'll soon make her do it." And marching to the bed, he rips away the mosquito net.

My wife cowers in her lair. She draws the sheets about her and pushes back her hair.

"If you refuse to please me," I say, "your beauty will wither and fade and in no time you'll become an old maid whose breath smells of curdled milk, who talks nonsense to cats and makes people stare in market squares."

As usual she treats me to her indifference.

Wouter stands before her.

"I hear complaints about you." His voice is stern.

My wife squats on her heels and hides her face in her hands.

"You do not comply," he says, "with the Captain-General's wishes in kindness."

Wouter leans forward and gives her a firm shake.

"Now, however, you will have to make up your mind."

She peers at him through her fingers.

"Either you will go the way of the others," he says, "or else you must do that for which we have kept the women."

Rocking back and forth, she cradles her head in her arms. Impatient, Wouter holds her wrists. "Come now, show the Captain-General your pretty face."

She struggles like a tomcat. But Wouter proves stronger. He has her about the waist, yanks back that lovely hair and puts one hand around her throat.

"Come now, Captain-General," he says, "give this maid a kiss."

My stubborn wife grits her teeth. I seek her with my tongue. Then, wearied by her lack of desire, I draw up a chair and order Wouter to break my filly in.

All at once he flushes and loosens his grip on Lucretia. Rubbing bruises on her wrists, she stares at me, imploring, beseeching. I notice she is shivering.

At a loss, Wouter looks from me to Lucretia again.

I clap my hands, signaling the performance to begin. But my puppets prove shy, unnerved by this twist to our game. Wouter even hangs his head in shame, he who has feasted and gorged on all of our women except, of course, until tonight the fair Lucretia.

"So. This time," I say, "it's your turn to disappoint."

His cheeks flame crimson.

I smile. Such bashful modesty, you would think this lad a virgin unmanned by the luminous naked innocence of first love.

When I pour us a triple tot of brandy, Lucretia makes a dash for the door. But, seizing her, Wouter flings her on the bed, where she lies sobbing.

He takes a deep swig of brandy.

"Is this an order, sir?" he asks in a low voice, giving my wife a quick, appraising glance.

"It would give me the greatest pleasure," I reply.

At last Wouter unbuttons his breeches, with fumbling fingers. He kicks off his boots and slowly unfastens his tunic and shirt.

I enjoy watching him and, for the first time in a long time, find myself stirring. There is much to admire in my lithe pagan faun. I ask him to parade naked before me wearing only the Commandeur's hat, instruct him to turn this way and that.

A mischievous grin begins to play at Wouter's lips; he struts back and forth, hands on narrow hips. Studying him, it seems to me that he too is aroused by the joyousness in this game, relishes the prospect of it being played over and over again.

Arms clenched around her knees, Lucretia has drawn herself into a tight ball against the wall.

Wouter the seducer, the stealthy, steals toward the bed. Sweat glistens in streaks across his taut muscled back.

At his approach, Lucretia screams.

"My dear boy," I suggest, "do not hesitate to use this to correct her."

I give him a sharp whittled stick, marked in places with cruel knots of rope and leather, which I have lovingly prepared for this very moment, the consummation of our wedding night.

And Wouter does. Again and again he does.

I relish the spectacle of this singular choreography. My wife bucks. Swiftly Wouter rides her. Sometimes I feel compelled to interrupt certain scenes, configure different postures, redefine roles. As in any tableau it is a matter of sketching perspectives, composing scenes; in short, establishing from the onset a protocol of ceremony.

ON THE THIRTY-SIXTH DAY, my wife lies on the bed, whimpering like a beaten dog.

Outside, there's a soft, warm wind blowing. I do believe she has been cooped up here long enough. Ocean breezes will do her good, bring the color to those sallow cheeks. It's time too that Carp laundered the bedding, the torn, stained sheets. For although my passion has waned, I care for her still.

I unbolt the door. Sunlight streams across the bed. Lucretia moans and shields her face with one hand as if warding off imaginary blows. I feel a sudden renewed surge of tenderness for this wife of mine. Never before have I seen her so defeated or alone. Gently I lift my bride in my arms and carry her outside. Overhead a bird whistles a long, shrill warning note. Lucretia makes no attempt to struggle. I am astonished at her lightness. If I were to let her go, she would float away, drift like thistledown above the scrub, her hair catching among the leaves.

I decide to set her down on my wooden throne in

the shade. When I begin to tie her hands, bind her feet with rope, she clasps her fingers behind her back, without protest, assisting me almost.

Although I secure her tight, I pull her sleeve cuffs over her wrists so that the rough cords will not chafe that delicate skin. See how I care for her.

Her eyes are huge and withdrawn, as if she has retreated into some dark, distant, secret part of herself. I can't bear to look at her face for long.

Later, footsteps scale the track. She stiffens and jumps at the sound of every twig snap.

Wouter must have mistaken the appointed hour, the violet hour when the light is calm and languorous shadows slant across the bed.

It is not Wouter, though, but the Predikant our unexpected guest. Who would have thought him so fleet, so light of foot? Why, this blubber of lard melts like a sorbet.

My wife stares at him, as if trying to remember, then she shakes her head and frowns.

At the sight of her, the Predikant stands stock-still. He seems to shrink a little in his gown as if all the breath had been punched out of him. Then he kneels at her feet and tugs the knotted ropes.

Queasy with desire, I wait for her to speak.

First she begins by rolling sounds around in her mouth. But my noble lady finds that words stick in her throat. She fairly retches on them. In the old world, they'd keep her straitjacketed in an asylum cell.

Still the Predikant continues to unravel the knots of her bondage.

"No, leave me," she finally manages to say. "This is where I now belong."

So my contrary wife has made her choice. Pity it's too late.

"They have murdered women and children," the Predikant whispers.

My wife opens her mouth to scream but no sound comes out. The Predikant folds her in his arms. First he lets her sob angry tears until she can cry no more and rests against his shoulder. They remain in this hateful attitude for some time until gently, with infinite care, he wipes her eyes with a soiled handkerchief.

Her tearstained face upturned, my wife believes him Jesus and herself his sheltering lamb.

Again the Predikant attempts to untie the ropes. Again she shakes her head and refuses his help. My clever wife's no fool. If the traders discovered her game, knew that all the while she had been accepting privileges denied to them, why they'd tear her limb from limb.

Watching the minister take his reluctant leave, I decide to arrange an entertainment of sorts, a celebration of our first month on this island. It is also a matter of keeping my boys occupied. They complain, turn fractious. Say the island offers little in the way of distractions.

Tonight the Predikant and his eldest daughter will

be invited to dine in my quarters. He will relish his meal, drink the wine, mop the sauce with bread. At my command, at the third tap of my forefinger against the brandy decanter, Wouter will slip to the Predikant's hut.

"Are you asleep?" he will call to the Predikant's youngest child.

Rubbing fearful, rabbit eyes, she will step outside.

"Will you do me evil?"

At this he will curl his lips into a seductive courtier's smile and put one arm around her.

"No, my love, not at all."

And the night will shriek with the thud of an axe.

THE PREDIKANT'S eldest daughter is called Judith. Fine Old Testament name. Those early biblical wives were tough, made of sterner stuff than these fair, placid Dutch maids. Docile long-lashed Judith sits beside her father and can't tear her eyes from the banquet laid on the table. Gull wings of course, stewed this time in a fragrant ragout of sorrel and fennel. Peeled turtle eggs dipped in aspic. Reef fish the size of trout, a good half-dozen skewered tail-to-mouth on a spit. A platter of sliced cured ham.

Cut adrift from the horizon, a young moon flails in webs of pagan constellations.

For the wines, we begin with an aromatic Portuguese red. Judith gapes in wonder, as if one of her saintly relics had shed blood for tears.

The Predikant, on the other hand, is jumpy as a cat. He takes no notice of the feast before him.

Carp serves the rich ragout. Ladles it with care into pewter bowls. I tell the Predikant to inhale that pungent steam, for Carp has become an excellent cook.

When a bowl is set before ravenous Judith, she

grabs a spoon and begins to slurp the sauce, gnawing and crunching the gull bones. In this she reminds me of my wife, who, refusing to share our celebratory repast, remains inside huddled on the bed.

Strange, but her day *en plein air* did Lucretia's constitution no good. The Predikant too failed to cheer with his visit. When at the appointed hour I carried her to the bed and rang the bell for Wouter, she ran wild with fevers and ravings. In a rage she quite forgot and spoke. Threatened to gouge out her eyes so she would never see my face again.

When Wouter had gone, she lit a taper and tried to burn down my quarters. But the wick sputtered, being salt-stained, and would not even light the hem of her gown. Still, I would not like my pretty wife to be reckless and damage herself.

How Wouter leers at his new bride. Pleased at my decision to save Judith, he refills her glass and salutes her robust appetite. Fastidious courtly De Beere fillets the fish with surgical skill. At Judith's smacking gulps, he casts disapproving looks. De Beere prefers his dainty, abstemious wife, now so emaciated I wonder how she lasts the nights.

The Predikant pushes his bowl to one side. Judith snatches it eagerly and gobbles his portion.

"Why, minister," I say, passing him the fish on a gold plate, "you seem poorly tonight. What can be the matter?" Fireflies dart and flicker among the candelabras.

The Predikant raises his heavy head. His eyes are fierce. Pupils dilated. This time I wonder if he's been pilfering the opium. I signal De Beere to bring me the brandy.

"You are feverish perhaps," I say, unscrewing the top of the decanter. "Lately the nights have been humid and there's thunder in the air. A tot of brandy will set you right."

At the first tap of my finger against the silver rim, Wouter nudges De Beere. Pelgrom drains his glass. At the second signal, my boys are on their feet, fastening cloaks around their shoulders. At the third, I grant them permission to leave.

I pour brandy for the Predikant, quite concerned by the sight of him. His face is ashen. Still Judith eats and licks her way around all the plates. I fear the Dominie will not be with us for long.

ON THE THIRTY-SEVENTH DAY, I am struck by the change in our Predikant—that gaunt face, those wild staring eyes. Such a fuss made about his mean-mouthed wife, whereas I would have thanked Wouter for the deed, which so I hear was not easy. For all her prayers and psalm recitals, the Predikant's wife was none too keen to meet her Lord. It took five blows of the axe, Wouter said, before her skull split like a coconut.

The Predikant should count himself one of the lucky ones; after all, the council has kept him alive.

Yet look at him now.

"They have strangled pregnant women, murdered men and children," he wails by the shoreline, blinking back tears in the sun.

Murder, don't make me laugh. These people have chosen their destinies. Even you, minister, deserve punishment for innumerable transgressions, your sly, stealthy prayers. You must think me a fool. You knew the council rules yet deliberately broke them. Tell me of one man in Amsterdam who would tolerate another's secret assignation with his wife? Yet unbidden you visited Lucretia. Why should you be exempt from regulations that in our place the Company would impose?

Besides, you don't understand. You're on borrowed time. Had the *Batavia* not run aground, you would have died over a month ago. The skipper was a man of his word. We'd made a contract. At first signal, the hatch would have been fastened, and I don't recall your name on my list. Imagine your terror at the sound of those first nails hammered into wood. Instead you've been spared and should be grateful for this extra portion of life. Yet you refused to admit that I was a good man.

Listen to the songs of this wind-strummed island, the hum of gulls on the wing and, from the main encampment, Wouter's ceaseless chant, continuous as the spill of sand in an hourglass.

"Who wants to be boxed on the ear?" he calls. "Who wants to be stabbed?"

At the sound of Wouter's cries, the soul-shriver's shoulders heave. Once again he resumes his lament.

"Judith and I went not knowing why to that hut like an ox in front of the axe."

My, all these tears, you'd think this desiccated scrub would bloom on them. There should be flowers the size of trumpets, stalks sap-filled, distillations of nectar to intoxicate bees.

"Judith I took with me not knowing why," he says.

Such labor in this tale.

"Murdered wife and children all together on that night and I—with Judith, my daughter." Finally he curses the empty heavens, the indifferent stars, the scattering clouds of terns at twilight.

I intend to have fun with the Dominie. Tonight he'll preside over the marriage of his only child.

～❀◎

"I've arranged an entertainment," I tell my wife, taking her bruised hands in mine. Lucretia has learned to fear those words, my ingenious devices to kill time— and *that* I have in plenty.

"Tonight, my dear," I confide, "you will be bridesmaid to Judith, the Predikant's daughter, soon to be Wouter's fair wife."

My wife cringes beneath the sheets and stifles tears.

"Were I to believe your God," I whisper, "I would call it a match made in Heaven."

I kiss her cold lips. She makes to strike me, but I catch her by the wrists and enjoy watching her struggle.

"Don't be jealous, my darling," I say, "it was agreed by all council members that the wives would be shared, even you, my pretty one."

～❀◎

Evening breezes ripple the gaily striped pennants stitched to Wouter's bridal tent. Fires are lit. Wine kegs tapped. Carp plucks a jaunty tune on his harp. There are gull feathers in his hair and blood speckles his shirt.

The boys busy themselves with their toilette. Indeed Judith is a lucky girl. How proud her dear mama would have been to see her eldest wed Wouter, this gifted youth from Amsterdam.

I escort my wife dressed in a white cambric evening gown to the councillors' quarters. By a fire on the shoreline, my disciples stamp their feet to a drum's wild rhythms. Judith is dragged before them, her frightened eyes blackened with kohl. And behind, the Predikant, a rope around his neck, once again led like an ox to the slaughter.

Afterward, such a ball as you have never seen. Wouter drunk on brandy. Judith teeters, trips on the damask hem of her gown. Carp serves champagne first to the ladies, then to the gentlemen. The Company would be proud of such a spectacle. Toasts to Holland and once again to the Governor-General.

ON THE THIRTY-EIGHTH DAY, the number of people on Traitor's Island has been reduced to a very few. Always I knew that I would succeed in my mission.

Would that Torrentius was here to share this citadel at the world's end. I've created the fantastical Eden which existed only in his dreams. How proud he'd be to see me spread his gospel to the four corners of the world. I have given true meaning to his creed to enjoy all without hindrance or censure. Only I, Jeronimus the chosen one, shared his vision. For he spoke the same language as I.

When he talked of pleasure, his flock saw bordellos, painted boys, masked flagellants, whereas here I have conjured wonders with his words. Torrentius was aware of my powers. He knew I would outstrip him in the end.

Strange that my aunts were the ones who first introduced me to my mentor. He had won a reputation among the ladies of Amsterdam for his miniatures, exquisite still lifes, detailed compositions of pheasant and fruits entwined with wild flowers. Delightful themes which always fetched a good price from my aunts, who paid regular visits to his studio in the center of town.

The first time they ushered me into his inner sanctum, a high-ceilinged room where the curtains were drawn against the windows—he suffered from a photophobic affliction, an acute sensitivity to daylight — Torrentius rose to his feet from a seat by the fire and extended both hands in welcome. All at once I felt his black, brilliant eyes on mine and I shrank from the scrutiny of his gaze.

While my aunts conferred in close whispers about the price they would offer on a motif of dogrose which had caught their fancy, Torrentius led me through a curtained door to a spacious antechamber.

Again his work lined the walls, but here the subjects were vastly different and much more to my liking: subtle arrangements of chains, whips, and bridles.

I was struck by one circular miniature called *Emblematic Still Life* which later, along with the others, the magistrates burned. It was a study of spurs, harnesses, polished bits, which gleamed darkly against a black velvet backdrop. In the foreground stood a pewter jug, the spout cruelly erect beside a wine flagon, nutbrown as a peasant's belly, its speckled glaze turned to the candlelight. In the center of the painting a silver wine goblet, studded with rubies at the stem, pinned down a fold of parchment on which I recognized the Lord's prayer written backward.

Standing behind me, my future mentor placed both hands on my shoulders.

"Tell me what you see," he whispered.

"The jug represents power, infinite and absolute," I replied. "The harness submission, the flagon sensuality."

He laughed at my untutored exegesis.

"You've been pampered by your aunts long enough," he said. "It's time for the rooster to leave the henhouse. You'll begin your life's work under my guidance."

My aunts were becoming frail and forgetful, mislaying boards of *petit point*, smelling salts, pocket handkerchiefs, their belts of keys. They seldom ventured outside and had taken to locking their bedroom each night, where I could hear them whispering fretfully, furtively.

Sometimes coming home from a tavern at dawn light, I would see a candle glimmering from their window and knew my aunts were lying side by side, fearful and awake, beneath the great patchwork quilt they sewed year after year when I was young.

At mealtimes I only had to clink my cup against the

saucer or drop a spoon, and they would jump up in alarm as if the parlor were afire with a fusillade of musket shell.

Looking at my aunts I would smile, reassure them that they had me, as master of the house, to protect them.

Then they would grow quiet and watch each other. They invented a dozen excuses to take trays to their room—they were tired, they would say, rheumatic; one would have a migraine, the other the onset of some chill—and in my last year with my aunts, I dined alone. Whenever I offered to treat their frequent maladies, they would smile nervously and always decline. I also noticed that no matter how febrile or frail, they insisted on superintending all domestic duties with anxious eyes—cook at her pots, some maid washing the plates—despite my repeated entreaties that their hovering watchful presence was not befitting to their rank.

"Yes, dear," they would murmur, allowing me to coax them up the stairs, but whenever my back was turned they scuttled down to the kitchen again. Often, contemplating their tired, weary faces, I wondered if age, the march of threescore years, were afflicting their minds, and again I would recommend some remedy, which only set them aflutter like roosting hens hearing the soft, steady tread of a fox circling their coop.

So when that night, as I packed a valise, my aunts

wept at the prospect of my departure, I knew they were secretly relieved. They could not refuse Torrentius's request to become my guardian, and agreed to relinquish all responsibility of their charge, now a tall, aristocratic stranger, no longer their darling cherub of a child but a headstrong youth of seventeen.

I joined Torrentius's disciples who were sworn to his secret sect. But I always felt myself to be alone, because I knew things and had to hint at things which others apparently knew nothing of and for the most part did not want to know.

Only my friend Torrentius was able to unravel the babble of tongues in my head. Often when his disciples had retired and only the embers in the grate stirred he invited me to share a digestif of armagnac in his study.

Those were the violet hours of many stories.

—⁂—

"All this was a long time ago, I remember, when with diamonds clinking in my pockets, I traded cedar boxes of frankincense and myrrh in deserts unknown. All this was a long time ago, when in a dry season of portents and comets, I traveled mile after mile across dunes, slippery and sinuous as raw silk. I remember a white high-walled city. Sand whistled through cobbled streets, banked against fountains in empty squares, spilled like shattered hourglasses down municipal steps.

"The city was deserted. The taverns abandoned. I hammered on their doors. Not even the sound of dice thrown on a table, the porcelain clink of jasmine tea, or a cantankerous porter to greet me. The silent city hummed in my ears.

"At last, I came to an inn, rustic in style, where three old men were playing a desultory game of backgammon. They told me they were journeying north from distant kingdoms, navigating their camels by one single star.

"They could not explain why the city was deserted nor their exact purpose here. But before they returned to their game, ever the salesman I spread my wares: untied my muslin sachets of sweetmeats, opened my spice boxes, uncorked my perfume phials. I noticed they watched me with interest for the first time. In the end, not bothering to haggle, they bought frankincense and myrrh at five times the price even I'd expected.

" 'Gifts,' they muttered, exchanging furtive glances, yet when pressed would say no more.

"We traveled together for a week or two until we crossed a cool verdant valley. I left them at a village which they had seemed anxious to reach. There were many people there, encamped in olive groves. The place had a festive atmosphere. The troubadour's ballads, the dwarfs' antics, the children garlanded with flowers reminded me of a circus or a traveling fair.

"In a barn, among the cattle, the three men kneeled and raised a stranger's squalling new-hatched babe to the heavens.

"Later, sitting cross-legged at the marriage feast in Cana, miserable chicken village it was, I warned the Holy Family dressed exquisitely in blue that their son would come to a bad end."

This was Torrentius's favorite story. Removing his green-tinted lorgnettes, the ones the doctors had prescribed, he wiped his eyes with a lace handkerchief.

"*Vous êtes un homme qui sait tout,*" he said, "*mais qui meurt jamais.*" How he flattered me in his courtly French.

There were other stories.

—✿

"Northern France, in a ripe season of vendange, I remember crouching by a flea-infested bed, whispering obscenities into a peasant's ear. Her name was Joan I think. She responded to my voices. It was I who cropped her flaxen hair, dressed her in armor like a chevalier. At the stake, just before the tapers were lit, she told the impressionable crowd she had been seduced by the Devil. I relished those rich tones rising above the mob, pungent as garlic on a fifth-generation cassoulet. Removing my executioner's mask, I bowed and thanked her for the gracious compliment."

 STRANGE THAT despite the national treasures, the Company's crates of gold, our Predikant has become the council's most valuable commodity, a prime asset representing living proof that we mean well, and without which all negotiations with the soldiers would be steeped in mistrust. When I explain to the Predikant that he must come with us on the raft to High Island, he begs to take Judith with him. I tell this fretful father to be reasonable. She's Wouter's wife. No longer his daughter. A fine handsome wife—although rather plump for my liking—to be shared communally with all council members. For I've always believed monogamy an outdated notion.

The Predikant kneels at my feet.

"Kill me and spare my only child."

This minister is a mournful, morbid man. As with many men of his profession, he suffers from an imagination enfevered by violent biblical fables, that popular fiction which in all schools should be banned. His constant talk of murder begins to get on my nerves, particularly when I've thrown him a wedding. In Amsterdam, his peevish daughter would have ended a spinster, yet here has found salvation in my boys. The Predikant must pull himself together.

ON THE FORTIETH DAY, I am dressed in all my finery. Breezes ruffle the plume in my hat. Wouter heaves the Predikant onto the raft. It was just as I had expected. Yet the soldiers seem almost too easy to woo. There's something lacking in the challenge.

Paddling me across, my boys are unnaturally quiet. Then Wouter smiles in delight.

"I have thought of a good new plan."

"What is that?"

He leans toward me, conspiratorial and eager.

"If a ship comes to rescue us, we should seize it and go pirating to Madagascar."

From this angle, sitting beside him, the nape of his neck looks vulnerable.

"Good thinking," I say, tousling his bleached blond hair. Sometimes I forget they are just children. Playing games of tag and dare.

Soon we will float over the wreck. Dare we look beneath the swell? Far below, the sunken ship wavers. Fractured masts hoist tiger weed for sails. Anemones seal portholes with their suckers. The Honourable Company's cargo carpets the sea floor, barnacles the rocks. Gold and silver coins spin in slow currents, sending to the surface an unearthly sheen of light.

Approaching High Island, I stare at the soldiers through my glass. They line the shore, piteous, half-naked. At the sight of the raft, they cheer. Hayes waves a white flag. They set fire to a timber pyre piled on the rocks. I am touched by these crude simple cere-monies, honored even, and I salute them.

De Beere spreads his cloak on the sand. I step ashore. The buckles flash on my polished calfskin boots. Soon my followers will have new council uniforms, embroi-dered with gold fleur-de-lis.

Hayes, my fellow conspirator, and several of his men stride toward me. The others continue to fuel the fire with handfuls of leaves and twigs. To my surprise some even rip off ragged shirts and throw them in the flames. And hoisted to a pole, the white flag flutters.

I was not expecting this pageant, a celebration on such a scale, and I'm flattered by their devotions.

At Hayes's approach, I extend both arms in welcome, longing to embrace my true friend. It is time I made a speech.

His men surround me. I bid them kneel. And when I speak, my voice roars like the noise of a crowd—

All at once the soldiers close in.

The glass is knocked from my hand and shatters at my feet—it is Hayes who wrestles me to the ground.

I shrink from the cold touch of his skin. Coarse oakum ropes tighten around my wrists.

There is a sound of rushing air and the unfolding of wings.

The islands of the sea will be terrified by this end.

That I, Jeronimus, a man of phials, Captain-General of coral shoals, should be so betrayed by Hayes, my only friend.

I mourn my lost empire encircled by its dark halo of terns. I hold in my heart an unspeakable sorrow. Even consider walking away, turning my back on it all, and marching into the scrub, the silence.

Call me mad if you will, but this citadel which I've created at the world's end is all I've ever desired, this plot of land surrounded by the seas all I've wanted, all I need.

If you asked me now, I would say this is the evil hour when the sun shrinks to a pinprick in the terrible blank expanse of cloudless sky, when it is difficult to remember and moments pass without explanation.

Then I see it. Etched on the horizon. Tremulous mirage. The rescue ship glancing the reef on a low tide.

PART
FOUR

Epilogue

THEY KEEP ME HERE, on my island, my lost empire, which they call Batavia's Graveyard, in a filthy pit separate from the others. Out of no love for me but fearful I should raise a mutiny. They are all spies. Both guards and prisoners.

And spare me the Commandeur. That peruked and epauletted officer, traitor to us all. How I despise his false sermons, his tight-lipped piety, the tremor in those soft white hands each time he turns a leaf of his precious calf-bound Bible.

⟡

This morning the Commandeur requested that I kneel and hear the word of God. But I said I would have nothing to do with the Dominie, his vicious, scurrilous lies, obscenities heaped against me, which the daily threat of trial by water forces me to confess. I will not submit to the foul filth of that funnel again. Confessions extracted under torture are vile and void. These are mock trials. Yet my guilt has already been decided.

Outside, the sound of nails hammered into wood. They are building a scaffold. I am to swing from salvaged planks and scraps of driftwood. They have given me three days to repent of my sins. When I heard, I spat in the Commandeur's face.

"Three miserable days," I said. "Did I hear right?"

He flinched and wiped the spittle from his lips with a lace handkerchief.

"Where's Wouter?" I cried. "Put him to the strappado—swing him by the arms and break every bone in his body with weights—and you'll soon hear the truth and learn of my innocence."

That silenced this masquerade of a court all right. They looked at me strangely, and I laughed and said that having committed no evil, I desired no grace. How dare they offer me the sacrament of baptism, declare I have the soul of a sinner, denuded of all humanity, letting flow innocent blood? What would they know of sin, of infinite pleasures to be enjoyed without censure or restraint?

Again, the dull knock of nails driven into wood. It's a wonder there's any left to be had.

When, finally, I was condemned by these executioners, refused a fair trial in the courts of Batavia, I demanded to be beheaded rather than hanged. I imagine it to be a clean, swift death, a single swish of a sword, a sharpened blade aimed at the nape of the neck.

That too was denied me by these murderous torturers, the Commandeur and the undersigned of the rescue ship's council.

Instead it was agreed that first they would cut off my hands, then punish me on a gallows with the cord until death.

Should there be a kernel of truth in any such spider web of lies, woven by hard-hearted godless men, would I, Captain-General of this isle, ever have orchestrated such a cruel, lingering end? No is your answer, even if many of my subjects here might have deserved it.

I spend the last night trying to master my fear. I cry out for Lucretia; sometimes I think I hear the rustle of her skirts, the halting tread of her footsteps outside, her voice calling to me. But no one ever comes.

I imagine the coarse cotton hood fastened on my head, the rough rope noose dropped around my neck, pulling me step after stumbling step. I imagine my hands tied and splayed, twitching on a slab of timber—no, I close my mind to this butchery, will not think of it.

I refuse to go silently to this death. They will drag me up the ladder, guide me to a platform, where, before I am pushed, gasping my last of this island's hoary, savage air, I will cry, Revenge, revenge.

THE END

Note

On his return to the Abrolhos in the rescue ship *Sardam*, the Commandeur, Francisco Pelsaert, conducted a trial of Jeronimus and his fellow mutineers there and then, fearing that taking them captive to Batavia would give them the opportunity to incite another mutiny.

After subjecting Jeronimus to water torture and extracting his full confession, Pelsaert condemned him to death. His fellow conspirators demanded that Jeronimus be hanged first, so *their eyes could see that the seducer of men had died*. On 2 October 1629, Jeronimus was taken to a makeshift gallows on Seal Island. Both his hands were held down on a block and amputated before he was hanged by the neck. His last words were 'revenge, revenge.'

Two of Jeronimus's supporters, Wouter and Jan de Bye [Carp], were reprieved and marooned on the Australian mainland on 16 November 1629 *in order to look into the opportunities of the land, be it gold or silver* until such a time as they were rescued by a passing ship. They were never seen again.

The *Batavia*'s skipper, Adriaan Jacobsz, was betrayed by the mutineers, who, under torture on the Abrolhos, had accused him of being one of the principal instigators in the plot to drive the *Batavia* off course, overpower the ship, and make off with the precious cargo. He was incarcerated in the notorious dungeons of Batavia. The last known record of him is a letter from the higher echelons of the Dutch East India Company: *Adriaan Jacobsz, skipper of the wrecked ship* Batavia, *on the strong indictment of having had the intention to run off with the ship, has been condemned to more acute examination and has been put to the torture.*

Pelsaert's earlier decision to leave the survivors and seek help in Batavia came to be viewed by the Dutch East India Company as a complete abdication of responsibility and led to his disgrace, despite his bravery in initiating the trial of the mutineers on the Abrolhos. Already sick with malaria, and unable to clear his name, Pelsaert was posted to Sumatra, where he sank into a depression from which he never recovered. He died some time between June and September 1630.

The soldier Wiebbe Hayes, who finally captured Jeronimus on High Island, was hailed as a national hero in bringing the mutiny to an end. His salary was increased by forty guilders a month. He was promoted to Standard Bearer and promised future promotions. There is no recorded trace of him after his arrival in Batavia.

The Predikant, Gijsbert Bastiaensz, married a bailiff's widow in Batavia in 1631. He died of dysentery in the Banda Islands two years later.

His daughter Judith was married and widowed twice. Following her second husband's death in 1634, she found herself destitute. The Dutch East India Company awarded her three hundred guilders *in consideration of her widowhood and to compensate for the affliction to which she had been submitted in the course of the* Batavia *tragedy*.

Lucretia van den Mylen, who was held captive as Jeronimus's concubine, arrived in Batavia only to find that her husband had died shortly before. She married Jacob Cornelisz Cuick, the brother-in-law of her own half-sister. The couple, who remained childless, returned to the Netherlands in 1635 and settled in Leiden. The last known record of her appeared in 1641—the baptism registry in a local parish when she became godmother to one of her young nephews by marriage.

꧁

Source: *Voyage to Disaster*, by Henrietta Drake-Brockman, first published in 1963 by Angus & Robertson, and in 1995 by University of Western Australia Press.